STITCHED UP HEART

COMBAT HEARTS #1

TARINA DEATON

TARINA DEATON LLC

DEDICATION

To the women who have served and still serve today.
Because not every G.I. is a Joe.

CHAPTER 1

*U*gh. How many times had she asked him not to park in the carport? Her house. Her spot. How hard was that to understand?

Bree stopped her SUV next to the walkway, giving Chad plenty of room to back out. She dropped her head to the steering wheel and banged it a couple times. One good thing about him showing up unannounced—now she didn't have to call him to say *we need to talk.*

Only she could go from planning on breaking up with a guy a month ago to being engaged to him. She lifted her head and sighed. "Time to put your big girl panties on, Marks."

Turning off the ignition, she grabbed her bag from the passenger seat and got out. She detoured into the yard to pick up the circular before trudging up the porch steps. Odd—the front door was unlocked. Why did he unlock the front door if he parked on the side of the house? Why wouldn't he just use the side door?

Bree stumbled and slammed her hip into the edge of the foyer table. "Ow! Shit." She looked to see what she had tripped over.

Those were not her stripper shoes. Even if she owned a pair of six-inch platform stilettos, those were about three sizes too small. What the hell?

"Chad?" She dropped her bag on the foyer table and walked through the foyer into the open concept living room, kitchen, and breakfast nook. His sports coat hung on the back of one of the kitchen stools. She turned left and walked down the short hall to the bedrooms. Just outside her room she heard his voice, "Oh, baby," followed by a high-pitched moan.

I swear, if he is fucking some bitch in my bed, I'm going to cut off his cock.

Bree closed her eyes and took a deep breath, trying to tamp down her anger as it rose up through her chest. Her fists clenched and unclenched in rhythm to the grunts and groans coming through the cracked door. She shook her hands to loosen the tension when she realized what she was doing.

"Orange is not your color. Orange is not your color," she muttered.

Bree pushed the door open to the sight of Chad thrusting into a pair of legs. She leaned a shoulder against the doorjamb and crossed her arms, drawing on the stillness deep inside.

"Hey, Chad, sweetie. Are you busy?"

Chad scrambled to a kneeling position, his eyes wide. He whipped the sheet around his lower body and exposed the girl under him. "Bree! Shit! What are you doing home? You're early. This isn't what it looks like."

"One, I live here, seeing as how it's my house and all. And two, you're really going to go with 'this isn't what it looks like'? Did you slip and fall and this lovely woman was nice enough to catch you with her vagina?"

The girl came up on her elbows and pushed her white-blonde hair out of her face. "You said you weren't married."

"Oh, we're not," Brianna said. "You've got about two seconds to get out of my house before I get my gun."

"What!? Me or him?" the blonde asked as she sat up fully.

"Uh, both of you. I sure as hell don't want you sticking around to chit chat after I just found you banging my boyfriend." Her piercing gaze shifted back to Chad. "Oh, wait. We're engaged now."

"Bree, honey." The asshat hopped on one foot, scrambling to pull his pants up. "This doesn't mean anything. She's just some chick I met at the bar last week. She's no one."

"You asshole!" Blondie slid out of the bed and grabbed her patterned leggings from the floor. "Don't believe a word he says. We've been screwing for months. Although now I understand why we always had to go to my place."

She finished dressing and stomped toward Bree. "I'm sorry. I didn't know he was engaged. I wouldn't have…" Her eyes glittered as she looked up at Bree and she swiped a hand roughly across her cheek. "I'm not that kind of girl."

Yeah, right. Shit. That wasn't fair. There's no telling what lies Chad told this girl. She seemed contrite. Ashamed even. It would be easy to blame her for Chad's fuck up. Bree ran a hand over her face and struggled against the urge to lash out at her. "Don't worry about it. I know whose fault it is."

Blondie gave her a little nod and brushed passed. Bree turned her attention back to Chad. "Get. Out."

His white button-up hung open and a sock stuck out of one of his pockets. "Bree, please. I'm sorry. It really didn't mean anything. It's just been stressful with some stuff at work and you won't set a date for the wedding."

She came away from the door frame, fighting to control her reaction as anger seethed inside. "Are you kidding me? Don't you fucking dare blame this on stress—" she emphasized with air quotes "—or me because I'm not in a rush to get married. This is all you."

"You're right. I know, you're right." Chad moved closer to Bree. "I love you so much, Bree. I see you pulling away and—"

"And you decide to fuck some chick in my bed to get my attention? What the hell are you even doing here? What would even possess you to bring someone here?"

"Sweetie, it wasn't like that. I came by to make you dinner and surprise you. She followed me and I couldn't get her to leave."

She gestured toward her bed. "And *this* was the best way you could think of to get her to leave?"

"That was what she wanted and I figured it'd be easier to get her out the door before you came home, but you got off work early." He tried to pull Brianna into his embrace.

She stepped back. "Do not touch me. You don't get that right anymore. I wasn't kidding when I told you to get out. I'll send any shit you have here to your place. I don't want to see you. I don't want to hear from you. We. Are. Done!"

Chad sighed. "Gran is going to be very disappointed."

It took everything in her not to throat punch him. "You are such a fucking asshole. Seriously? You're throwing my eighty-five-year-old grandmother in my face? Believe me, she'll be okay with me kicking your ass to the curb when she knows why."

"You're going to tell her?" Chad's voice rose in panic along with the flush that crept up his face.

Had he always been this stupid and she had just ignored it, or was this a new development? How had she gotten to this point? Why had she let it go on for so long?

She spoke slowly. "Yes, Chad. I'm going to tell my family why I'm breaking off the engagement. We're done here." Bree stormed out of the room and down the short hall to the kitchen, where she tore his suit jacket off the back of the kitchen stool. Grabbing his shoes by the heels she opened the door, stepped onto the wide porch that ran the entire front of her house and threw all his things onto the walkway.

"Bree! That coat cost eight hundred dollars!" Chad jogged down the steps to pick up his things.

"Well, that's just ridiculous." Bree stormed back into her house, slammed, and locked the door behind her.

She leaned against the door and took several calming breaths. "Stupid fucking asshole." She snatched her purse off the table and dug around for her phone. Still muttering curses, she dialed as she walked into the dining room.

Denise answered on the second ring. "What up, chica?"

She opened the corner hutch. Empty. "Do you have any alcohol?"

"I might. What do you need?"

"Vodka. Or whiskey. Both if you've got it."

"Uh...do I need to bring a shovel, too?"

Brianna let out a short laugh. "No. I avoided doing anything that would land me in jail. Just come over when you can and I'll fill you in then."

"Dude. You gotta give me a clue. You never drink liquor."

"Oh no, you're going to want to hear this in person." Her wine rack was bare as well. "Where is my wine? How do I not even have any wine?"

"Pretty sure we drank it last weekend. I'm heading out the door now. Don't break out the mouthwash before I get there." The phone disconnected.

Where the hell are Charlie and Polly? She set her phone on the counter and opened one of the French doors. Her two dogs, Charlie and Polly, came running from across the wide lawn. Bree sat in one of the loungers on the deck and leaned against the back with her legs on either side of the long seat, feet on the floor. Polly jumped up onto the lounger and lay down with her head on Bree's hip, staring up at her. Bree scratched Polly's ears. "Well. That sucked." Polly raised her head. "I know what you're thinking. I should have broken up with him a long time ago." Polly lowered her head back to Bree's hip and huffed. "Especially since he never really liked you and Charlie. Should have been all the warning I needed."

Charlie bound up the steps of the deck. He stood with his paws on the armrest of the lounger and tried to lick the side of

Bree's neck. "Eww! Gross. Quit." Bree pushed him off the chair. "There's no telling what you've been eating out here. Where's your ball? Go get your ball!" Charlie leaped off the deck in search of one of the many tennis balls in the yard. She threw the ball until Charlie spread out in the shade of the large magnolia tree her grandfather had planted when he built the house for her grandmother.

Bree let out a sigh and pushed up from the lounger. The dogs trailed after her as she returned inside to her bedroom. She stood on the threshold of her room and stared at the bed. She didn't want to touch the sheets, but there was no way in hell she was ever going to use them again. Later. After she'd had a few drinks and checked to see whether Amazon sold hazmat suits. She changed her scrub top for a t-shirt and her yoga pants for cut-off shorts. Back in the kitchen, she poured a glass of water and made sure the dogs' bowl was full.

The side door opened and closed. "You here?"

"In the kitchen."

Denise walked around the corner holding a brown shopping bag. "I wasn't sure what you were in the mood for so I got you mandarin Absolut, Jameson, and, in case it's a particularly bad night, a bottle of Baileys."

"Well, I don't have any cranberry juice for the vodka, so whiskey."

Denise set both bottles on the counter. "You mixing it with soda or Bailey's?"

"It's a cut-my-alcohol-with-more-alcohol kind of night."

"Right. So, what happened? And why is your car in the front of the house instead of on the side?" Denise pulled her long, honey-blonde hair into a bun and secured it with a hair tie.

"Chad. Chad happened." Bree spared no detail as she poured their drinks. By drink three, she'd managed to fill Denise in on all the gory details.

"I have to ask again, because I'm having a hard time with this. In your bed?" Denise asked as they lounged in the living room.

"Yup."

"What a dick. What was wrong with his place?"

"I have no idea. He said he came over to surprise me, she followed him, and one thing led to another."

"How the hell does one thing lead to another?" Denise's voice rose. "And how did she not realize a woman lived here? This house doesn't exactly scream bachelor pad."

"Your guess is as good as mine. Maybe he told her he had it decorated. I can't work up the energy to care at this point."

"What did she look like? Please tell me she didn't look like you?"

Brianna considered the lock of her long, dark auburn hair she was twisting around her finger.

"Nope. She was short. Like, oompa-loompa short. She barely came up to my shoulders. Fake blonde hair and her boobs were fake."

Denise gave her a crazy look. "Is that a guess or did you see more than you needed to see?"

"Oh my god. She had no shame. Chad whipped the sheet around him like he was Caesar on the Ides of March and left her naked as a jaybird. No one's boobs are that perky unless they have supporting infrastructure. That chick had more plastic than a Hasbro factory."

Denise laughed so hard she nearly toppled off the couch. "Oh my god, stop. All I can picture are her boobs in the shape of toy trucks."

Denise's laugh was infectious and Bree joined her. Then Denise snorted and they both lost it.

"The worst part is they were screwing on my favorite set of sheets." Bree's laughter faded to chuckles. "I'm going to have to buy a whole new mattress now."

"Did you already burn the sheets?"

Bree dropped her head back against the sofa. "Ugh. I could barely look at the bed when I changed clothes. I'm going to need a full hazmat suit to get rid of them."

Denise smiled before asking, "How're you really doing?"

"I should have cut bait a long time ago. Hell, I never should have said yes when he proposed." Bree raised her head back up.

"Kind of hard to say no when he blindsides you at your gran's big birthday bash in front of all your friends and family. What I don't know is why you didn't break up with him before then." Denise raised her eyebrows as she looked at Bree over the rim of her glass.

"Honestly, I don't know either. Laziness?" She shook her head. "I've been trying to figure out a way to break it off for a while without being a complete bitch about it." Bree sighed and sipped her drink. "I didn't want to cause a big scene at Gran's birthday."

"You really think she would have cared?"

"No," Bree admitted. "But I panicked when he got down on one knee. Plus, he drove."

"Hmm...I can see how that would have been a problem."

"Yeah. I'm not even hurt. I'm fucking pissed. It's just so freaking disrespectful. Seriously. Who does that shit?"

"Uh, a narcissistic asshole."

"True story." Bree finished off the rest of her drink. "We're not doing this. I refuse to sit around and brood over what an asshat he is. Let's go out."

"Go out where? It's eleven o'clock and I did not come dressed to go out and drink your cares away. I dressed to bury a body in the backyard."

Bree looked at the cut-offs and t-shirt she had on. "We'll go to The Deck. No need to change clothes. And I would never bury a body in my own backyard. That's just asking to get caught."

"The biker bar? Are you nuts? There's a stabbing there every night."

"Don't be dramatic. I'm sure it's only every other night."

"Ha ha. Not the point."

"Come on. My old boss used to go there and was always trying to get me to go. He said it was a cool place to chill and hang out."

"He told you that because he was trying to get in your pants."

"Yeah, well, I've got no argument for that. Get your shoes; I'm getting us an Uber."

"Fine." Denise let out a disgruntled sigh but grabbed her shoes. "Who knows...maybe you'll find the love of your life tonight."

Bree stood and pointed at Denise. "Don't jinx me."

CHAPTER 2

*J*ase set the parking brake on his truck and switched off the ignition. He sighed and stared at The Deck.

Fuck, it'd been months since he'd been here. Probably closer to a year. He didn't want to be here now, but Brandon had asked him to come celebrate his separation from the Army. The promise he'd made himself warred with his desire to be anywhere else but here. But a buddy called. He answered. Even if it was to go to a bar.

He shouldered the door open and slammed it, thumbing the lock button on the fob over his shoulder. Gravel crunched under his boots as he crossed the parking lot. He took the steps two at a time and yanked the door open.

Nate rose from the tall stool with a grin. "Jase, my man." He grabbed his hand and slapped him on the shoulder. "Haven't seen you in forever. Where've you been hiding?"

Jase smiled to hide the wince from the pounding he took. "Getting my company off the ground. Staying out of trouble."

Nate sat on the edge of the stool, one foot on the floor. "I heard about that. You still looking for guys to help you on trips?"

"Yeah. Anytime you're interested, let me know."

"I'll give you a call next week. We've got block leave coming up before we head out next month."

"Where're you going this time?"

Nate stood and nodded behind Jase. Jase stepped to the side as a guy and two women, all dressed in riding leathers, held out their IDs. Nate checked them and handed them back to the group. "Have a good night, folks." He sat back on the stool. "The HOA. Six month rotation."

Horn of Africa. "Fuck, man. Stay safe."

"Easier to do in Africa than Afghanistan."

"Yeah. I'll let you get back to work."

Nate stood again, taking the ID held out to him. "Good to see you again."

Jase waved and strode into the bar. He scanned the crowd, looking for Brandon and Gary. The bar wasn't to capacity yet. Brandon, Gary, Evan, and Nick were easy to spot standing around a couple of tables in the middle of the room. It helped they were one of the few groups not dressed in riding leathers. Brandon spotted him and raised a hand. Jase waved back and pointed to the bar.

He hooked a foot over a stool and waited for Brian to notice him.

"Holy shit! Jase — where've you been hiding?" He held out his hand.

He shook Brian's hand. "Out in the woods. How've you been?"

"Livin' the life. What can I get you?"

"Killian's. Draught."

"Sure thing." Brian knocked on the bar and pushed away.

Jase spun on the stool and scanned the crowd. He recognized a few faces. Recalled fewer names. It hit him in a rush — he didn't miss this place at all.

A flash of blonde caught his peripheral vision and he turned. Tight jeans and a cropped halter showed off all her assets, leaving little to the imagination. They'd had a few hot and heavy nights when he'd been partying all the time. *Shit. What was her name?* Something that ended with a 'y.' Maybe an 'i.' Only stripper names were coming to mind.

She pushed her way between his legs. "Jase, where've you been?" Her red lips pouted as she ran her hands up his chest.

"Popular question tonight." He kept his hands on his thighs. He had no desire to encourage her. Literally, none.

"I missed you." Her long nails, painted to match her lips, pinched his nipple.

He curved his chest and covered his chest with a palm, dislodging her hand. That's right. She liked to pinch.

"Jase," Brian said behind him.

Thank god. "Sorry to hear that." He put his hands on her hips and pushed her back far enough so he could turn on the stool.

He stood and reached in his back pocket for his wallet.

Brian waved him off. "First round's on me. Welcome back to civilization."

"Thanks." He pulled his credit card out and threw it on the table. "I'll start a tab anyway. Put Brandon's drinks on it." A small hand roamed up and down his back, full breasts pressed to his side.

Still no reaction. If he hadn't jacked off in the shower that morning, he'd think something was wrong with him. He stepped away from her touch and turned. "Good to see you again." He lifted his glass as he walked away.

"What?"

He doubted a guy had ever walked away from her, but he didn't do random anymore. He walked across the bar, feeling the weight of her gaze the entire time. *Mandy? Candy? Cindy with an 'i'? What the hell was her name?*

He set his glass down on the table and Brandon grabbed him for a back-thumping hug. "Glad you made it."

"Congratulations." Jase thumped him back.

"I see Tiffany found you." Brandon thrust his chin out, using it to point across the bar.

Tiffany. He spared a glance over his shoulder. She was running her hands over the chest of the guy now sitting in front of her, in much the same way she had with Jase. She glanced up, found Jase, and licked her lips. He turned his back to her. "Yeah. She found me."

"Dude. As soon as we sat down she came over and asked about you. It was like she had Jase-dar or something."

Jase grinned. "Gary, your California is showing." Gary threw his head back and laughed.

"You here for the night or just popping in?" Evan asked.

"The night."

Brandon raised his empty bottle, catching the waitress's attention. "You gonna drink or just nurse?"

"Your night. You wanna drink, I'll drink with you."

The waitress stopped at their table, tray and pad at the ready. She pulled a pen out of her ponytail. "Ready for another round?"

Brandon flashed her a smile. "We sure are. Another for everyone."

She looked at the table, then scribbled notes on her pad. She pointed at Jase's glass. "You want another?"

"Please." He leaned close to her ear. "I gave Brian my card. Put the first few rounds on my tab."

"Sure." She shoved the pen back in her hair and picked up the empty glasses, setting them on her tray. "Be right back, boys."

"You driving?" Nick asked.

Jase shook his head. "I'll take a cab to Chris's. He's still out of town."

"I texted him, told him we'd be here. Didn't hear back," Brandon said.

"He's not due back for another couple of weeks."

"Bummer. I was looking forward to seeing him again." Gary nudged Carlos. "Dude, what are you lookin' at?"

THE SULTRY SUMMER air wrapped around them when they got out of the car in front of the bar. Bree stepped up onto the large, covered wood deck the bar took its name from. Small groups and couples lounged against the wood railing. Denise pulled open one of the double doors, sidestepped to allow a couple to exit, and led the way over the threshold. They stopped just inside the front door and showed their IDs to the bouncer. He gave them a once over, dragging his gaze down their bodies and back up, his expression inscrutable.

Bree looked down at her feet, then back at the bouncer. "What?" Bree asked.

He smirked and handed their IDs back. "Have a good night."

Denise tucked her ID in her back pocket. "What was that about?"

"I have no idea."

The Deck had an old barn feel to it — wide open with lots of wood and sawdust on the floor. To the right of where they stood, a small U-shaped bar was set up for patrons to watch the TVs hanging over the bar. To the left, an area with tables and chairs for the restaurant, which was closed. The back half of the building was mostly open with round, high-top tables and stools positioned along one side of the room, with another bar running along the opposite side. Large garage doors opened onto the deck at the back of the building, and a large fenced-in courtyard made the building appear even larger.

"Front bar or back bar?" Denise asked.

Bree glanced to her right. Almost every stool was occupied. "Let's go to the back bar."

Bree threaded her way through the throng of denim- and leather-clad bodies. Every few steps, she shook a foot to dislodge the sawdust that had worked its way between the soles of her feet and thin flip-flops.

Denise leaned close to her ear to be heard over the loud rock music. "We seem to have missed the memo on the dress code."

"You mean you don't subscribe to the Ladies of Leather newsletter?" Bree asked over her shoulder.

"Just imagine how many cows had to die to make all the leather these people are wearing. We are way underdressed."

"Better than being overdressed, I think."

"Probably."

Bree stopped short, causing Denise to run into her.

Holy hotness, Batman. "Oh my god. I just creamed my panties." Bree nudged Denise and tilted her head in the direction she was looking.

"Sweet, merciful Jesus, that man is a walking orgasm. How tall do you think he is?"

Bree's eyes traveled down the well-muscled expanse of chest to lean hips, slouchy jeans, and scuffed boots. "I don't know...six-three? Six-four, maybe?"

"You could wear heels and not have to worry about bending over to kiss him."

"I'm pretty sure that's one of the reasons I was going to break up with Chad. All my heels are four inches."

"Just like Chad," Denise said.

"Erect Chad." Bree tore her gaze away from the walking orgasm. They stared at each other a moment and burst out laughing.

"Oh my god, we crack me up." Denise wiped at the tears in her eyes.

Bree grabbed Denise's hand. "Come on, let's get a drink."

"You're buying, just so you know."

"How am I buying? I'm the one who has to buy a new mattress," Bree asked.

"One, you're loaded. Two, because you dragged us out looking like shite, but I will concede your point. First round is on me."

"How very gracious of you," Bree replied.

CARLOS NODDED TOWARD THE DOOR. "Check it."

Two women stood toward the front of the bar, heads thrown back, laughing and holding onto each other. They stood out in their causal clothes as if they'd given little thought to their appearance. The redhead caught his attention. Her smile sparkled, full of joy. Full of life. They wove through the crowd close to the bar. When they reached it, she hiked up a leg and rested her foot on the bar close to the floor. He caught a glimpse of long legs and nicely rounded ass before someone stepped in the way.

The desire that'd been lacking earlier made itself known. Nope. Nothing wrong with him at all.

Evan let out a low wolf-whistle. "Damn. Don't see chicks like that in here. I call dibs."

"The fuck you do." Jase put his glass down hard, setting off for the bar.

THEY BELLIED up to the bar and Denise raised her hand, credit card held between her fingers.

The bartender leaned over the bar, closing the distance. "Ladies. What can I do you for tonight?"

"Two vodka cranberries with a lime, please," Denise said.

"Sure thing." He winked and pushed away from the edge.

"He's cute," Bree said.

"And flirty."

"I'm sure it helps with the tips."

"I've got a tip for him." Denise wiggled her eyebrows.

"I'm sure he's got a tip for you too. Just the tip, if you know what I mean."

"Nice." Denise held up her hand and Bree high-fived her. "Thank god your mind is as dirty as mine."

The cute bartender returned with their drinks.

"Put it on my tab, Brian," a deep voice said.

The hair on the back of her neck stood on end and shivers raced down her spine. *Please be the walking orgasm.* She couldn't get that lucky.

The bartender nodded. "Sure thing, Jase."

Bree and Denise made wide eyes at each other as they grabbed their glasses and turned to—. She could get that lucky. A well-defined chest and biceps straining the fabric of a faded blue t-shirt greeted them. Her gaze drifted up, and up, over a short, trim beard surrounding full lips, past a slightly crooked nose, straight into the hazel eyes of the walking orgasm.

Wow. He's even better looking up close.

Bree took a sip of her drink and imagined running her hands through his dark, curly hair.

"Ladies. Haven't seen you here before."

Bree choked on her drink. *Wrong pipe.* "Really," she strained through the burn. "You're going with 'come here often?'"

The sex god smiled. "Well, that wasn't my intention, but if it works..."

Holy hell, that smile. She shifted her weight in an effort to ease the sudden throb between her legs.

"I'm Jase," he said. "Are you meeting someone here or is it just the two of you?" He looked directly at Bree, a flirtatious smile teasing at his mouth.

What was the question? She'd been staring at his mouth. Saw it move. Imagined sucking on that full bottom lip.

"Just us," Denise said. "Spur of the moment decision. As you can see, we weren't aware of the dress code."

"Dress code?" Jase turned his attention to Denise.

Bree rolled a shoulder, pulling out of the lust fog clouding her mind. "I think she's talking about the fact that we aren't wearing any leather." She waved a hand. "Inside joke."

"Oh yeah. Bikers like their leather. Since you're not meeting anyone tonight, would you like to join my friends and me?"

Bree glanced at Denise, who gave a little shrug. "Sure, why not?"

"I'm Bree, by the way. This is Denise." Bree indicated to Denise with her drink.

"Nice to meet you. Follow me." He took Bree's free hand and led them toward the group of guys he had been standing with when they first noticed him. Bree turned to Denise and mouthed *oh my god* as he led them to a couple of tables set against the far wall. All the guys were good-looking, well-built, and hovering around the six-foot-tall range. It was like a real-life hot-guy calendar shoot — just with more clothes. Jase introduced Bree and Denise to the guys standing around the two tables.

"This a normal Friday night for you guys?" Denise asked.

Nate leaned a tattooed arm against the table, turning full to Denise. "Brandon's celebrating separating from the Army."

Gary leaned around him. "We're here most Fridays."

Bree bit her lip, watching the subtle posturing as the two guys fought for Denise's attention. This should be interesting. A hand slid across the small of her back and a hot body stepped close to her side. The top of her head barely reached his chin. Used to being the same height as, if not taller than, most men, standing next to Jase she felt...dainty.

"Do you want another drink?" he asked.

She looked at her almost empty glass. "Think I'll switch to beer. We've already had a few." She peeked up at him through her lashes. Nervousness fluttered in her belly.

Jeez, he's hot.

When was the last time a guy had flirted with her? Really flirted with her, not just came on to her?

The waitress came by and Jase added a beer to the order.

"You seriously never heard of Papa's Pizza?" Denise's question caught her attention.

"What about Papa's Pizza?" she asked.

Denise pointed a finger between two of the guys. "They were at Victory around the same time we were."

"Really?"

"The only pizza place was the crappy one at the exchange. You sure it was on Camp Victory?" Gary asked.

"Swear." Denise raised her hand, palm out. "We went every Sunday for lunch. Hand-tossed, deep dish."

"Where on Victory?" Brandon challenged her.

Jase's hand brushed against the side of her neck, pushing a strand of hair off her shoulder, and she lost interest in conversation again. Tingles raced along her skin, chasing after his fingers. It was becoming a familiar sensation. He'd found little ways to touch her since he took her hand at the bar. A hand smoothing along the curve of her hip. Leaning down to speak softly in her ear. Every simple touch felt like a brand on her skin. It left her hot. Needy.

"You're kidding," Evan said.

Bree pulled her attention back to the group. "What's up?"

"The brawl between the third country nationals behind the chow hall," Denise explained.

"Oh yeah," Bree said. "It was like something out of a movie. Pans, knives, chains, metal pipes. All that was missing was Michael Jackson's Beat It playing in the background."

"Seriously?" Jase said.

"Yup. Took security forces close to an hour to break it up," Denise said. "Two guys ended up dying."

Bree set her glass on the table. "Excuse me. Need to use the facilities. You need to go?" she asked Denise.

"I'm good. Unless you need me to guide the way."

"Big neon sign. Think I can find it."

A blonde in a cleavage-baring halter top left the bathroom as she pushed open the door. She gave Bree a once over and sneered.

Bitch, please.

She washed her hands and tucked a strand of hair behind her ear. Her cheeks were flushed and her eyes were bright. It could've been the alcohol, but more likely it was the sensual foreplay that had been going on since Jase had pulled her away from the bar. She tended to shy away from being touched by strangers. Hugging and touching was reserved for friends and family, but something about Jase's touch had every nerve in her body singing. Every brush of his fingers had sent shivers down her spine and raised goosebumps on her skin. She'd soaked it up. When was the last time a simple touch had caused desire to coil low in her belly? *Not since before Afghanistan.*

Bree shook that thought away. Tonight was not the night for those thoughts.

She left the restroom after drying her hands. Jase caught her in the hall leading back to the bar. He backed her against the wall and braced his forearms slightly above her head, caging her in but holding himself away from her. He leaned down and brushed his lips gently against hers, then stopped.

Was he asking permission? Bree grasped his hips and hooked her middle fingers in the belt loops of his jeans. She bit the corner of her lip.

"You've been biting your lip all night, Bree. It's my turn." Bree's gaze darted from his mouth to his desire-filled eyes, just before his tongue laved the center of her bottom lip. She pulled her fingers out of Jase's belt loops and stepped closer. She slid one arm around his back and the other around his head, her fingers threading through his hair. Jase wrapped his arms around her, bending at the knees and pulling her up onto her toes. He pushed her against the wall, fitting their bodies so close together Bree could feel the hard press of his cock against her abdomen. The kiss quickly turned carnal, tongues dancing together in an intimate tango as their breathing became heavy. Had she ever been kissed with that much heat...that much passion...that much desire?

The clearing of a throat broke the spell. Jase pulled away

slowly, sucking on her bottom lip as he lifted his head. They stared at each other a moment before turning their heads to see Denise standing a couple of feet away trying to look anywhere but directly at them.

"Hey, sweetie." Bree pushed at Jase trying to create some space between them. He was reluctant to let go, but he released the tight hold he had on her.

"Sorry to interrupt. Got a sec?"

"Sure." Bree looked at Jase. "I'll meet you back at the table?"

Jase stared, still holding the back of her neck. "Yeah."

He bent down and gave her a quick, hard kiss before nodding to Denise and leaving them in the hall.

"Holy hell, that was hot and I wasn't even the one being kissed," Denise said. "I'm not sure if I should high-five you or hose you down."

"No need. My underwear is already soaked." Bree fanned her face with her hands. "Am I red? I feel flushed. Am I flushed?"

"You're fine, gorgeous as ever." Denise reassured her. "I'm going to head out."

"Oh, okay. Let me go tell Jase we're leaving." She hadn't given any thought to what was going to happen at the end of the night. Maybe she could— No. She was not going to be a crappy friend.

Denise shook her head. "Oh, no. No, no, no. You're going home with the walking orgasm. I wouldn't be any kind of battle buddy if I dragged you out of here because I'm beat and have to get up early in the morning."

"Our deal is we come together, we leave together."

"Not tonight it's not. Tonight it's you go home with the hot guy and make up for all the boring sex you've had for the last year."

Bree bit her lower lip as she struggled with her indecision. She really wanted to go home with Jase. That kiss. She felt the tips of her ears growing warm as she remembered it. With Chad, kissing had become...perfunctory. If that kiss with Jase was anything to go by, the sex would be phenomenal.

"Are you sure?" she asked.

"Honey, I'm sure. You two looked like you were going to go at it against the wall in front of the entire bar."

"It wasn't that bad."

"Uh, yeah it was. And again, it was hot."

"Whatever." She looped her arm through Denise's and headed back to the bar. "Let me make sure Jase is good with giving me a ride home before you leave."

Denise stopped walking, pulling Bree to halt.

"What?" Bree asked.

Denise tilted her head and gave Bree a look. "You're kidding, right?"

"What? I don't want to be presumptuous."

Denise rolled her eyes and walked straight over to Jase. "I'm leaving. Bree's not. You fuck with her and I will hunt you down, chop you up in my meat grinder, and feed you to my dogs. The cops will have to dig through their shit to identify your DNA. We good?"

Jase gave her a bemused look. "Yeah, we're good."

"Good." Denise turned to Bree and gave her a big hug. "Do everything I would do if I had a guy like that looking at me the way he's looking at you," she whispered.

Bree smiled and whispered, "Love your face."

"Love yours more."

Bree watched Denise make her way to the door.

Jase gave her a level look when she turned back to him. "You want to get out of here?"

"Yes."

"Good."

*J*ase grabbed her hand and led her to the front doors, giving head nods to his friends as they left. Outside they walked straight to a taxi parked in front of the bar.

"That's fortuitous," Bree said.

Jase gave her a lopsided grin as he opened the back passenger side door. "I called him while you were talking to your girl."

"Now who's being presumptuous?" Bree mumbled as she slid into the back seat.

"What's that?"

"Not important."

Jase gave the driver an address as he slipped in next to Bree. He slammed the door closed and looked at Bree with a raised eyebrow.

"What?" Bree tugged on the material of her t-shirt before tucking a strand of hair behind her ear.

"Too far away, darlin'." He hooked his arm behind her waist and pulled her across the seat until she almost sat in his lap. He ran his other hand under her hair at the nape of her neck, grabbing a handful as he brought his mouth to hers. The kiss picked up where it left off in the bar. His tongue invaded her mouth. His teeth nipped at her bottom lip. She moaned into his mouth, trying to get as close as the confined space of the backseat would allow. Finding the edge of his t-shirt, she ran her hand up the wide expanse of his back. Hard muscles under smooth skin. Her fingers curled in, nails biting. He answered with a groan and lifted her leg over his. The kiss lasted an eternity and was over in an instant.

The driver cleared his throat. "We're here."

Bree pulled back with a small gasp and tried to catch her breath. She'd forgotten where they were. She met Jase's gaze and licked her lips. He looked at her mouth before pulling his wallet out of his back pocket and paying the driver. He took Bree's hand and opened the door, pulling her out behind him.

"Thank you," Bree said to the driver on her way out of the car.

Jase led her to the front door of a suburban house that looked like every other house on the street. He unlocked the door and threw his keys on the low table to the right of the door. Bree glanced around the small living room as Jase shut the door. She kicked off her flip-flops out of habit and dropped her keys on the table.

"Do you…" She gasped as Jase placed his hands on the outsides of her upper thighs, lifted her and held her against the wall next to the door, forcing her to grab onto his shoulders for balance.

"Wrap your legs around me," he said.

She did and felt his hands slide under the cuff of her shorts, digging his fingers in the fleshy part of her ass.

Bree melded her lips with his in an open-mouth kiss that left her breathless. There was a moment of weightlessness when she come away from the door as Jase pushed off and carried her down a short hall to a bedroom. She let out a small scream when Jase all but dropped her on the bed. The laugh that followed was cut off when Jase found her mouth again. She groaned when he rubbed his erection against the junction of her thighs. The friction sent pulses down her legs. She hooked a knee over his hip, seeking even more contact. His hands found the hem of her shirt.

She lifted her arms over her head and he pulled it off. He pressed his mouth to her neck. His fingers hooked into the straps of her bra. A quick tug exposed her breasts. He tore his mouth away from hers and sucked on her nipple as he fumbled with the back of her bra.

"Front clasp," she gasped.

"Do it." He moved his mouth to her other breast.

Bree released the clasp of her bra and let it fall open on the bed. She reached for his shirt, helping Jase pull it up over his head. As soon as he was free of it, he returned his attention to her nipples. Bree arched her back and ran her hands over his well-defined shoulders and upper back, reaching for any inch of skin she could find. She grabbed fistfuls of his hair and hissed through her teeth as he sucked painfully at her nipple.

"Too much?" he asked as he gazed up at her.

"A little."

"I'll ease up. A little." He laved her sore nipple with his tongue and she moaned at the sensation. She'd never gone for nipple play before, but his mouth and tongue were magic. He switched back to the other side, scraping his teeth across her sensitive skin. Bree let out another moan as the tingling in her nipples traveled down to her already throbbing clit. She dug her nails into his shoulders and undulated her hips trying to get more friction where she really wanted it.

"Patience. I'll get there." He moved his mouth down her stomach, leaving a trail of hot fire in his wake as his hands found the button of her shorts.

"Screw patience." Bree continued to move her hips rhythmically.

Jase chuckled. "I've wanted these shorts off since you crawled into the cab." He unzipped her shorts and pulled them down her hips and thighs, taking her panties with them. Bree kicked her legs free as soon as he gave her room. He wedged his shoulders between her thighs, forcing her legs apart. His hot breath blew across her clit before he flicked the tip of it with his tongue.

"Seriously?" Bree demanded in frustration. "I want to come."

"Oh, you will. You're going to come all over my face. Then you're going to come all over my cock as I bury it deep inside this pretty pussy."

"Oh my god." She lifted her head to look down her body at him. Her core clenched at the sight of his head buried between her legs. "Are you going to fuck me or talk me to death?"

Jase looked up at her from his position between her thighs. "I'm going to find something more useful for that dirty mouth to do, you keep it up." She watched as he extended his tongue, again barely touching the tip of her clit, never taking his gaze off her. Bree dropped her head back and rocked her hips, forcing the contact she wanted. Apparently, it was exactly what Jase wanted as well. He finally covered her sensitized pussy, flicking and circling his tongue around her clit. His short beard tickled the soft skin of her inner thighs, adding to the sensation of his mouth and tongue. Bree rode Jase's face as she felt her orgasm gathering in her core.

"Oh god, right there, please don't stop. I'm gonna come."

She bucked when Jase pushed two fingers into her, rotating them around and hooking them slightly as he retreated. Bree's orgasm careened through her. She grabbed a handful of Jase's hair and forced his mouth even closer. The other hand flew above her head using the wall to give her the leverage she needed. She couldn't control her body's response. Primal need had her rolling her hips. Her entire body shuddered when she felt his mouth leave her with one last, long lick.

Jase continued to fuck her with his fingers, drawing out her orgasm. Through hooded eyes, she saw him rip a condom wrapper with his teeth. Somehow he managed to sheath his cock before removing his fingers. Talk about talented. He lined up the head of his cock with her core and thrust forward in one hard move. He stretched and filled her with his thickness. She sucked in a quick breath. It was almost painful. If she hadn't already come, been so wet, it might have hurt. Instead it just felt exquisite.

"Shit, you're tight. And wet," he ground out. "I can feel you pulsing around me. I need you to quit doing that, darlin' or I'm not going to last very long."

Bree was still breathing heavy. His thick cock entering her, stretching her, had set off a mini orgasm. She would have sworn the pulsing was him. "I don't have any control over it at the moment since I think I'm still coming."

"Well, let's see if we can make sure you're coming." Jase rose up and sat back on his heels, pulling Bree's legs over his thighs as he spread his knees slightly. Bree gasped at the angle. He grabbed her hips, retreated and thrust, hitting deep. Deeper than Bree had ever felt. Long, hard strokes; pulling almost all the way out before smoothly driving all the way back in.

"Fuck, darlin', you're so fucking hot spread out like this. I'm not going to last long. Play with your tits. Pinch your nipples; make them hard." Bree tugged at her nipples. "Yeah, just like that." It was almost too much. She hovered at the brink of another orgasm. Again? Could she even?

"I'm close," he warned. "I want you to come again." Jase placed a thumb on the top of Bree's clit, rubbing the nerve cluster of the hood.

"Oh shit." Fingers dug into his thighs, using them to pull herself even harder on Jase's cock as he drove into her. She threw back her head and let out a shout as her second full orgasm ripped through her. Her fingers and lips tingled, like he had zapped her with a bolt of electricity.

Jase shifted over her, bracing his hands on either side of her. Bree wrapped her legs high up on his hips. He growled as he thrust hard, no longer controlling the pace or speed of his movements. One final thrust and he shouted, burying himself deep. He collapsed forward, resting his head in the crook of her neck as his body shuddered. His hot mouth grazed the sensitive skin below her ear. Zaps of electricity continued to pulse through her body, keeping time with her heartbeat. Or his throbbing erection, she wasn't sure which. Bree ran her hands through his hair, unable to even open her eyes.

All too soon, Jase lifted his head to look at Bree. "Need to get rid of the condom, babe."

"Mmkay," Bree mumbled. She moaned a little when he pulled out. He licked the valley between her breasts and pushed himself off the bed. She gave a small groan, rolled to her side, and fluffed the pillow under her head. She was almost asleep when she felt Jase get back in the bed and pull her close.

THE DULL THROB in her skull woke her. She burrowed her head further into her pillow. Why were her sheets so scratchy? She cracked open an eye, then lifted her aching head to stare at the plain blue fabric under her face. These were not her sheets. She turned her head and saw Jase's muscular, naked body sprawled on his stomach next to her.

The previous night came rushing back to her. *Shit. This is going to be awkward.* When was the last time she'd had a one-night stand? Crap, she'd still been an airman on her first tour in the Air Force. She peeked at her watch–a little after six in the morning. *Stupid internal alarm clock, it's the weekend.*

She glanced at Jase again. He really was mouthwatering. His arms were tucked under the pillow and his head turned away from her. The sheet rested in the small of his back, exposing the wide expanse of his back and the tattoos covering it. Even asleep, he was ripped. A slight variation in the tan line on his arms and neck suggested he spent a lot of time outdoors, with and without a shirt. Did he say what he did last night? She couldn't remember. The lust fog must have been really thick.

She hovered a finger over a quote tattooed on the left side of his ribs. *For he today that sheds his blood with me shall be my brother.* She smiled. Shakespeare. Henry V. The top and edge of a battlefield cross, a rifle set in a pair of combat boots topped with a helmet, was visible on his left shoulder. She bit her lip. She'd seen that one too many times in real life. His entire upper back was covered with a large gray-and-black mural depicting scenes from a modern-day battle. Beautiful, almost photo quality. She frowned as she ran her finger along a two-inch jagged scar just under the mural.

Jase stirred slightly, adjusted his head on the pillow and let out a small sigh. She jerked her hand back and held her breath. She shifted on the bed, sliding toward the edge and hopefully to her clothes. Jase had thrown them all over his head after he'd gotten them off her. She clenched her thighs together when she remembered Jase stripping her. Maybe she should stick around and see if he was up for another round.

No, that would lead to the awkward stage of pretending what happened wasn't a one-nighter. Better to go while he was still asleep and avoid the whole cliché.

Bree gathered her clothes from the floor and got dressed. She checked her shorts pocket where she found her debit card and phone still in the back pocket. She pulled up a taxi app and ordered a pickup. She sent a silent thanks to the inventor of the GPS because she had no idea where she was. She eased the bedroom door open and tiptoed down the short hall into the living room. Her flip-flops and keys were still where she'd left them.

"Don't do it." A deep voice came from the couch.

Bree jumped, barely holding back a small scream.

"Son of a biscuit," she hissed. She glanced over to see a guy stretched out on the couch, covered by a plaid blanket, his eyes closed. He looked familiar. Was he at the bar last night? He hadn't been with their group, she knew that much.

"Don't do what?" she whispered.

"Don't take off without waking him up and telling him you're going."

"He's asleep and I have to get to work."

"He's not that asleep, believe me. He's not going to be happy when he wakes up and finds you snuck out." He opened his eyes and looked at her. "Wake him up, he'll drive you home."

"He doesn't have a car."

The guy centered his head back on the pillow and closed his eyes. "I drove his truck back last night. Wake him up."

"I honestly don't have time to wait. I've already called a cab to come get me."

"Don't say I didn't warn you."

What? Bree scrunched her face up in his general direction. "Okay. You warned me. Later."

"Yup."

Bree walked around the corner and waited for the taxi just in case Jase woke up and came out after her. She had a few more hours before she needed to be at the retirement community where she volunteered. Maybe she'd be able to get a couple more hours of sleep before starting her day. She flagged down the taxi coming down the street.

She gave the driver her address and leaned her head against the head rest. Staring out the window, not seeing the scenery flashing by, she thought about last night. The way Jase had kissed her. Touched her. The way she had responded. She chewed the cuticle of her thumb. She could have at least left him her number. Maybe she should... She looked out the rear window. No. It's better this way. Too bad, really, because Jase was someone she could get used to.

CHAPTER 4

The faint smell of jasmine and vanilla lingered on the sheets, reminding Jase of the woman in bed with him. The scent triggered his morning wood, all too happy to respond. He adjusted his hips and rolled to his side. The hand he ran across the sheets kept going, finding nothing but an empty bed. His eyes popped open.

She must be in the bathroom. If her mouth was as dry as his, she probably needed some water. He rolled to his back and folded the pillow under his head. He'd give her a few minutes, but he had plans for her luscious body. Her laughter echoed in his head, sending another rush of blood to his hard-on. He stroked his cock, trying to relieve some of the pressure. Damn, this woman had him wound up. He hadn't brought a chick home in more than year. The couple of women he'd dated in that time hadn't lasted more than a few months at most. Even then, he'd never woken up aching for them. Hell, he'd never woken up with them.

But Bree…every asshole in that bar had eye-fucked her and her friend as soon as they hit the floor. Hard to miss them, dressed in cut-offs and t-shirts. Not the usual biker babes and Special Forces groupies that hung around The Deck, looking for a quick thrill. That kiss in the hall had made him feel something for the first time in a long time. He'd barely refrained from fucking her in the taxi. The only thing that stopped him was the audience. If he'd been sober enough to drive, he probably wouldn't have gotten further than the cab of his truck.

That had been one of the hardest orgasms he'd ever had. Her long auburn hair, tangled from his hands, had been spread out on the bed, and he'd been ready to go again. He groaned remembering how she tasted coming in his mouth.

What the hell was taking her so long?

He got out of bed, pulled on his boxers, and headed down the hall past the dark, empty bathroom.

Where is she?

Jase walked into the dim living room. Her shoes and keys were gone.

"What the fuck?"

"She bailed, dude," Chris said as he sat up on the couch, digging the heels of his hands into his eyes before running his hands back and forth over his head. "She left about an hour ago."

"You didn't try to stop her?"

"Short of tackling her and hog-tying her until you woke up, what did you want me to do?"

"Wake my ass up."

"Why were you asleep in the first place? Fine piece of ass in my bed, I wouldn't have been sleeping."

"Don't call her a piece of ass. Your place was closer."

"Didn't want to wait the half hour drive to your place?"

"No."

"Figured. Wash my sheets." He got up and headed to the kitchen.

"Yeah, sure. I thought you were going to be gone for another week." Jase collapsed on the recliner.

"Got a break. Wrapped it up early."

"Get the bad guys?"

"Always."

Jase stared up at the ceiling fan as it spun in a slow, hypnotic circle. "Fuck. I need to go get my truck."

"Had one of the guys drop me at the bar. Brandon said you took a cab, so I grabbed your truck."

"'Preciate it."

Chris paused in the process of scooping grounds into the coffee maker. "Did you get her number?"

"Fuck. No." Jase put both hands over his face, scrubbing his beard and running them up into his hair.

"Did you get her name?"

Jase dropped his hands to the arms of the recliner and glared. "Yes, jackass, I got her name."

"Her whole name?" Chris asked.

If Chris weren't such a good friend, he'd knock that shit-eating grin off his face. "She mentioned it at one point."

"But you don't remember it." Chris started to laugh. "You're screwed, then."

"I'll call Tim, see if he can do anything."

"You're really going to call your brother to track down a chick? Must have been one sweet pussy."

"I don't think I've ever blown my load that hard in my life." He adjusted his shorts as his body responded to his memory. "And don't refer to her as pussy again."

"I said sweet pussy."

Jase growled.

"Chill, dude, I'm just giving you shit. Must have been one hell of a ride though, to have you this strung out over a chick leaving the morning after. Hasn't been your MO in a while, bringing home a woman you just met in a bar." He reached into the fridge to grab some eggs before turning back to Jase.

"Shit, I don't know what the hell it was. It was just...different. The way she handled herself last night. You know how we can be, especially when we're drinking. Loud and obnoxious."

"You mean drunken jackasses."

"Yeah, basically. She and her friend didn't blink. Just rolled with the punches. She didn't take anyone's shit." Jase trailed off as he rested his head against the back of the chair. "Christ, I sound like a chick."

"Keep it up and I'll have to confiscate your man card," Chris said, pointing a spatula at him. "You really want to find her?"

"Dude, I just said I was willing to call my brother and deal with the ration of shit he's going to give me because I'm asking for a favor. Yeah, I want to find her."

"Well, I might be able to help you."

"How's that?" Jase pushed out of the chair to grab a cup of coffee.

"She seemed familiar."

Jase closed the cabinet door hard. "Familiar how?"

"I haven't slept with her, if that's what you're thinking. She looked familiar. Maybe on a deployment? It'll come to me."

Jase gave him a small head nod.

"You need help with class today or are you going home to sulk and pine over your girl?" Chris asked.

"Asshole."

Chris smirked. "Is that a yes?"

"Yes."

"Just checking. You want some eggs?"

"Sure," Jase headed back to the bedroom. "I'm gonna grab a shower."

"Put my sheets in the wash, fucker," Chris called out at Jase's back.

JASE STACKED the hay bales used behind the targets on his 10-acre property near Haven Springs, twenty miles south of Raleigh, North Carolina.

"We're going to have an extra guy today," he told Chris.

"Last minute addition?"

"Yeah. One of the guys already signed up called and asked if he could bring his buddy along."

"You good with that? Has he been vetted yet?"

Jase sighed. "No. He said he's turned in all the paperwork and he's just waiting on the shrink to sign off on it. We're using blunt tips today anyway."

"Still bleed like a motherfucker if a guy manages to shoot you with an arrow," Chris said.

"I know, but I can't turn a guy away."

Chris gave a curt chin lift. "Yeah."

They worked together without saying anything more. Jase appreciated Chris's willingness to help him out with the archery classes. Most of the other volunteers were willing to help on the trips because they got to go out and hunt or fish, but they didn't like the mundane part of the business. Maybe if his funding came through he'd be able to actually hire some guys to help out on a regular basis.

"Trucks are coming up the drive," Chris said.

Jase and Chris introduced themselves to each guy as they arrived. Ryan introduced himself as the extra.

"You understand you're going to have to share equipment with your friend, right? I usually limit beginner classes to six."

"That's no problem. And I really appreciate you working me in. The doc at the VA said my paperwork should be faxed to your office no later than Wednesday."

"I'll keep an eye out for it."

They walked over to the group and Jase began his introduction. "Okay, let's get started. Welcome to V.E.T. Adventures. This is an introduction to using a hunting bow, so when you are able to go on a hunting trip, you'll actually bag a kill. Chris is going to help me demonstrate the basics: stance, proper posture, aiming, and release. Everyone here went through Combat Arms Training so it should all be familiar. Are there any questions before we begin?"

"Why a bow and not a rifle?" Robert, one of the students, asked.

"Really it comes down to preference. I think a bow requires more skill, more patience, and more concentration. Much harder to bring down a deer with an arrow than it is with a rifle. Anything else?"

When no one responded, Jase took them over to the small tables set up about eighty feet from the targets. He walked them through the different parts of the bow before he had Chris demonstrate the proper stance.

Jase stood close behind him to adjust his support arm. "Hey now, you just got you some last night," Chris said.

"Shut it, asshole."

The group spent the next hour trying to hit the circle targets pinned to the hale bales. Jase kept an eye out for when guys became frustrated. One guy, a below-the-knee amputee, seemed to be having the hardest time.

"Hey, what's your name again?" Jase asked.

"Rob." He dropped his arms with the bow and arrow still gripped tightly in his hands.

"Okay Rob, tell me what's throwing you."

"Everything. My balance is off and it's throwing everything else off."

"How long have you had your prosthetic?" Jase asked. He didn't mince words. Ignoring the ugly baby didn't make it less ugly.

"I got fitted about a month ago," Rob said.

"And how long did it take you to learn to walk after you healed up?"

"Shit, I was in rehab for eighteen months."

"Right. It took you eighteen months to learn how to walk again, so you're not going to learn archery in an hour. It's a new skill. It's going to take practice, just like anything else. Don't get frustrated. You get frustrated and it's just going to mess you up even more. What service were you in?"

"Marines."

"Okay, so this should sound familiar. Slow is smooth, smooth is fast."

Rob smirked. "Yeah, it's familiar."

"Same principle. Focus. Find your balance. Take your time."

Rob closed his eyes, took a deep breath and let it out. Jase stepped back to give him room. Rob shifted his weight between his prosthetic and his leg, finding his center of gravity. He raised his arms and pulled back on the string. Jase could see the moment, on the fall of Rob's exhale, when he released the arrow. It flew forward and landed on the outer ring of the target with a dull *thunk*.

He clapped Rob on the shoulder. "Good job, man."

"Thanks." Rob picked up another arrow, a small smile on his face. Jase walked down the line, leaving Rob to his victory. Small as it may be, for a lot of guys those small victories were all that kept them going some days.

By the end of the class, each student was hitting the target four out of five times. It wasn't until they were putting the equipment away that he noticed the extra guy, Ryan, hadn't been using an arm guard.

Jase grabbed Ryan's wrist and turned it to look at his forearm, noticing the extensive scars that ran from the back of his hand all the way up to his bicep. "Man, your arm is going to be black tomorrow. It's already bruising. Why didn't you say anything?"

Ryan ran his fingers over his forearm as Jase released his wrist. "I don't have a lot of feeling from my elbow to my wrist because of the scarring. I honestly didn't know it was happening."

"Sorry, man. I would have fixed something up if I had known."

"Really, it's no problem. Although my physical therapist is probably going to ream me a new one tomorrow."

"He a dick?" Jase asked.

Ryan laughed. "It's a she and she's gorgeous. Usually nice as can be, but I've seen her lay into guys before when they weren't sticking to their program. She scares me a little. She used to deploy with Special Ops guys and doesn't put up with anyone's bullshit."

Jase smiled. "Well, if she gives you too much shit, give her my number and I'll take the brunt of it for you."

"Ha! Don't think I won't. I wasn't kidding when I said she scares me."

After the students left, Jase and Chris returned the hay bales to the metal shed, stacked the equipment on the racks, and locked everything up. Chris took off with a wave to go back to his place, and Jase headed to his house on the other side of the property.

Jase turned off the ignition and sat in his truck. Even while running the class, he couldn't get Bree out of his head. Every breeze seemed to carry a hint of her perfume, the only trace she'd left behind. He tapped his phone against his thigh, thinking about calling his brother, a cop on the Haven Springs police force. He felt kind of stupid doing it. He could just imagine how that conversation would go. *Hey, man can you put out an APB for a woman I took home last night? I only got her first name.* His brother would never let him live that down. Plus, what could Jase really tell him? He knew her name, knew it was short for Brianna. Knew she had long, red hair that felt like silk running through his fingers. Knew her sapphire-blue eyes sparkled when she laughed and got dark when she was turned on.

He hit the steering wheel. *Fuck.* He couldn't believe she had just taken off that morning. He yanked the keys out of the ignition and slammed out of his truck. He had nothing to give his brother. Nothing.

CHAPTER 5

*B*ree let out a small moan, rolling her hips. She whimpered, trying to reach fulfillment. The alarm sounded and her eyes opened abruptly. Her arousal faded along with the erotic dream teasing the edges of her subconscious.

Dammit!

She slapped the snooze button and groaned. The unfulfilled orgasm lingered, leaving her edgy, frustrated, and downright grumpy. She'd dreamed of Jase every night for the past week, always waking just before climax. She couldn't get him out of her mind. To make matters worse, the memory of his hot mouth trailing down her body would suddenly burst into her mind and she would get hot and flushed. Patients saw her reddened cheeks and asked her if she was feeling well. She thought about driving by his house, but she didn't want to be that girl. How embarrassing would it be if she showed up and he didn't remember? Or had another girl there?

Her phone binged on her nightstand. She glared at the offending device. Chad had texted every morning since she'd kicked him out. *I'm sorry. Please forgive me. I didn't mean to hurt you.*

I miss you. She deleted the text without reading it. Day late and a dollar short, asshat.

With a groan she got out of bed and got ready for work. An hour later she strolled into the physical therapy clinic.

Her first patient of the day was already in the waiting room.

"Morning, Ryan. I'll be with you in a few minutes."

"No worries, Doc. Feel free to delay the abuse as long as you need," he replied with a grin.

Bree rolled her eyes at his exaggeration. "Don't be such a baby."

She stored her bag in the locker and logged on to her computer to see if there were any changes to her schedule. One of her afternoon appointments had cancelled, but a call-in had quickly taken the spot. She sighed and adjusted her neck. There were just too many patients and not enough providers.

She pulled up Ryan's record to review. Extensive injuries to his left side during an Improvised Explosive Device attack in Iraq had left his arm nearly mutilated. The surgeons had managed to save it, but the damage to the underlying muscle and tissue limited his range of motion. Bree read her notes from his session two weeks ago–his treatment plan was right on track.

She picked up her phone and dialed her assistant's extension. "Cindy, can you bring Ryan back?"

"Sure, Dr. Marks."

"Thanks." She hung up the receiver and covered the table with a new sheet.

"Hey, Ryan. You know the drill."

"You know, Doc, just once it'd be nice if you had me lie down for a reason other than to torture me."

Bree patted Ryan on the head. "Oh. That's sweet you think you could handle me."

Ryan laughed.

"Let's see if we can break up some of this scar tissue and increase your range of motion." She turned his arm over, palm up.

"What the hell is this?" She brushed her thumb over the black and purple bruise covering most of the inside of his forearm.

"Oh, that. Archery."

"*Oh, that,*" she repeated. "I need more detail. I can't work on you with this kind of bruising."

"Why? It's not like I can feel it."

Bree sighed in exasperation. "You might not be able to feel it because of the nerve damage, but what I do still affects the underlying muscle and fascia. This is a lot of bruising, which means a lot of trauma happened to the area. What were you doing?"

Ryan sat up. "A buddy of mine invited me to go to an archery class for wounded veterans. It's part of a prep course to go on a bow-hunting trip. I was a last-minute addition, so they didn't have enough arm guards for everyone. The guy who was running the training reamed me a new one, if it makes you feel better."

Bree looked at him for a moment. She could yell at him for being careless, but that would only shut him down. She depended on communication with her patients to determine their pain level and appropriate treatment. And she didn't want to discourage him from doing something he enjoyed. "Did you like it?"

"Shooting with a bow? Yeah, it was cool. Different than shooting a rifle, you know? Took a lot more concentration."

"Were you able to straighten your arm all the way or did you have to compensate somehow?"

"I couldn't straighten it all the way. I kind of had to cock my elbow and lock the muscles around it to hold the bow steady. It was awkward."

Bree gave Ryan a small nod. "Lay back down; I'll go easy on you today."

"Thanks. Sorry, Doc. I even told the guy you were going to yell at me when you saw it."

"Are you going on a trip soon?"

"I'm not sure. My buddy's going in two weeks or so. The trips are Thursday through Sunday, so I have to see if I can get off work."

"What's the name of the company?"

"Vet Adventures. They organize hunting, fishing, and camping trips. One of the guys running it said their main goal is to get guys back out and be part of a team again, even if it's just a few days."

"It sounds like a good program." Her thumb palpated the inside of his elbow, searching out knotted tissue.

He winced when she found an especially tender spot, but didn't react otherwise. "I think that's one of the things I miss most about the Army, you know?"

"What's that?" she asked.

He turned his head to watch her work his arm. "The camaraderie. Just being with a bunch of guys who get you. They don't ask stupid questions or want to know how many bad guys you killed. They just get it."

Bree gave Ryan a small smile. She got it. It was one of the reasons she applied only to military hospitals after she completed her degree.

At the end of his session, she handed Ryan a list of exercises to do at home to help strengthen his shoulder muscles. "Do me a favor? Be more careful next time. Ask for something to protect your arm."

"I will. Thanks, Doc. See you in two weeks."

SHE TOOK a bite of spinach salad before typing "Vet Adventures" into the internet search engine. The first link was a website for Veteran Excursion Team (V.E.T.) Adventures that listed a North Carolina address. She clicked on the link and navigated to the contact page. Grabbing her phone, she dialed the number listed. An off-hook tone sounded in her ear, as if the receiver on the other end hadn't been set in the cradle properly. She'd try again in a little while. Maybe they'd figure out that their phone was off the hook.

"Dr. Marks?" Cindy knocked on her open office door.

"I'm almost done eating. Is Mr. Barns here already?"

"The ER just called up. Mr. Barns was admitted a little while ago and when they looked him up in the system, they saw he had an appointment today."

"Did they say why he was in the ER?"

Cindy cringed a little. "He fell and broke his other hip."

Bree's face fell. "Please tell me you're kidding."

Cindy shook her head.

She tossed her fork into her almost empty plastic container. "Why doesn't anyone listen to me? I told him and his wife if he continued to overdo it, he was going to fall again."

"Also, your four o'clock had to reschedule."

If she left after her three o'clock appointment, she could probably make it to V.E.T. Adventures before they closed. She'd check their hours before she left, just to be sure.

"Block off that time slot for me, please. I'm going to run some errands this afternoon."

"Sure. Also, Chad's called four times today. He didn't leave any messages," Cindy said.

"Is he calling my line or the main line?"

"The main line."

Bree scrubbed her hands over her face. She had told him not to call her at work unless it was an emergency. He knew that. She was going to have to open a door in her wall of silence to tell him to fuck off and quit bothering her.

"Do you know if we can block numbers on the office phones?"

"I don't know. I can find out." She wrung her hands and shifted her weight. "Can I ask?"

"I caught him cheating on me."

"Oh. That's...what the hell? What a shitty thing to do. Especially to someone as nice as you."

"Thank you, I really appreciate that," Bree told her.

"I'll call IT and see if we can block numbers."

"Thanks. I'll handle it if we aren't able to, but I don't want to have to talk to him if I can avoid it."

"I understand." Cindy went back to the reception desk.

Since she had some time to spare, Bree tried to call V.E.T. Adventures again. Same busy tone. The website provided only basic information. She copied the email listed and sent a message introducing herself and requested information on the services they provided. Some of her patients would really enjoy the things this company offered. Many of them reminisced about their time in the service during their appointments. They missed the brotherhood or sisterhood of the military. If this company could give them a small sense of that again, she'd send them all the business they could handle. Hell, she'd even make a donation.

She tried to call one more time with the same results. What the hell, it was on the way home—she could just drive by this afternoon after her last appointment.

BREE PARKED in front of a nondescript shopping mall where V.E.T. Adventures occupied the corner storefront. She opened the glass door and entered the small reception area. It looked like the waiting room of a dentist's office.

An older woman with a small bouffant hairstyle looked up from her computer. "Hi, welcome to Vet Adventures. How can I help you?" she asked in a thick, North Carolinian twang.

"Um, hi. I'm Brianna Marks. I'm a physical therapist at the Wounded Warrior Unit at Fort Bragg. One of my patients mentioned this place and I was hoping to get more information, maybe set up some kind of referral system for some of the vets I work with."

"Oh honey, that's wonderful. Jason, the owner, is on a conference call right now and he has an appointment lined up right after that. Let me pull up his schedule and see when he's available."

"That would be great, thank you." Bree pulled out a business card and gave it to the woman. "I didn't catch your name."

"Oh lordy! Where are my manners? I'm Carol. I do all the scheduling and phone answering around here." She extended a well-manicured hand.

Bree smiled at Carol's Old South charm and shook her hand.

"Oh, speaking of answering phones, I think yours might be off the hook. I tried to call a couple of times, but got that weird busy signal."

Carol glanced at the phone on her desk and pushed on the handset. "Well, darn it. How long has it been like that? No wonder it's been so quiet today. Thank you."

"You're welcome."

"All right, let me see… What's your schedule like?"

Grabbing her phone from her purse, Bree pulled up her calendar app. "I have some time blocked off Tuesday morning."

"Is nine o'clock good?"

"That works." Bree added the information to her calendar then put her phone in her back pocket.

"Thank you so much for your help. It was lovely meeting you."

"You too, honey. I'll give Jason your information as soon as I can pin him down."

"Have a good afternoon."

Bree's hand was on the door when the office to her left opened. She glanced over as Jase walked out of the office, his attention on the papers he was shuffling in his hands.

"Ms. Carol, can you..." Jase trailed off when he looked up and caught sight of Bree standing at the door.

Shit. Jase. Jason. Jase. Holy hell.

Bree stared wide-eyed as he handed Carol the papers in his hand and marched toward her. Too late, she took a step back.

"Not this time." Jase bent, put his shoulder to her stomach and lifted her up in a fireman's carry. He turned and stalked back to his office.

"Jason Michael Larken! Your mother raised you better than that!" Carol hollered. Bree raised her head to see Carol come around her desk, stand with her hands fisted on her hips, and stamp her foot. If she wasn't in shock from being thrown over his shoulder and carried off like some caveman's conquest, Bree might have laughed at the sight of the genteel, southern lady stamping her foot.

Jase slammed the door to his office and turned and hefted Bree off his shoulder just enough to get an arm under her ass and brace her against the wall. His other hand went to the nape of her neck where he forcefully grabbed a handful of hair.

Bree didn't know whether to be scared or turned on–maybe a little of both. Okay, maybe a lot of both. She wiggled her hips, trying to get her feet on the ground.

"Let me down," she demanded.

Jase ground his pelvis into hers to stop her movements.

"Be still," he ordered her. "You're lucky I don't bend you over my desk while I spank your pretty ass for bailing on me."

"Like hell." She continued to struggle, but her mind and body betrayed her. The image he put in her head ramped up her slow-burning arousal to Mach speed. Her legs spasmed and he pressed their bodies impossibly closer. She gave in and, rather than let her legs dangle uselessly, wrapped them around his hips.

"Yeah?" Jase breathed against her neck while he rocked his hips into hers. "You like that idea? I would have done that to you Saturday morning. Spanked your ass pink then kissed every silky inch of your body. But you left. Without leaving your number. Why'd you leave, Bree?"

Jase's words turned her blood into molten lava in her veins. Bree arched her neck back, giving him room to drag his teeth up the sensitive column of her neck. She was senseless to everything except the orgasm that had been building for close to a week from dreaming of him. And he wanted her to think? Now?

Jase stopped moving his hips and used the hand in her hair to force Bree to look at him, his gaze intense and demanding.

"Answer me, Bree."

"I don't do that. I don't go home with guys. It was awkward."

Jase started moving his hips again, rubbing the seam of his jeans against her sweet spot, continuing to build the friction. "Does this feel awkward?" he asked in a low voice.

"No," Bree whispered on an exhale, doing her best to ride his hips.

"Are you going to come for me Bree?" he whispered against her lips.

She felt like a horny teenager, dry humping on her parents' couch. Except she was pinned to a wall and her legs were wrapped around Jase's trim waist. Yes, she was going to come.

Jase engulfed her mouth. His tongue invaded and she groaned as her orgasm exploded through her. *Finally.* Her legs tightend around his waist and her hips surged against his. The kiss–deep, claiming–continued for what seemed like hours, but was probably only a minute before Jase pulled back enough to look into her eyes.

Before he could say anything, a buzzer sounded on his desk and Carol's voice came over the intercom in a staged whisper. "Jason Larken, I don't know what you're doing to that poor girl, and I don't want to know, but you quit it right this instant and get your hiney out here 'cause your four-thirty appointment is here."

Bree pressed her lips together to suppress her laughter at six-foot-four Jase being scolded by little bitty Carol.

"It's not funny."

Bree smiled. "It kind of is."

"We're not done with this conversation," Jase said.

"We didn't actually have a conversation. You just threatened to spank me and made me come."

He quirked an eyebrow. "Did you get my meaning?"

She narrowed her eyes, unwilling to give him the satisfaction of an answer.

He smirked. "We had a conversation."

Bree rolled her eyes and started wiggling in earnest, trying to get down. "Let me down, Captain Caveman."

His smirk turned into a grin and he stepped back from the wall. "I'm letting you down only because I don't have time to bend you over my desk."

He released her legs, keeping her pressed close to him as her feet finally touched the ground.

She couldn't believe he had just dry humped her in his office and now he acted like he did her a favor by letting her down. Bree glared at him, causing him to smile even wider. He bent to kiss her, but she turned her head to the side in irritation. She wasn't going to give in again. He scraped his teeth along her neck where his mouth landed. Bree grabbed the backs of his biceps and tilted her head to give him more access. Damn her traitorous body.

"Yeah, you got me," he said with a self-satisfied grin.

Bree growled and turned to leave. *Conceited ass.* Why did it have to be so sexy?

Jase grabbed the back of her shirt and pulled her against him. "Wait for me to get done with my meeting. Don't even think about taking off again."

Bree tilted her chin up slightly at his warning.

"I'm going to take that as your agreement that you'll wait for me." He placed a quick kiss behind her ear.

He reached around her and opened the door to his office, giving Bree a small push to get her moving ahead of him.

Bree walked into the reception area and glanced at Carol sitting behind her desk. She winked at Bree.

"Ms. Carol, make sure Bree is comfortable until I'm done with my meeting."

Jase turned his attention to the older gentleman in the waiting room.

"Richard, come on back. It's good to see you again." Jase held open his door and let the gentleman in ahead of him. Before going into his office, he pointed at Bree in warning. He entered his office and closed the door behind him.

Bree looked at Carol. "Is he always this bossy?"

"Oh honey, you have no idea. That boy's been wearing bossy pants since he was knee-high to a gnat's knee."

Bree couldn't help but smile at Carol's analogy. "You've known him that long?"

"Oh yes. He and my son were best friends since they were in diapers." Carol's look turned wistful.

Bree saw the folded flag on the shelf over Carol's shoulder. "I'm sorry for your loss."

"Thank you, honey. It was a few years ago, but I still miss him every day." She gave a small smile and then schooled her features. "Now, if you're going to skedaddle, you need to skedaddle."

Bree raised her eyebrows. "You're not going to try to keep me here?"

"Brianna honey, the chase isn't going to be any fun for either of you if you don't actually run."

Bree grinned slowly; she really liked Carol. "Thank you, Carol."

"I'll see you later," Carol replied with another wink.

JASE WALKED out of his office to an empty reception area. Impatiently, he walked Richard to the door before turning to Carol.

"Please tell me she's in the bathroom," he demanded.

"Jason Larken, don't you use that tone of voice with me," Carol scolded him for the second time that day.

Jase hung his head like he used to when she chastised him as a child. "Yes, Ms. Carol."

"Now," Carol went on. "I couldn't very well hog-tie her to keep her here, now could I?"

Jase threw up his hands. "What does everyone have against hog-tying her? Don't suppose she mentioned why she was here?"

"Well, I suppose she wanted to talk to someone about setting up a referral system for some of her patients. She's a physical therapist."

"Don't suppose she happened to leave her contact information, did she?"

"I suppose I might have her business card right here on my desk," Carol told him with an evil smile.

Jase smiled and took the card from her outstretched hand. *Brianna Marks, DPT.* And it had her cell phone number on it. His smile stretched into a grin.

"Love you, Ms. Carol."

"Love you too, Jason. Go get her."

Jase pulled out his cell phone and called his brother. "Hey man, can you do me a favor?"

CHAPTER 6

Bree parked on the side of the small ranch-style house her grandparents had built early in their marriage. They had raised their children here; then later, her. After her grandfather passed away, her grandmother moved to a retirement community and deeded the house to Bree, along with the acre and a half of property they still owned.

Bree entered through the mudroom and laundry off the kitchen and set her bag on the counter. Her dogs scratched at the French doors in the living room leading to the back yard. She grabbed a beer from the fridge on her way to let them in. Glass crunched under her shoes as she crossed the threshold into the living room.

"What the hell?" She looked down. A framed picture had fallen off the wall and shattered on the floor. "Crap. How did that happen?" She stopped before going farther into the living room. More pictures lay shattered on the floor in a pile. She glanced around the room. Only the pictures of her and Chad had fallen—or had been thrown.

She turned and froze. The front door stood slightly ajar. She hardly used the front door. She might live in the country, but she always made sure to lock her doors when she left.

Why are the dogs outside? They should be inside, where they usually had free roam of the house.

She listened to the house. "Chad?"

She retraced her steps back to the kitchen to get her phone out of her bag and dialed 9-1-1.

"9-1-1 operator. Please state your emergency."

"This is Brianna Marks. I'm at 5335 Lakeview Drive. Someone broke in to my house."

"Ma'am, do you think someone is still in your house?"

"I don't know. I haven't gone past the living room."

"Ma'am, for your safety, please exit your house. Do you have somewhere safe you can go? A neighbor, for instance."

"Not really; I'm out in the country."

"Do you have a working vehicle you can lock yourself in?"

"Yes, I can do that."

"All right ma'am, a sheriff's unit is on its way. I'll stay on the line with you until they arrive."

"No, thank you, I'm good. I'll just keep my phone on me."

"Ma'am, you should really stay on the line until the sheriff arrives."

"I'll be fine. I'll go wait outside."

She heard the operator's sigh on the other end. "Call back if you need to."

"Thank you." Bree disconnected. A hand grabbed her upper arm. She let out a scream, wrenched her arm away and spun. She dropped to a knee as she turned and punched out at the attacker, connecting with his crotch.

"What the fuck, Bree," Jase ground out as he dropped to his knees.

Her hands flew to her mouth and her eyes widened at the sight of Jase crumpled in front of her. "Oh my god." She dropped her other knee. "I'm so sorry. Are you okay?"

He dropped his head on her shoulder, curling in on himself. "Fuck no. What did you do that for?"

She ran a hand through his hair, petting him, and tried not to smile. She shouldn't laugh. She felt bad, but he kind of deserved it for sneaking up on her. "I thought you were whoever broke into my house."

"What the hell do you mean someone broke into your house?"

"Someone broke into my house," she repeated. "What more explanation does that need?"

"Did you call the cops?"

"Yes, I called the cops. A sheriff is on the way."

His head came up off her shoulder. "Why are you still in your house?"

"I was on my way out when you grabbed me."

"Well, let's go," he said as he carefully stood up.

Bree rolled her eyes. Could he be any bossier? She led the way out of the front of her house.

A sheriff deputy's car pulled into the drive as they went down the porch steps, a Haven Springs police car close behind. A uniformed officer got out of each car. She fell in county jurisdiction, so why did Haven Springs PD send a car?

"What are you doing here?" Jase demanded.

Bree looked askance at Jase, who stared at the Haven Springs officer rounding the hood of his car. *Who talks to a cop that way?*

"The very address you asked me to look up not thirty minutes ago goes over the net for a B and E and you don't think I'm going to show?" the Haven Springs officer asked as he joined them on the walkway.

"It wasn't me, jackass. I got here after she called the cops."

"Is that true, ma'am?" The Sheriff's deputy joined them.

"Yes," Bree replied.

"Why are you limping?" the cop asked.

"I ran into something," Jase said.

"What was that?"

"My fist, for scaring the crap out of me," Bree said.

The cop threw his head back and laughed. The deputy coughed into his hand.

"Not funny, man," Jase grumbled.

Bree finally noticed the similarities between the cop and Jase–same height and build, similar facial features but with some slight differences. "Are you two related?"

"Jason here is my baby brother. I'm Tim."

Bree took his outstretched hand. "Bree. Do you always give out women's addresses to anyone who asks?"

"Uh, no?"

"Are you asking me if you do it all the time, or telling me you don't?"

"Telling you I don't do it all the time?"

"You're still answering in the form of a question. Do I look like Alex Trebec?"

"You gave out someone's personal information?" the deputy asked.

Jase looked down at Bree. "You know I could have found you on the internet, right?"

"You know that's not the point, right?"

Jase winked at her. Her eyes rolled again. If she kept doing that, she was going to get a headache.

The deputy stepped forward, hand outstretched. "Ma'am, I'm Deputy Grant. Is it all right if I take a look around your house?" Jeez, he was young looking. Was he even old enough to be a cop? He was probably fresh out of the academy. It was just a break-in; it wasn't like he was investigating a murder.

"Go for it. Door's open," she said. "Shit, I need to call a locksmith." She pulled out her phone and opened her internet search app.

"Do you want me to go with you?" Tim asked.

Deputy Grant raised a hand. "No, I got it."

They watched the deputy enter the house. "Did you notice anything missing?" Tim asked Bree.

"No, but I didn't really take a good look around, and I never went beyond the living room."

"Why did you think the house had been broken into?"

"The front door was open and there were some pictures that looked like they had been thrown on the floor," she explained.

"Only certain pictures were broken?" Tim asked.

"Yes, just the ones of me and my ex." She looked sideways at Jase to judge his reaction.

"How long ago did you break up?" Tim asked.

Bree cringed, stealing another glance at Jase. "A little more than a week ago." One of his brows lifted, but he didn't say anything.

"Was it an amicable split?" Tim continued.

"Uh, no. It was in no way shape or form amicable."

"Did he threaten you?" Jase asked, in a low, controlled voice.

Bree let out a small laugh. "No, I did the threatening. I found him screwing a living Barbie doll in my bed and told him if he didn't get out of my house, I was going to shoot him."

"You own a gun?" Tim inquired.

"Yes, I own a gun. It's in a gun safe, locked with a biometric lock and six-digit PIN. No one is getting in that safe except me."

Tim let out an impressed whistle. "I kind of want to see that gun safe."

Bree grinned. "It's all sorts of awesome."

"Ma'am," the deputy called out from the porch. "Your house is clear. You can come in and see if anything is missing."

Bree led the way back to her front door. They entered the foyer and walked through to the living room where the sheriff was standing.

"Do you mind checking to make sure all your valuables—computers, laptops, jewelry—are accounted for?" Sheriff Grant asked.

"Everything of value is in the spare bedroom I use as my office," Bree said.

"There's also quite a mess in the master bedroom."

"What kind of a mess?" Bree asked.

"It looks like someone ripped up the bedding."

Jase held Bree back by grabbing her hand. "Hold on. I'll go with you." All three men followed her to her bedroom.

Feathers. Feathers everywhere. The down comforter was shredded, as were her pillows and mattress.

"I'm assuming from the lack of blood, no one sacrificed a chicken in here," Jase said.

"Down comforter."

"Don't those get hot in the summer?"

"Not as much as you would think."

"If you two are done playing Martha Stewart, you want to check your gun safe?" Tim asked.

"It's fine," Bree said.

"You can't know that unless you check it," Tim mansplained.

"Considering I can see it from where I'm standing, I actually can know that."

"Your gun safe is in your bedroom?"

"In plain sight." Bree walked over to the full-length mirror attached against the far wall of her bedroom, next to the walk-in closet. She found the keypad on the top edge of the mirror and entered her PIN, then placed her hand on the upper right-hand corner of the mirror. With a soft whir of moving parts and a click, the mirror came away from the wall on a hinge, revealing her three rifles and two handguns.

"All weapons accounted for." She turned and faced three stunned men standing in the doorway of her bedroom.

"That's cool." The deputy stared wide-eyed at her state-of-the-art safe before giving himself a small shake. "Uh, ma'am, I need to get some information from you to write up my report, if you don't mind."

"Yeah, we can go into the kitchen, if that's okay."

"I'll meet you in there," he said.

"No problem." Bree turned back to her gun safe and closed the mirrored door, locking it again by reentering her PIN. When she turned, she was alone with Jase.

"You think it was your ex?" he asked.

She walked toward him. She couldn't get a read on him. Was he upset about the thought of her having a recent ex? Did he think he was just a rebound and that was why she took off? She wished he would give something away.

"I don't think so. This doesn't seem like something he would do. Send me twelve dozen roses even though he knows I don't like them, or some over-the-top gift, sure; but this is angry. Personal. And I think it's a little weird that nothing else in the house was touched." Bree crossed her arms over her chest, hugging herself as she looked at the shredded bedding. "Whoever did this came into my personal space and attacked it. It's creepy."

Jase closed the distance between them and wrapped his arms around her, pulling her into his embrace. "You don't like roses?"

"Hate them. Too cliché."

"What's your favorite flower?" he asked, rubbing small circles on her back.

"Calla lilies." She turned her face into his neck. She liked this side of him. It reminded her of the guy she met in the bar. Sweet. Attentive. His hands on her back soothed her in much the same way petting her dogs helped her calm down when she was anxious.

He bent his head and whispered in her ear. "I can't tell you how hot it is that you have guns. And that safe is cool as hell."

And there was the guy she met this afternoon. Bree smiled against his neck, inhaling the hint of aftershave lingering on his skin. "Don't get too excited. I haven't been shooting since before my grandfather passed away–it was our thing to do together."

"Still hot." His hand drifted down to the cheek of her ass. She titled her head and opened her mouth against his neck.

"Y'all comin' sometime today?" Tim yelled at them from the hall.

"I would really like it if people would stop interrupting right when things are getting interesting," Jase grumbled.

Bree smiled. "Come on. I need to let my dogs in."

She pulled back and looked up at him. She rose up on her toes and kissed him briefly, his beard tickling her face. "Thank you."

Jase grabbed her face with both hands and deepened the kiss, sweeping his tongue into her mouth before raising his head. "You're welcome." Back to sweet.

They made their way down the hall into the family room and open concept kitchen. Deputy Grant sat at the angled bar. Tim had made himself comfortable at her small kitchen table tucked into the breakfast nook.

"Ms. Marks," the deputy began.

"Dr. Marks," Jase said.

The deputy looked at Jase, then back at Bree.

"Bree is fine," she said. She grabbed a glass from the cabinet and poured herself some water from the pitcher on the counter.

"Yes, ma'am. What time did you leave your house today?"

"Seven o'clock. Give or take a few minutes."

"Is that what time you normally leave in the morning?"

"Yes."

"There's no sign of anyone tampering with your locks. Are you sure you locked the door on your way out?"

"Yes. I always check the front door and leave through the door off the mudroom."

"Who else has a key to your house?" he asked.

"My grandmother, my best friend, and my ex. I'm sorry, I'm being rude. Would anyone like something to drink?"

The deputy shook his head. Tim and Jase copied the gesture when she looked at them.

"No one else has a key? No cleaning service or pet-sitting service?"

"No. I don't use either. Is it okay if I go get my dogs' beds and bring them in here? I don't want them walking in the living room until I can clean up the glass." she said.

The sheriff nodded as he made notes in his note book. She retrieved the two beds from the living room and dropped them against the far wall in the family room.

"Has your ex made any threats against you?" the sheriff asked.

She opened the back door and let in her dogs. "Not that I'm aware of, but I've been deleting any messages without listening to them or reading them." Sensing Bree's heightened anxiety level, Polly sat down at Bree's feet and whined up at her. Bree ruffled her ears and closed the door. Her pit bull's butt wiggled in excitement as he made a beeline for Jase, now sitting with Tim at the kitchen table.

"How'd he lose his leg?" Jase asked.

Bree looked up from scooping dog food to find Jase petting Charlie.

"He got hit by a car. I found him on the side of the road and took him to the vet. He wasn't chipped and no one came forward to claim him, so I kept him."

"Ma'am, is there anyone who might hold a grudge against you or your ex?" the deputy asked, drawing Bree's attention back to him.

"My ex, maybe, against me. I caught him cheating on me. I'm pretty sure it wasn't the only time." She shook her head and mumbled, "Jackass."

"Did you know the woman you caught him with?"

Bree shook her head. "I'd never seen her before and didn't bother with introductions."

"Did she say anything to you? Threaten you or your ex?"

"Mostly she just called my ex an asshole. She seemed embarrassed more than anything. Told me she was sorry and left as quickly as she could."

After writing a few more notes, he flipped the notebook closed and placed it in the breast pocket of his shirt. "I think I've got everything I need. You can request a copy of the report in a week or so for insurance purposes."

"Thank you, Deputy Grant. I appreciate you coming out."

"No thanks necessary, ma'am. Just doing my duty."

Bree walked him to the door and shook hands with him as he left. When she came back into the kitchen, Tim smiled at her while Jase glared.

"What?" she asked.

"You're not staying here. Pack a bag with a few days' worth of clothes," Jase ordered.

"Why?"

"You're not staying here."

"You said that already. It'll be fine. I'll sleep in the guest room until I can get my room cleaned up."

He crossed his arms over his chest and leaned back in the chair. "No. You won't sleep in your guest room. Not until you get your locks changed and have an alarm installed."

"That's ridiculous." Bree put her hands on her hips. "The locks still work and an alarm system can take days to get installed. I'm not staying in a hotel that long, especially with my dogs, and Denise lives in a one-bedroom loft apartment above the kennel, so that's out."

"You're staying with me."

"No. I'm not."

"Yes. You are."

She threw her hands up. "Why are you insisting on this?" In her peripheral, she saw Tim try to hide his smile as he watched them argue.

Jase leaned forward and put his elbows on his knees. His eyes narrowed. "Because someone broke into your house, shredded your bedding and selectively shattered pictures of you and your ex. As you pointed out, this was personal. You're not safe here by yourself."

Her breath caught when she remembered the sight of the ripped bedding. As creepy as it was, she could still take care of herself. "I have a gun, and the dogs will let me know if someone comes into the house."

"Not if they're outside, they won't." Jase stood and took a few steps toward her. Bree crossed her arms and tilted her head back a little to keep her gaze with his.

"I don't leave my dogs outside; they're always in the house unless they have to go out." Bree was becoming annoyed with Jase for pushing the issue. This was her house, dammit. She wasn't going to be scared out of it.

"They weren't today," Jase pointed out.

"They were when I left."

"Wait. What?" Tim interjected. He wasn't trying to hide a smile now—he was frowning.

Bree looked at Tim. "I left the dogs inside this morning, like I always do."

"Did you put them out when you called the police?"

"No. They were outside when I got home. I figured Chad came by, let them out while he was here, and forgot about them. He's not their biggest fan."

"But you don't know that for sure," Jase said.

Bree looked between Jase and Tim's matching serious expressions. "No," she said in a soft voice.

"They're friendly dogs." Tim scratched Charlie behind the ears. "Anyone could have let them out the back door to keep them out of the way while they were in your house."

Bree's chest tightened as what Tim insinuated finally sank in.

Jase drove the point home. "They could have done something else to them to get them out of the way."

It was the threat to her dogs that finally made Bree agree to go to Jase's. She could have taken them to Denise's and gone to a hotel, but she preferred to keep them near, and Jase was offering her a solution. Maybe not the best solution, but after what happened in his office, then later in her bedroom, a part of her wanted to learn more about this man who could be both demanding and sexy, sweet and attentive. She just wasn't willing to examine that part of her too closely yet.

JASE WENT through her house and made sure all the windows and doors were locked. He examined the lock on the front and kitchen doors. It didn't look like someone had pried the doors open. He'd pick up a couple of deadbolts from the hardware store this weekend and change her locks for her, whether she liked it or not.

Grabbing the broom and dust pan from between the washer and dryer in the laundry, he cleaned up the majority of the glass in her living room. He studied one of the pictures of Bree and her ex. The guy was clean-cut–white dress shirt, tan blazer, styled hair. He had an arm thrown around Bree like she was a prize. She looked stiff and uncomfortable with both her arms in front of her, elbows tucked into her sides, holding a drink in front of her like a shield. The dress she wore was black, sleeveless, and clung to her body. She was beautiful. He set the picture on the coffee table with the others.

He walked over to the bookcases, checking out the other pictures scattered on the shelves. Her and an older woman. Her and Denise. Pictures of her in scrubs and different Air Force uniforms, including one of her and Denise in their battle rattle–helmet, body armor, loaded down with weapons and ammunition. It was like looking at a different person–open and friendly, smiling and laughing. He didn't yet know what the deal was with her ex, but Jase was pretty sure he didn't have anything to worry about.

He turned as Bree came down the short hall with a duffle bag thrown over one shoulder.

"Is that all you're taking?" he asked.

She glanced at the duffle bag. "I wear scrubs for work, so I only need a few changes of clothes for the week. I need to bring Charlie and Polly's beds, their bowls, and their food."

"Why don't you grab the food and bowls while I put their beds in my truck?" He took the strap of the duffle off Bree's shoulder, then grabbed the two dog beds from the family room.

He went out through the mudroom and put everything in the back of his pickup. By the time he went back in, Bree had dragged a small bin into the mudroom. He hefted it up and led the way out. He watched carefully as Bree locked the door, making sure he heard the bolt slide into place.

He loaded up Bree and her dogs and drove the twenty minutes to his house. Turned out they were practically neighbors. Since he had convinced her to leave her car at her house, she was stuck. He was already thinking of the night to come. No way in hell she was sneaking out the next morning. She was also going to answer some questions. Like why the hell she had gone home with him the day she broke it off with her ex.

Jase pulled up in front of his garage, turned off his truck, and looked at Bree. She hadn't said much during the drive other than to ask how far away he lived.

"Where are we?" Bree asked.

"My house."

"This isn't where you took me last week."

"That was my buddy Chris's house. He was supposed to be out of town."

"He was the guy on the couch?"

"Yeah."

"Well, that's embarrassing."

"Don't worry about it. You good otherwise?"

"Other than being mortified that we had sex in your friend's bed and being overwhelmed thinking about everything I need to do this weekend, sure. I'm just peachy."

"I washed his sheets. Can't go back in time and bring you here instead. What do you need to do this weekend?"

"Well, I have to work in the morning, so you're going to have to take me to my car." She gave him a pointed look. "Then I need to buy a new mattress and clean up my house, set up a time for the locksmith to change the locks, and call an alarm company. It doesn't seem like a long list of things to do, but it's all time consuming."

"My schedule is flexible so I can get your locks changed and meet the alarm company if you have to work. We'll figure it out," Jase promised.

CHAPTER 7

e'll figure it out.

Chad would have told her not to stress about it, that she'd figure it out, and he would have left it to her. He would have helped if she'd asked, of course, but he wouldn't have offered. He wouldn't have asked what he could do to make things easier for her.

She'd waited too damn long to break things off with him.

"You ready to in?" Jase asked.

"You okay with the dogs coming inside?"

Jase looked over his shoulder at the two dogs panting in his back seat. Charlie leaned his head forward and licked Jase's face.

"Yeah. They're good."

Bree laughed, opened her door, and hopped down. They unloaded the truck and let the dogs down. They immediately sniffed around the yard and relieved themselves before following their humans inside.

Jase led her to a covered walkway, which connected the colonial-style house to the much newer-looking oversized two-car garage. A small porch opened into a breakfast room with an old-fashioned potbelly stove tucked into the corner.

67

"Do you actually use that?" Bree asked, looking at the stove.

Jase glanced to where she was looking. "Sometimes, during the winter. My bedroom is right above us, and the chimney goes up through the wall, so I use it for heat instead of turning on the thermostat."

"Doesn't that make the rest of the house kind of cold?"

"Don't really use the rest of the house. There are two more fireplaces if I need them. I cut enough wood to get me through the winter. It's not like we're up north and I'm battling negative degree temperatures."

"Good point."

"Come on. Let's get your mutts settled and get dinner started. I'll take the rest of your stuff up in a bit. The family room okay to put their beds?"

"Wherever we'll be spending the most time is fine."

"Feel free to take a look around." Jase carried the large dog beds down a short hall and disappeared around the corner.

Bree glanced around. The U-shaped kitchen opened into the breakfast area. Rather than follow Jase, Bree went through the door to her left, which led her to the dining room. Built-in hutches occupied two corners of the room. Judging by the thin layer of dust on the table, Bree guessed Jase ate all his meals in the kitchen. Formal double doors to her right led her to the foyer. Straight through was a formal living room with one of the two fireplaces Jase had mentioned. Through a set of large pocket doors was a large family room where Jase had arranged the dog beds in the back corner, next to the second fireplace. A large framed drawing hung above the dark wood mantel.

Bree stared at the picture. It was the same one tattooed on his back. A black and white montage of battle scenes. It looked like it was drawn in pencil or charcoal. The detail was exquisite.

At the back of the family room, a short hall led to a full bath and a bedroom, which Jase used as a home gym. On the right, stairs led to the second floor. She kept walking around to the right and found herself back in the breakfast area and kitchen. Jase was pulling food out of the refrigerator, and she could smell onions and peppers sautéing on the stove.

"Fajitas okay?" Jase asked when he noticed her come back into the kitchen.

"That sounds good. You chopped up those onions while I was walking around? Are you a culinary wizard?"

Jase chuckled. "The exact opposite. I hate chopping onions so I buy them pre-sliced."

"Huh. I'm assuming you have beer," she said.

He pointed a wooden spoon at the refrigerator. "Yeah, I have beer. Help yourself."

"You want one?"

"Sure."

Bree grabbed a couple of beers from the fridge and opened one for Jase.

"Do you want some help?"

"I got it. Sit down and relax." She sat at the table and watched Jase move around his kitchen. His butt filled out his jeans nicely, especially when he bent to get another pan out of a lower cabinet.

"How old is your house?" Bree asked, trying to distract herself.

"Court records said early 1920s. There were some renovations done in the late 70s, early 80s, but it was in pretty bad shape when I bought it."

"I was going to ask if any of it was original. The brick in the living room is gorgeous," she said.

The sound of sizzling meat hitting a hot pan filled the kitchen. "My best friend Tony and I spent a little more than a year renovating after I bought the place," he explained. "We had both just gotten out of the Army and just wanted to relax a little. Have a place away from people."

"How much land do you have?" she asked.

"Almost ten acres."

"That'll get you away from people."

"Tony didn't adjust so well after getting out," he said. Jase looked at her, something in his eyes. A haunted look. One she had observed in many of her patients. Guys who'd seen too much, done too much, and sacrificed more than anyone should ever have to. A look she'd seen in her own mirror.

"Anyway, we gutted the place, top to bottom. A couple of guys we knew from the service did the electrical and plumbing for me, but we did the rest ourselves."

"You did a really good job. I like that you kept the original structure–all the rooms–and didn't try to make it open concept," she said.

Jase stirred the meat in the cast iron pan before looking at Bree. "Your house has an open concept."

"Only for the family room and kitchen. I renovated it after my gran deeded it to me. I did the demo myself, but everything else a contractor did. Had the bay windows put in the dining room and kitchen nook and opened up the kitchen–it was tiny before. Combined the two back bedrooms into the master and put in an ensuite."

"That was cool of her, to deed it to you," he said.

"It got to be too much for her after my grandfather passed away."

"Where is she now?" He moved the meat off the pan.

"In a retirement community in Haven Springs," she said.

"She's close then."

"Oh yeah, I see her every Saturday. I volunteer there. What about your family? Are they local? Other than Tim?"

"They were," Jase said. "My parents retired to Wilmington a couple of years ago. I have a sister out in Colorado." He pointed to a drawer across from the stove. "Can you grab silverware out of that drawer there, and some plates? Dinner'll be ready in a few minutes."

Bree got silverware and plates, grabbed some paper towels, and set the table. Jase set a platter piled high with meat and vegetables on the table. Charlie and Polly moved from where they were sitting next to the stove watching Jase prepare dinner to under the table on the off chance some food might make it to the floor.

"They'll stay on their beds if they're bothering you," Bree offered.

"They're good."

Bree smiled. So different from Chad. He'd hated when Charlie and Polly sat under the table and always insisted she put them in their kennels whenever he was over for dinner.

They sat at the small table and piled their plates high with food.

Bree spread sour cream on a tortilla. "Who did the picture over the fireplace in the living room?"

"Uh, Tony did it."

"It's beautiful. He's very talented."

"Yeah, he was."

Bree hesitated for a moment, not sure she wanted to ask the next question. "What happened to Tony?"

Jase paused in the act of raising his food-laden fork to his mouth. He put it back on his plate and leaned back in his chair.

"You don't have to tell me," Bree said.

"PTSD."

Bree set the tortilla and knife down.

"Really bad. He didn't like therapy. Hated the drugs they had him on. Said it put him in a fog, so he didn't take them for more than a couple of days at a time. One doc prescribed him some sleeping pills, but he didn't like them since they didn't actually help him sleep. He'd just walk around like a zombie and lose days. About two weeks after we finished the house, all the major stuff anyway, he downed the entire bottle and chased it with a bottle of bourbon."

He paused, staring down at his plate as he pushed his food around with his fork.

"The only time I recognized the guy I grew up with was when we were hunting or fishing. He said being out in the woods was the only time he found peace. The only time his mind and soul were still." Jase's swallowed, his throat working more than necessary. He grabbed his beer and took a long pull as if he were trying to force the bitter memory back down.

"Anyway," he continued, setting his beer back down and going back to his food. "I started V.E.T. Adventures a few months after that. I figured if Tony could find peace out in the woods, other guys could, too. Been slowly building it up by word of mouth since then."

He looked at Bree, putting on a brave face, but she could see the agony he buried deep.

She reached forward and placed her fingers in the palm of his hand resting on the table. His hand closed around hers, so tight her fingers pinched together. Her thumb brushed across his fingers, doing what little she could to ease his pain. She had no words that would erase his hurt or express her sympathy, so she didn't offer any.

They finished dinner in silence, lost in their own thoughts, but never letting go of each other's hands.

After dinner, Bree helped Jase clear the dishes and load the dishwasher, then fed her dogs. Once everything was put away, Jase took her hand and led her out the front door onto the screened-in porch. He pulled her onto a large rope hammock and gathered her close. He tucked her into his side with one arm, the other going behind his head. Bree rested her head on his shoulder, tilting it up to look at Jase, who looked back down at her.

"You ready to finish the conversation we started in my office?" he asked.

"What if I say no?"

"Then we do it anyway."

Bree scrunched up her face and glared at him.

Jase kissed the tip of her nose. "You're adorable, but we're still talking."

"Fine." She let out a disgruntled sigh. "What do you want to know?"

"How over it is with your ex, for starters."

Bree turned her head into the pocket of Jase's shoulder and rubbed her face on his t-shirt, letting out another sigh. "One, I wouldn't be here if it wasn't extremely over," she told him firmly. "Two, it should have been over a long time ago. I was more pissed that I had to get new sheets and get tested than I was that he was cheating on me. Honestly, I never should have agreed to marry him."

"You were engaged?"

She titled her head back. "Yes."

"For how long?"

"Engaged? Less than a month."

Jase pursed his lips. "How long were you together before that?"

"Eight or nine months, I guess."

"Why did you say yes when he asked?"

She moved her head back into the pocket of his shoulder. "He proposed at my grandmother's eighty-fifth birthday party. Did the whole speech and got down on one knee in front of everyone. It caught me off guard. I didn't want to embarrass him or myself in front of all my friends and family."

"Wow, that's..."

"Underhanded?" Bree suggested.

"I was going to say an asshole move, but sure, we'll go with underhanded. Why'd you stay engaged?"

Bree traced a small circle on the t-shirt stretched across his chest. "I didn't actually see him more'n a couple of times between when he asked and when I caught him."

His fingers rubbed back and forth across her shoulder. "You never set a date?"

"No. He wanted to. I didn't see the rush. The more he pushed, the more I resisted."

"Why?"

"Why did he push it or why did I keep putting it off?"

"Both," Jase said.

"Money."

"You're going to have to give me more than that, darlin'."

"Sooo...there's a stipulation in my grandfather's will that says I won't receive the entirety of my inheritance until I'm married."

"That's kind of old school," Jase observed.

"It was my grandmother's idea. She fell in love with my grandfather when she was fifteen years old and married him when she was seventeen. She wanted the same fairytale for me that she had. And yeah...she's kind of old school about some things."

"So how much money are we talking about?"

Bree hesitated. She hated telling people how much she was worth. Their attitudes changed as soon as they found out she was wealthy. People she thought of as friends would either start ignoring her, making assumptions about her because she had money, or start sucking up to her.

Jase squeezed her gently. "Now I'm kind of scared to know. If you don't want to tell me, you don't have to."

Bree bit her bottom lip, then decided to go with her gut and trust Jase. "That I get? Slightly more than five million dollars," she said quietly.

He let out a whistle. "Shit, darlin', you are loaded. And you don't get any of that until you get hitched?"

"I get a portion of the interest as a living stipend."

"Do I even want to know?" Jase kiddingly asked.

"It's more than I need to live on and more than enough so I don't actually have to work," she said.

"What did your grandfather do? Win the lottery?"

"He was a cryptographer and statistician during World War II, then designed cryptography programs for the CIA after he got out of the Army. After he retired from the CIA, he sold a bunch of programs to big-name tech companies."

She smiled. "When I say he was smart, I mean genius-level IQ smart. He'd analyze data for hours, just for fun. Right before the stock market crashed in '08, he pulled out all his money. People told him he was crazy, but he just said 'watch and see.' He reinvested everything right after the crash and a couple years later had tripled his investment. Raised all sorts of flags with the SEC, but he kept all his data, all his charts and graphs. They offered him a job," she said with a small laugh. "By that time he had already been diagnosed with terminal cancer. He set the trust up right after he found out."

"You miss him."

"Yeah."

Jase squeezed her again. "What happens if you don't get married?" he asked.

"Well, my grandfather was not as old-fashioned as my grandmother. I can leave it to any children I may have down the road, or it can go into the endowment fund I asked him to set up with most of the money."

"Five million wasn't most of the money?" Jase asked.

"No, it was about a fifth of it."

"Holy cow. And you don't get any of that until you get hitched?"

"Nope."

"And you're okay with that?"

"Sure, why not?" She shrugged. "I really don't have to work if I don't want to. The interest is more than enough to live on, especially here in North Carolina."

"How old are you?" Jase asked.

"You know it's rude to ask a lady her age," Bree said, looking back up at him.

He just gave her another squeeze.

"Thirty-two. What about you? Are you really old? Is your beard covering up all the wrinkles on your face?"

"Thirty-four, smart ass."

Bree grinned up at him before tucking her head back onto his chest.

"Was last week a rebound?" he asked.

"No." She felt Jase release a breath as if he had been holding it, waiting for her answer. "I had no intention of hooking up with anyone on Friday. I just didn't want to sit around my house drinking and whining about what an asshat Chad was. I can't even remember the last time I had a one-night stand."

"Then why'd you leave? You didn't even give it a chance."

"You don't exactly seem like the kind of guy who's lacking for female companionship. I didn't want it to be awkward with you pretending like you'd call and me pretending like I believed you were going to. It was just easier to leave and not deal with the whole thing."

"I haven't been a monk." He wrapped his other arm around her, shifting them so they were face to face. "But I haven't taken a girl home with me in longer than I can remember. I woke up with your perfume in my nose and the taste of you in my mouth," he said as he ran his nose up the side of Bree's neck. "I was pissed when I woke up and you were gone."

He moved a hand under the hem of her shirt. The warm night air caressed her stomach as he exposed her skin on his slow path up to her breasts.

Bree's breath caught in her throat. His words, combined with his touch, fueled the slow burn of her desire.

"I want another taste, Bree." Jase's tongue traced her bottom lip before taking advantage of Bree's gasp, diving in and tangling his tongue with hers. His hand traveled back down her side, over her hip, and grabbed her thigh. He pulled her leg over his waist, nestling his rigid length against her core. With no one to interrupt them, their hands roamed freely, lifting shirts, unbuttoning buttons, and skimming goose-pimpled flesh.

Jase tried to roll Bree under him, forgetting they were in a hammock, and nearly toppled them out of it. He put an arm out to break their fall, but his momentum propelled him out of the hammock and onto the wooden deck of the porch.

Wide-eyed, Bree stared down at Jase. "Are you okay?"

"Yeah," Jase said as he got to his feet.

Bree laughed a deep, full-belly laugh as she rolled back into the center of the swaying hammock.

"It wasn't that funny," Jase told her.

"Yes, it was," she told him through her laughter.

"That's it."

Bree let out a shriek as Jase bent at the waist and grabbed her, throwing her over his shoulder yet again.

"Seriously with the Neanderthal?"

"Me Tarzan, you Jane." He opened the door and headed straight back to the stairs leading to the unexplored second story.

Bree held on tightly to his waist as he ascended, giving her a precarious view of the steep hardwood steps.

Jase took a sharp left turn at the top of the landing and stalked to the king-sized bed. He tossed her gently onto the bed, standing above her as she scrambled to brush her hair out of her face. Jase reached behind his neck and pulled his t-shirt over his head, throwing it in the direction of the far corner.

Bree's eyes traveled down his well-sculpted chest and stomach, noting the tattoos on his chest she hadn't been able to see the last time he'd been naked. Jase shifted his weight to toe off his work boots and she licked her lips as he slowly pulled down the zipper of his unbuttoned pants. The anticipation might have just killed her as she waited for him to push them down his hips. He stopped, his thumbs hooked in the sides of his briefs.

Her gaze shot to his.

"Like what you see?"

She smiled, remembering his pick-up line at the bar. "That's almost as bad as 'Come here often?'"

"What can I say? I like to stick with the classics." He ran his thumbs under the elastic of his underwear, teasing Bree with a glimpse of short, dark curly hair.

"Are you going to take those off?" she asked, a challenge in her voice. "Or do you need help?"

Jase removed his hands from his hips. "I think I need help."

Bree sat up and scooted to the edge of the bed. "Let's see what we've got to work with."

She grabbed the outside seams of his jeans just above the knees and yanked hard, pulling them completely off his hips but leaving his boxer briefs in place.

Bree swallowed hard. Wow. His impressive hard-on strained the confines of his underwear.

We're not going to fit.

"We're going to fit, darlin'," came Jase's amused reply.

"Shit. I said that out loud?" She slapped her hands over her face.

"Yeah, you said that out loud." He pulled her hands from her face and kicked free of his jeans. Moving over Bree, he scooted her back on the bed. He repositioned her so her head was on the pillows, bracing his arms on either side of her and resting his pelvis in the cradle of her hips. "Did you forget we already fit once?"

Her face felt like it was on fire. "I didn't really take the time to look last time. You're very, uh...proportional." God, that was lame. She had basically just told him she forgot they had sex. If the bed would swallow her up right now, she would be eternally grateful.

Jase dropped his head into Bree's neck as he laughed. "I'm hoping that's a compliment."

His beard tickled as he spoke, sending small electrical pulses along her skin. She ran her hands up his triceps, over his shoulders, one going into his hair and one going down his side and around to his equally defined ass. Maybe she didn't need the bed to swallow her after all.

"Yeah, it was a compliment." She ran her nose up his neck, inhaling his spicy aftershave.

"You done being nervous?" Jase lightly ran his tongue up the side of her neck.

"For the most part," she breathed. "You are really well endowed."

She felt him smile against her neck again. "Don't worry, I'll make sure you're ready for me."

"How do you plan on doing that?" she asked, the challenge back in her voice.

"First things first, we need to get you out of these clothes." Jase pushed up so he was straddling her thighs. He curled his fingers into the hem of her t-shirt and slowly drew it up over her head, tossing it over his shoulder.

He ran his fingers over the lace edge of her bra. "I like this," he said in a low voice. "Front or back?"

"What?"

"The clasp. Front or back this time?"

"Back." She arched her back, thrusting her breasts into his hands on the pretext of giving him room to remove it.

He unhooked her bra and eased the straps down her arms, exposing her breasts inch by aching inch. He scooted down the bed, quickly removing her shorts and exposing her matching lace-trimmed bikini briefs.

He placed his mouth over the thin cotton and tongued her clit through the fabric, causing Bree to groan at the contact.

"Now this," he said, peeling her panties down. "This I've dreamed about."

Bree panted at his words.

His warm breath caressed the most intimate part of her. "Sweet. Juicy. Heaven on my tongue."

He pulled Bree's legs over his shoulders as she ran her fingers through his hair, burying them in the soft curls. He didn't tease this time. His fingers dug into the soft flesh of her upper thigh as his tongue swirled and flicked. Flicked and swirled. It seemed like Bree's orgasm crashed over her in mere seconds.

Jase quickly removed his briefs and rolled on a condom. He positioned his cock at Bree's wet entrance when she placed her hands on his hips.

"Wait!"

"What? What's wrong?" Worry created a furrow between his brows.

"I wanna suck your cock first." She bit the edge of his jaw.

"Holy fuck, woman, I thought I had hurt you." Jase thrust hard into Bree's slick heat. "Next time. Before you've just come all over my face in all of ten seconds."

"It wasn't that fast," she argued. His thickness stretched and filled her. Slightly uncomfortable, but exquisite at the same time. She wrapped her legs high around his waist and tilted her hips, taking him even deeper.

Jase withdrew and thrust forward again. "I counted. You came so quick for me last time I wanted to see if it was a one-time thing or if you're always that responsive."

"Are you counting this time?" she asked, meeting him thrust for thrust, stroke for stroke. Each time he drove forward, he caressed her clit. Forward and back. Never enough contact to push her over the edge, but just enough to slowly ramp up her arousal again. If he would only prolong the contact with her clit, she could get there. She wrapped one hand under his arm and around his back. The other reached low, grasping and releasing his ass in time to his thrusts. Spurring him on.

"Darlin', I'm doing everything I can not to blow my load before you can come again."

"That's going to be soon."

"Thank fuck." He rotated his hips while he was sunk deep, rubbing her clit on the downward stroke.

"Right there. Like that." He did it again and she came apart in his arms, digging her nails into his back and ass, and biting his shoulder.

Jase threw his head back and shouted his own release, thrusting hard once, twice, and staying buried the third time. He collapsed most of his weight on her, breathing hard while running his mouth along the hollow of her shoulder.

He raised his head to look down at her. "You doing that on purpose?"

"Doing what?"

"Pulsing around my cock."

"Aftershock," she explained as she licked the base of his neck.

"It's gonna make me hard again," he said.

"Okay."

Jase groaned, causing Bree to grin against his neck.

"I need to get rid of the condom."

"'Kay," she whispered, reluctant to loosen her hold.

He pressed his lips firmly to hers while gently easing his body from hers. When he returned from the bathroom, Bree was curled up under the covers, drifting quickly toward sleep.

The bed shifted as Jase pulled back the covers on his side and got into bed, jolting her from the edge of sleep. He pulled Bree close, tucking her back to his front as he kissed her exposed shoulder and buried his face in the base of her neck. His sigh caressed her neck and his weight became heavy at her back. She would never have taken him for a cuddler. She smiled and let her eyes drift closed, giving herself over to sleep.

CHAPTER 8

"GET DOWN! GET DOWN!"

The sharp, whip-crack sounds of M-4 rifles were answered by the low, rat-a-tat of AK-47s. Bree scanned the road ahead of her, looking for pressure plates or uneven pavement that might indicate a secondary device. Bree raised her head over the driver's side hood of the Humvee, scanning the insurgent positions.

"Cover me!"

"God damn it, Marks, get your ass back here! Fuck! Cover her!"

Go! Go! Go! Running in a crouch, rifle pointed down, Bree raced across the open space—a perfect moving target for the enemy. Rounds ricocheted off the rough concrete. She slid on her knees behind the rear bumper of the Humvee that had taken the brunt of the IED explosion, tearing up the hard plastic of her knee pads. A round caught the corner of the mangled metal, missing her by millimeters. She flinched, small pieces of shrapnel stinging her face. Slinging her M-4 around her back, she pulled on the lever of the two-hundred-pound door. The passenger side had taken the force of the blast and the door swung open without any resistance. She glanced up to assess the soldier sitting behind the driver. Blood flowed freely down the front of his face as he fumbled with his seatbelt.

"Hold on. I'll get you out of there."

He turned his head. The right side of his face was gone. Nothing but a gaping hole. "Help me, Bree."

She stood and took a step back, staring at the carnage in front of her.

"Don't leave me here, Bree."

She shook her head and took another step back. A fist clenched the sleeve of her uniform and yanked her around.

"What the fuck do you think you're doing, Marks?"

Thwack!

A bullet tore through the side of his head, blowing out a good chunk. Something warm and wet hit her face. She reached up to brush it away. Her hand touched a furry muzzle and a warm tongue threaded between her fingers.

She jerked her head away and her eyes flew open. Polly licked her cheek, following Bree's movement.

You're safe. You're safe. You're not there. It's not really happening.

Her heart pounded, blood rushing so fast and hard it affected the pressure in her ears. Breathless, as if she had just finished a marathon, she concentrated on slowing the rise and fall of her chest. She looked to her right–Jase was on his stomach, still asleep. She must not have called out, or he was a deep sleeper.

Bree pushed the covers off, eased from the bed, and padded into the bathroom, Polly by her side, and closed the door. Easing the latch into place, she placed her back against the door and slid down to sit on the floor. Dim, pre-dawn light filtered in through a small window, creating ghostly shadows of the vanity, toilet, and free-standing bath. Polly wiggled herself onto Bree's lap and let out a low whine.

"Shh, don't wake up Jase." She hugged Polly close and scratched her ears. "Thank you, sweet girl. Did you leave Charlie downstairs by himself? What do you think brought that on? You haven't had to wake me up in months. Do you think it was Jase's story about Tony? Maybe it was because someone tore up my room. Lots of stuff happened today, huh?"

She petted Polly and whispered to her for another few minutes. "Okay, girl. I think I'm good." She moved her dog off her lap, used the toilet, and washed her hands before she eased back out of the bathroom. Edging onto the bed, she lay facing Jase. She moved as close as she could without touching him. Polly jumped onto the bed and took up position at her back. Watching Jase's chest rise and fall, Bree matched her breaths to his.

BREE LET OUT a small moan and rolled her hips as her orgasm built. She whimpered, trying to reach fulfillment. This dream was so much better than the nightmare. She could feel Jase's beard tickling her inner thighs, his fingers gripping her ass, pulling her closer to his mouth, his breath hot as he licked her aching center. She reached down to bring herself to orgasm and found a head of hair instead. Her eyes flew open. Jase's mouth was between her legs and she was going to come all over his face–again. Her back arched as her orgasm rolled through her, not as strong as the one last night, but just as satisfying.

Jase kissed his way up her stomach, stopping at her breasts to suck on her nipples before moving up to her mouth. She could taste herself on his tongue. He gathered her close before rolling to his side. He pulled her leg over his hip, keeping them intimately connected and tucked her head under his chin. Bree pushed her face into the hollow of his throat.

"Morning," she said.

"Morning." She could hear the smile in his voice. "Hope you don't mind the early morning wake-up call."

"Nope. Nice to actually wake up to your mouth between my legs instead of my alarm clock interrupting me," she said.

Jase drew his head back to glance down his nose at Bree. "What do you mean?"

Heat bloomed in her cheeks. She couldn't believe she had just said that. She tucked her head back into his neck and mumbled, "Nothing."

Jase pulled away and tipped her chin up to look at him. "What do you mean 'instead of your alarm clock interrupting'?"

Bree cleared her throat and looked at his chin. "I may have dreamed about you doing that a couple of times over the last week."

A shit-eating grin spread across his face. "Yeah? How many times?"

Bree forced her head back under his chin and mumbled her response into this neck.

"What? I didn't catch that."

Bree reared her head back and practically shouted, "All of them. Jackass."

Jase responded to her declaration with a hard, long, open-mouthed kiss that ended with him back on top of her, cradling her head between his hands.

"I hope the reality was better than the dream."

"I came, didn't I?"

"Yes, you did."

"What about you?"

"Depends. What time do you have to be at work?"

"I usually show up around eight o'clock or so. I don't have any set time, but if I'm not there by eight-thirty, the bocce ball crowd gets a little ornery. They like to get an adjustment before they start—says it improves their game."

"Really?"

Bree shrugged. "Who knows?"

"Unfortunately, I don't think we have time. It's a little before seven. You can make it up to me tonight."

Was he for real? He was passing up an orgasm. Chad would never—

No, she had to quit doing that. There was no comparison. In the short time she'd known Jase, he'd shown himself to be caring and unselfish. Bossy and a little overbearing, but still unselfish. Everything Chad had never been. She just had to stop judging Jase against the low standard Chad had set. The low standard she had accepted for far too long.

"Why don't you take a shower," he suggested. "I'll fix us something to take with us and take you to your car."

"Crap. I forgot you kidnapped me. I forgot about my house." She stared at the ceiling. Bossy and overbearing at the forefront of her mind.

Jase leaned down and nipped her chin. "Don't worry about it. Do what you gotta do this morning. I'll handle your locks for you."

Bree searched his face. "You sure?"

"I wouldn't have offered if I wasn't sure," he said. "Get dressed so we can go and you don't get assaulted by a bunch of old people."

Bree leaned up and brushed her lips against Jase's. "Thank you."

He rubbed his nose against hers before getting out of bed. She watched his naked butt as he grabbed a pair of boxers from the floor. "Thirty minutes, woman," he said as he left the room.

Bree grinned and looked over the edge of the bed for Polly. Her dog raised her head and gave Bree a puppy grin. "Like he would leave me."

She glanced around his bedroom, taking in everything she had missed last night. The bed had a simple distressed wood slat headboard that looked like it was made from reclaimed barn wood. Two solid night stands and a large, antique-looking dresser. Her duffle bag sat in a worn leather recliner tucked into a window alcove. None of it matched, but oddly it all worked together. She got out of bed, dug through her bag for her shower items, and headed to the bathroom.

Bree stopped, the antique high-back porcelain claw-foot soaking tub taking up the wall under the small window calling to her. Her shoulders dropped—no time for a bath. She closed her eyes and envisioned herself leaning back against the cool porcelain; scented bubbles piled high around her shoulders.

Her vision shifted. Jase sat behind her, one hand caressing her breast while the other played with her clit. She shook her head and opened her eyes. *Seriously woman, get a hold of yourself. You'd think I'd never had sex before.*

Not good sex, apparently.

Whose side are you on?

And now she was arguing with herself. She shook her head again at her unusual flightiness and opened the shower door.

Thirty-five minutes later, she walked into the kitchen. Charlie and Polly were finishing the last of their food. Both glanced up at her and gave her happy grins, then went back to finishing their kibble.

"Thanks for feeding them," she said.

"No problem. One scoop each, right? That's what you gave them last night?"

"Yeah." She stood in the center of the kitchen with her hands on her hips, staring at her dogs.

"What's wrong?"

"I want to take Polly with me today, but that means leaving Charlie at the house by himself."

"Leave him here."

"Really?"

"Yeah, why not? He seems to be housebroken. I have stuff to do to get ready for next week so he can hang out here. No big deal."

It was a big deal. Charlie and Polly were her fur babies.

"Thanks."

Jase gave Bree a head tilt and finished pouring coffee into two travel mugs. "Sugar is on the table. Milk is in the fridge. I don't do that flavored crap."

Bree smiled at the idea of Jase waiting all year long for eggnog-flavored coffee creamer. "Just milk."

They finished making their to-go cups and headed out to Jase's truck. The drive to Bree's house seemed much quicker now that she was paying attention. Jase really didn't live that far from her. Twenty minutes in the country made them practically neighbors. They had probably passed each other on the road, in the store, in any number of places over the years without ever realizing it.

Jase pulled in behind Bree's SUV and put his truck in park. "You got an extra house key?"

Bree took her keys out of her purse and removed one from the ring. "Kitchen door."

Jase grabbed her behind the neck and pulled her to him, giving her a hard kiss. "I want you back at my house tonight. Don't make me track you down again," he warned.

Bree gave him a baleful look. "You have Charlie."

Jase grinned. "Oh yeah. Look how that worked out."

"Jackass."

～

"BRIANNA, honey, can you take a look at my hip? I keep feeling a click when I walk."

"You were shagging again, weren't you, Ms. Mary?" Bree asked, referring to the Carolina dance similar to the swing.

"Well, you know William just won't take no for an answer," Ms. Mary said.

"Uh huh. And it had nothing to do with the jive competition I saw flyers for last week?"

"I couldn't very well let someone else take my title. Janice

Wilkinson told Emily she and David could take me and William. She may be five years younger than I am, but she couldn't shag her way out of a broom closet."

Bree couldn't help but laugh at the unintended double meaning of what Ms. Mary said. "Let's take a look at you and make sure you didn't actually throw out your hip. You need to take it a little easier. You're not five years younger, you know."

Ms. Mary lay down on the portable massage bed Bree had set up in one of the unused offices. "Oh honey, when you stop dancing through life, you may as well stop living. You're only as old as you think you are. In my mind, I'm still twenty years old and driving boys crazy on the Strand in Myrtle Beach."

"Well, you might want to have your mind talk to your hips, because they're in their eighties."

Bree saw three more people that morning suffering from the consequences of the shag competition, as well as a few regulars. At noon, she looked down at Polly, who had spent the day lying in a sun spot in the corner. "You ready to go find Gran?"

She meandered along the paths through the manicured lawns and found Gran reading on the patio of her villa. A wide-brimmed hat shaded her face from the afternoon sun while she read. Polly trotted ahead of Bree and nudged Gran's hand with her nose. Gran's head tilted back, revealing her bright green eyes. The scene reminded Bree of a movie from the 50s or 60s. Even at eighty-five, her grandmother exuded class and style.

"Hey, Gran." Bree leaned down to give her a kiss on the cheek.

"Hello, dear. You brought Polly with you." Gran placed a bookmark between the pages of her novel and set it on the small table next to her.

"I had a bad night. I needed her close today." She reached down and laid a hand on Polly's head.

Gran gave her an assessing look. "I have chicken salad for lunch, is that okay?"

"Did you make it with your spicy mayo?"

"Of course."

Bree smiled. "Then, of course."

They made small talk over lunch, discussing Ms. Mary defending her title at the shag competition and other gossip from around the community.

Bree was clearing the dishes when Gran said, "Something is different about you."

"How do you mean?" Bree glanced over her shoulder.

"I'm not sure. I expected you to be more somber, since you said you had a bad night, but your spirit seems lighter."

"My spirit is lighter?" She couldn't stop her grin. "Have you been visiting that psychic again?"

"Tease all you want, but she told me you were destined for great things and look at all you've accomplished," Gran said.

"I haven't done anything spectacular, Gran."

"How many lives have you saved?"

"I was just doing my job. Anyone would have done the same in my position."

"There were other people in your position who didn't do what you did. I don't like it when you sell yourself short."

"Okay, Gran. I won't sell myself short." There was no use in arguing. She shot a glance at the framed medal and citation sitting on Gran's mantle, centered between her grandfather's World War II service picture and her own service picture. "Why do you think my spirit is lighter?" she asked.

"You just seem happier." She took a small sip of her herbal tea. Hot tea, even in the heat of the afternoon. "Have you and Chad set a date?"

Bree took a deep breath and let it out. "I have bad news about Chad."

Gran set down her cup. "I think you would have told me by now if he had been in an accident or hurt, so you must have finally broken off your engagement."

"What do you mean 'finally'?"

"Dear, Chad was never the man for you. I realized that fairly early on. I just kept waiting for you to realize it, too."

"I did," Bree admitted.

"Why on earth did you say yes when he asked you?"

Bree tossed the dishtowel on the counter and leaned against it. "I didn't want to cause a scene at your birthday party."

"Darling." She conveyed so much in that one word. "Do you really think I would have cared?"

"I cared." Bree crossed her arms. "And I was completely shocked when he asked. Not one of those times I was able to think fast on my feet."

Gran took a sip of her tea. "Should have just told him no."

"Well, it's over, so water under the bridge and all that."

Gran raised an eyebrow. "But that isn't why you're happy."

Bree ducked her head and scuffed her heel on the floor, afraid if she gave voice to her budding feelings for Jase, she might jinx it somehow. "I met someone. It's still really, really new and really early, but I like him. He's..." she tried to think of a way to describe Jase. "Strong."

Gran smiled at Bree. "I liked your grandfather from the first moment I laid eyes on him, too. He was so handsome and confident. I knew, almost from the very beginning, I was going to spend the rest of my life with him. When your heart knows, your heart knows. Just don't go letting your mind talk you out of it." She gave Bree a pointed look.

Bree smiled and shook her head at her fanciful grandmother. She wasn't sure where it was going with Jase. It had really only been two days since she'd met him, not counting that first night. It seemed like it had been so much longer, but she had only run into him again the day before. How had so much happened in such a short amount of time? Her house had been broken into, she'd willingly let Jase manipulate her into staying with him, and he was pretty much holding her dog hostage to guarantee she returned to his house. His high-handedness should infuriate her, but it was actually kind of nice. She had always felt like the dominate personality in a relationship. She liked that Jase had taken charge, packed her up, and made sure she was safe.

Gran interrupted her thoughts. "What's your new young man do?"

"He runs a non-profit for veterans. He organizes hunting, fishing, and camping trips."

"Did you meet through work?"

"Kind of. One of my patients mentioned Jase's company and I went by to see if I could get some information for referrals." It was partly true, anyway.

"That's lovely. You're both passionate about helping others. When are you seeing him again?"

"Tonight. I actually need to run by the grocery store. I'm cooking him dinner at his house and I'm not sure what all he has."

"Well don't let me keep you, my dear. I'm sure that will be much more interesting than spending time at the old folks' home," Gran said as she stood.

"Don't be silly, Gran. You know I love coming to visit."

"I know, dear, but if I were you, I'd rather spend time with a stud muffin than my grandmother."

Bree laughed. "Gran, no one says 'stud muffin' anymore."

"What do they say?"

Probably not appropriate to say she and Denise had called him a walking orgasm. "I'm not sure. I just know it's not 'stud muffin.'"

"Well, whatever it is, go spend time with him."

Gran sent Bree off with a kiss and a hug and waved as she drove away. Bree pulled out her phone as she walked into the grocery store. She had left it in the car while she was at the retirement community. Twenty-three texts from Chad.

"Ugh. Take a hint." She selected them all and hit the delete button. She received three more texts by the time she was finished shopping. Disgusted, she turned off her phone and threw it in her purse.

CHAPTER 9

Jase woke slowly, his hand already stroking his morning hard-on. Why stroke himself when he had a lush, willing woman in bed who could do it for him? He smiled to himself and reached for Bree. His eyes snapped open, blinking against the early morning light, when he found the bed empty. He glanced toward the bathroom—the light was off and there were no sounds coming that might indicate Bree was in there.

"Son of a bitch!" He scrambled out of bed, searching for his jeans and shirt he had discarded the night before. He glanced around the floor, looking for his shirt. He yanked open a drawer and grabbed a new one out of the dresser. He couldn't believe she'd taken off again. What the hell? He thought things were going well.

When she'd come back to his house yesterday, he'd been out in the yard playing fetch with Charlie. He'd been Jase's shadow all day and his company actually made the day easier. It'd been nice having someone to talk to, even if it was just a dog.

Bree had made stuffed peppers and salad for dinner. He couldn't even remember the last time someone had cooked for him—other than his mom on holidays. It was nice. Easy. They had relaxed on the hammock after dinner for a while before going to bed. The sex was phenomenal. Not so rushed, but Bree was still the hottest thing he could remember. She was so responsive and eager. Unselfconscious and, shit, when she came around his cock it was like a vice grip.

He turned the corner at the bottom of the stairs and stopped short as he came into the kitchen. Bree stood at the stove in his shirt—the one he couldn't find. The smell of sautéed onions and mushrooms mixed with bacon and coffee filled the room, while the dogs sat perfectly still by her side, watching her every move.

She glanced over her shoulder, the smile she had for him fading as she caught sight of his thunderous look.

"What? What's wrong?"

"You weren't in bed." His heart was pounding.

"I couldn't sleep. And I was hungry, so I figured I'd come down and make breakfast. I was going to bring it up to you."

Jase stalked toward her, backing her into the counter as she turned to face him fully. He leaned close, his mouth barely brushing hers.

"Wake me up if you can't sleep. Then we'll come downstairs."

"You were sound asleep," she told him. "I tried waking you up and you didn't budge."

"Get creative next time. I guarantee I'll wake up with the right incentive."

Bree's eyes flashed in what he could only describe as a devilish look.

Jase grinned and swept an arm around her waist, pulling her close while avoiding the spatula she held. He kissed her deep, the taste of the coffee she'd had still on her tongue. Shit. If he could get enough caffeine from kissing her, he'd give up drinking it altogether.

She pulled back slightly, her gaze on his mouth. "The eggs are gonna burn," she whispered.

"I have more eggs." His tongue darted out to lick her full bottom lip.

She pulled her head back again. "You don't have more bacon and if that burns, I'm going to be upset."

Jase relaxed his tight hold and straightened to his full height. "Only because it's bacon." He gave her a quick kiss before releasing her to get a coffee mug. He turned in time to catch sight of her lace panties as she bent to remove a cookie sheet from the oven.

Fuck the bacon, he thought as he put the empty mug on the counter. A knock at the kitchen door waylaid his plans to drag her back upstairs. He walked over and unlocked the deadbolt and let his brother in.

"Bad timing, man," he said with a growl.

"Seems like perfect timing to me. Ooh, bacon." Tim snagged a piece off the cookie sheet on the stove before stepping fully into the kitchen and grabbing the empty mug off the counter. "You using this?" He didn't wait for Jase to answer before filling it.

"You here for a reason?" Jase asked.

Tim turned around and leaned against the counter, his face serious. "Unfortunately, yes. I actually need to talk to Bree."

"About the break-in?" she asked. "On a Sunday morning?"

"We're not actually sure. I need to you look at a picture for me." Tim pulled his phone from his pocket.

"O...kay." Bree turned off the stove and moved the omelets she had finished folding onto plates.

Tim pulled up a photo of a woman and passed his phone to Bree. "Do you recognize her?"

"Yeah, I do," Bree said.

Jase heard the surprise in her voice.

"She used to be a neighbor. One house down, on the other side of the street. She and her husband moved four or five months ago. Sold their house to a younger couple with two kids. Her name was...shoot, it begins with a 'J', but it's escaping me right now." She handed Tim back his phone. "Why, what happened?"

"Her name was Jaelynn and she's dead," he said solemnly.

"Oh no! Was she in an accident?" Bree asked.

"She was killed."

"What does this have to do with Bree, other than this woman used to be her neighbor?" Jase asked.

"I need to show you something else." Tim swiped across the screen of his phone. "A letter was found with the body. It was addressed to Dr. Brianna Marks. We thought at first it was from the victim, but it doesn't appear to be from her." He hesitated a moment before handing his phone back to Bree.

She kept her eyes on him as she took the phone. Jase wrapped an arm around her waist, pulling her close to him. Polly whined low and moved to Bree's other side, leaning against her leg. She finally looked down at the screen.

Typed in bold, block print letters on a standard sheet of white paper was: HE SHOULDN'T HAVE CHEATED. YOU DESERVE SO MUCH BETTER.

"I don't understand." Bree handed Tim back his phone.

"You said you discovered your ex-fiance cheating on you and that was the reason you broke it off," Tim said.

"Yes."

"Was that...? Do you know...?" He stumbled on the question.

"Was that the only time he fucked around on me?" Bree finished.

"Yeah."

Bree took a deep breath and let it out. "Honestly, I had my suspicions. Especially about Jaelynn. She'd always come over asking if Chad could help her with something around the house when her husband was out of town. Or, she'd invite us over for lunch or drinks when I had something going on, and Chad would go by himself. I asked him about it a couple times and he always brushed it off. Said she and her husband were having problems and she just needed a sympathetic ear. It seemed kind of sudden when they moved away."

"Have you heard from your ex lately?" Tim asked.

"He's been texting me several times a day, but I've just been deleting them."

"Do you have your phone handy? Can you see if he's tried to contact you in the last few hours?"

Bree shrugged. "Sure, it's upstairs. I'll go get it." She placed her hand on Jase's arm as she moved out of his hold. Polly followed her, keeping close to Bree's side as she made her way around the corner.

"How serious is this?" Jase asked in a low voice.

"We aren't sure," Tim said.

"What do you mean, you aren't sure?" Jase's voice rose.

Tim glanced toward the hall leading to the stairs. "The note was found beside the body. She had been stabbed several times. She had rope marks on her wrists and, best we can tell, she had been tied to a rocking chair in her living room."

"What's the threat to Bree?" Jase asked, cutting to the chase.

"Man, I wish I could tell you she wasn't in danger, but we really don't know. We don't know who did this or why. We're pretty sure it's not the ex, but we also don't know why the letter was addressed to Bree. We've got the department shrink looking at it to get his take on it."

Jase wanted to ask more questions but stopped when he heard Polly's claws clicking on the wood as she followed Bree down the stairs. Thank fuck, she'd put on some shorts.

Her phone pinged incessantly in her hand.

"I had it turned off, so all the text messages are coming in all at once," she explained.

"How many do you have so far?" Jase asked.

"Far as I can tell, I have three from Denise, two from a couple of out-of-town friends, and eighteen so far from Chad." She pursed her lips in annoyance as she waited for her phone to stop pinging.

"What do they say?" Jase crossed his arms and leaned his hips back against the counter.

"Same thing they've said for the last week. 'I miss you.' 'I messed up.' 'Give us another chance.' Blah, blah, blah." Her phone stopped pinging.

"You haven't responded back at all?" Tim asked.

"No. You'd think he'd have gotten the hint by now. I really don't want to have to change my number. I've had it for almost ten years."

"When was the last time he texted you or tried to call?" Tim asked.

Bree scrolled through the display. "Um, this morning around —" *ping* "—right now." She glanced up from her phone at Tim. "Do you want me to call him?"

"Yeah, if you don't mind. See where he is."

Bree hit the button on her phone to call Chad and switched to speaker phone so Tim and Jase could hear. It rang once before Chad answered. "Bree, sweetie, I'm so sorry."

Bree cut him off. "What do you want, Chad?"

"I just want to see you. If I can just explain, I know we can work this out."

Bree rolled her eyes and hit the mute button on her phone. "Do you want me to agree to meet him?" she asked Tim.

"No," Jase said, at the same time Tim said, "Yes."

Tim looked at Jase. "He may have information we can use."

Bree glanced at Jase as she put the phone back on speaker-phone. "Meet me at my house in an hour. We can talk there."

"I can be there in fifteen minutes. I'll fix you french toast and we can talk over breakfast."

Bree rolled her eyes again. "I'm not there, Chad. And I don't like french toast."

Jase smiled at her irritable tone and stared at his feet. She'd obviously told her asshole ex that a few times.

"Oh, well, I can let myself in and I'll make you some eggs or something," Chad said.

Bree mouthed *locks*. Jase nodded.

"You can't. I had the locks changed."

"Why did you do that?"

"You're kidding, right? Look, I need to go. Meet me there in an hour. We'll talk then and you can get the rest of your stuff." She hung up without saying goodbye.

"How long were you with that guy?" Tim asked.

"Too long," Bree said.

She picked up one of the plates, taking a bite of omelet before continuing. "I'm going to take a shower. He'll probably be there in about fifteen minutes and wait for me to show up. Denise is meeting me at ten to help me clean up my house anyway."

Jase raised an eyebrow. "When were you going to tell me you were meeting Denise?"

"Probably around the time we ate breakfast." She took another bite of eggs without breaking eye contact.

Tim came away from the counter and drained the last of his coffee. "As interesting as I think this conversation is going to get, I'm going to head out. I'll meet you at your house." He snagged another piece of bacon on his way out the door.

"I'm going with you." Jase reached around her to pick up his plate.

"I figured as much. I'll be in the shower when you're done eating." Bree placed her plate in the sink and turned on her toes. She pulled Jase's shirt over her head as she rounded the corner, leaving him with a glimpse of the elegant line of her back.

Jase wolfed down the rest of his omelet and threw his plate in the sink.

CHAPTER 10

Jase pulled into Bree's drive and parked along the side of the house. He rounded the hood of his truck just as Bree hopped down from the passenger side, leaving Charlie and Polly in the truck until they dealt with Chad. Bree closed the door and he pressed her against the side of the truck. His left hand ran up the back of her t-shirt, drawing her close, while the fingers of his other hand thread into her hair at the base of her neck.

"You could wait for me to come around and open your door," he said.

"I could, but I'm a big girl. Been opening my doors by myself for a while."

Damn, he loved her sassiness. "I know you can." He ran his nose alongside hers. "It's a matter of me wanting to do something for you and you letting me do it because it makes me happy."

Her eyebrows rose. "Opening my door for me makes you happy?"

He wasn't old fashioned, but there wasn't a lot he could give Bree she didn't already have. It was going to have to be the little things. "I think doing anything for you is going to make me happy."

She didn't say anything for a few heartbeats. "I don't know what to do with that."

"Don't have to do anything with it." He gave her a gentle kiss before taking her hand and turned to walk around to the front of her house.

He'd seen the guy sitting on Bree's porch when they pulled into the drive. He came down the steps as they rounded the corner and took the path that led to the wide porch steps. Pressed white dress shirt, khakis, and loafers with no socks. Jeez, if this was Chad, he even dressed like a tool.

He ignored Jase and headed directly toward Bree. Jase let it play out until Chad made to pull Bree into his arms. She stepped back and closer to Jase, tightening her hold on his hand. Jase pulled her ever so slightly behind him, making it difficult to get at her.

"Bree, honey, who is this guy?" Chad asked.

"This is Jase."

Chad looked between Jase and Bree before asking, "Okay, but who is he?"

Before Bree could answer, a silver sedan tore into the drive. The car screeched to a stop, a hair's breadth from Jase's truck. The driver's side door flew open and a large man barreled toward them, losing a flip-flop along the way. Jase pushed Bree behind him and backed her up a few steps, but the guy went directly to Chad and laid him out with one punch to his face. He straddled Chad on the ground and continued to land punches as he shouted at Chad.

"You killed her, you son of a bitch! You killed her!" Chad struggled to cover his face with his arms while the guy continued to pound on his face.

"Jase!" Bree pushed on his back. Jase looked over his shoulder at the concern on her face. He stepped forward and grabbed the guy on top of Chad, pulling him off.

Shit, he wasn't going to be able to hold him without subduing him. Jase tapped the back of the guy's supporting knee with his, causing it to buckle and taking him to the ground. Jase wrapped his long legs around the attacker's torso and rolled onto his back, pulling the guy on top of him so he couldn't brace himself on ground and push back up. Jase hooked one elbow around the guy's throat and clenched his hands together, cutting off blood to his head.

A Haven Springs PD cruiser pulled up behind the silver sedan, lights flashing. An officer jumped out of the passenger side and ran toward Jase and Chad's attacker, still struggling on the ground. Tim stood from the driver's side, talking into a radio.

"Aren't you going to help?" Bree yelled.

"Jase's got it," Tim said.

Jase looked up at Bree as he rolled Chad's semi-conscious attacker off him with help from Tim's partner. "I'm good, darlin'."

Jase stood as the cop rolled Chad's attacker onto his stomach and cuffed his hands behind his back. Chad lay groaning on the ground, both hands holding his bleeding nose. Jase went to Bree and cradled her head in his hands, bending at the knees so they were eye level.

"You good?" He peered intently at her to gauge her reaction.

Bree grasped his wrists lightly as she leaned her forehead against his.

"Are you going to think I'm absolutely nuts if I tell you that was really hot?" she whispered.

Jase let out a bark of laughter before he hooked an arm around the back of her head and kissed her forehead. He leaned close to her ear. "You can show me how hot you thought it was later."

"I can do that." She wrapped her arms loosely around his waist and watched over his shoulder as Tim squatted down in front of Chad. She glanced at the other guy, still lying on the ground.

"That's Steven," she said.

Jase pulled her tight to his side as he turned them to face the action on her lawn. "You know him?"

"He's my old neighbor. Jaelynn's husband."

"Should I have brought popcorn instead?"

Bree and Jase turned as Denise sauntered across the lawn holding two large iced coffees. Her SUV was parked along the curb, and a huge dog hung its head out of the rear window.

"Oh! Love your face." Bree pulled out of Jase's hold and reached for one of the coffees.

"I know. Right?" Denise replied with a smile. "So, what's going on?"

"Well," Bree took a long sip of her coffee. "The guy in cuffs is Steven, my old neighbor. He tore into the drive and almost hit Jase's truck before attacking Chad. The cop talking to Chad is Tim, Jase's brother, purveyor of illegally obtained address searches, and I'm guessing the other cop is his partner."

"You ever going to let that go?" Tim asked as he helped Chad to his feet.

Bree shrugged as she sipped her coffee. "We'll see."

Jase grinned. It was nice to see his brother getting shit from someone else for a change.

"Why is Chad here?" Denise asked.

"Mmm, that's a little more complicated."

"You killed her, you son of a bitch!" Steven was struggling against Tim's partner's hold, trying to get at Chad even with his hands still cuffed behind his back.

"I don't know what you're talking about, you crazy asshole," Chad shouted back.

"You screwed her and now she's dead because of you!"

"I don't know what you're talking about." Chad held the bridge of his nose, trying to stem the bleeding.

"Jaelynn, you bastard! She was killed because of you. They told me! They told me it was because you were sleeping with her." Steven's voice broke, a sob tearing through him at the end.

"I never slept with Jaelynn," Chad said. He looked at Bree. "Sweetie, I swear there was never anything going on."

Steven turned toward Bree. "I hired a P.I. I have pictures."

"Is that why you moved away?" Bree asked

"I told her we either sold the house and left or I filed for divorce. But she kept seeing him. I filed a month ago."

"Bree, it wasn't anything. You know it didn't mean anything," Chad said.

"You carried on an affair with a married woman for how many months and it didn't mean anything? A lot of things don't mean anything to you, do they?" Acid dripped from Bree's voice.

"Bree…"

"Why don't you come over here with me so I can get your statement about what happened," Tim said. He pulled Chad none too gently toward the police car.

"I loved her. I still love her." Steven sat heavily on the ground, his legs splayed out in front of him, torso hunched forward, as if he no longer had the strength to hold himself together. He shoulders shook as he sobbed quietly.

Bree handed her drink to Denise and stepped toward Steven. Jase moved to follow her, but Denise stopped him with a cold coffee against his arm.

"She's got this."

Bree sat close to Steven on the ground, pulling her knees up and wrapping her hands around them. She leaned her head back and said something to Tim's partner who stood over them. He shook his head at whatever Bree said. She placed a hand on Steven's raised knee and he collapsed his head on her shoulder, his body shaking as he cried.

She sat and talked quietly to Steven until Tim returned to talk to his partner. Bree looked at Tim, then whispered in Steven's ear. He nodded a few times and wiped his face on his shoulder. Bree stood and helped Steven to his feet. Tim's partner took his elbow, walked him to the cruiser, and helped him into the back seat.

Jase and Denise joined Tim and Bree. "...didn't want an ambulance," he heard Tim say.

"Doesn't surprise me. I don't think he has health insurance," Bree explained.

"Chad or Steven?" Denise asked.

"Chad," Bree replied.

"He also wants to press charges against Steven for assault, so we have to take him in. Hopefully, the judge will go easy on him. Extenuating circumstances and all that," Tim continued.

"I hope he doesn't get in too much trouble."

"We ran a background check," Tim said.

"On Steven?" Bree asked.

"No, Chad."

"Oh. Shit. What don't I know?"

Tim hesitated.

Bree closed her eyes and shook her head. "Just tell me."

"He's two-hundred fifty thousand dollars in debt. Gambling," Tim said.

"What?" Denise and Bree exclaimed at the same time.

"He apparently likes to bet on the games he covers," Tim explained.

"What a dumb ass," Denise said.

"Did he ever have access to your money?" Jase asked.

"What money?" Tim asked.

"You told him?" Denise asked at the same time.

Bree answered Denise first. "Yes, I told him." She looked at Tim. "I have a rather large inheritance."

To Jase she said, "Chad has never had access to my money. Other than conveniently forgetting his wallet if we went out. Most of it's tied up with the estate or the foundation, anyway."

"Could all this be connected to his gambling debts?" Jase asked.

"It's an angle we're looking at," Tim said.

"Is what connected to his gambling debt?" Denise asked.

Bree took a deep breath. "Jaelynn, Steven's wife, was murdered. Somehow it's connected to either me or Chad. Or both, they aren't sure."

Denise looked between Tim and Bree. "Say what?"

"I'll explain while we're cleaning."

"I'm going to need to take a statement from you both about the attack. Give me a minute to call in to the station," Tim told Jase and Bree. "I may have to come back after we take Steven in. We still need to question Chad about Jaelynn. How long are you guys going to be cleaning?"

"It shouldn't take too long, but I need to go get a new mattress," Bree said.

"Hey, Tim. This guy is refusing to go to the station," Tim's partner called out.

"Of course he is." Tim left them to question Chad. Jase led Bree and Denise up the porch steps and unlocked the door before handing the new keys to Bree.

Denise took in the mess in the living room as they walked through to the kitchen. "They only broke the pictures of you and Chad?" she asked.

"Yup," Bree said.

"That's just weird."

"Yup."

"I'm going to go talk to Tim before he takes off," Jase said. "If you can help me get your mattress into my truck, I'll take it to the dump while you're cleaning, then we can go to the mattress store."

"Can you bring Charlie and Polly back in with you?" Bree asked.

"While you're out there, can you let my dog out of my car and bring her in with you? She'll follow Charlie and Polly in," Denise requested.

"Sure." Jase leaned down and gave Bree a quick kiss before heading back outside through the laundry room.

CHAPTER 11

*D*enise watched Jase leave through the kitchen. "I like him," she said.

"I hear a 'but'," Bree said.

Denise leaned against the counter. "It's been a week."

"Really, when you think about it, it's only been two and a half days."

"That's fast." Denise raised an eyebrow. "It took you, what? Three, four months before Chad was this involved in your life? Although, given how that's turned out, maybe it's a sign Jase is involved so fast."

"It's—" Bree shook her head. "I don't know what it is. It's a lot."

"How's the sex?"

A flush crept up Bree's neck and she opened the cabinet under the sink to get the garbage bags. Why was she embarrassed to talk about how good Jase was in bed? Denise knew way more personal details about her.

"That good, huh?"

Bree stood and blew a strand of hair out of her face. "In a word, yes." She tore out two bags and tossed the box back under the sink. "He kept Charlie while I went to Gran's yesterday."

"Wow, really?"

"Yeah. He was playing fetch with him when I got back to his place. And he changed the locks for me."

"That's why he had the keys."

"Yup." She twisted the bags in her hand. "Is it too much?"

"That depends, sweetie. How much do you want?"

Bree's answer was delayed by the sound of the side door opening. Charlie, Polly, and Denise's large English Mastiff mix, Sprocket, trotted in ahead of Jase.

"You know, you're supposed to be zoned for a farm to keep horses," he said. Sprocket let out a groan as she sprawled in the middle of the kitchen floor and yawned.

Denise reached down and rubbed Sprocket's head. "She's not a horse. The laziest dog in the world, maybe."

"I want to get the comforter off before we take the mattress out. I think just folding up the sheets around it will prevent most of the feathers from flying everywhere," Bree said.

Denise paused just inside the door and took in the carnage. "That's a lot of feathers."

"No kidding. I'm going to be finding them for days."

They carefully bundled up the sheets and comforter and got them into the garbage bags without too many more feathers escaping. Jase grabbed one end of the mattress, and Denise and Bree grabbed the other. Between them they hauled it out of the house and onto Jase's truck. Bree grabbed the vacuum out of the hall closet on her way back to the bedroom.

"You rearranged your dresser," Denise said, when Bree turned off the vacuum.

"What? No, I didn't." She walked over and stood next to Denise. There wasn't a lot on her dresser–a metal dish for loose change, a small crystal vase with a single porcelain rose she bought while in Italy, a small wooden jewelry box her grandfather had made her, and a few pictures of her and her grandparents.

They had all been rearranged. Before the pictures had been on one corner of the dresser. Now they were spaced evenly along the length of the dresser, the other items placed between the photos.

"That's creepy," Denise said.

"I told you."

"Do you think the cops should dust for prints or something?"

"Maybe? I'll get Jase to call Tim and ask."

The phone call to Jase, already on his way to the dump, was brief. In less than five minutes, Tim called Bree to let her know a crime scene technician was on the way and Tim would be joining them after he finished at the station.

Denise went to answer the door when the doorbell rang, leaving Bree to examine the rest of her bedroom and office. She was in the closet when Denise led the tech in.

The tech set his kit on the floor and knelt next to it. "Is the dresser the only thing you noticed was out of place?"

"And my closet. A few of my clothes are out of place."

He paused with a canister in one hand and a large brush in the other. "How can you tell?"

"She color-codes her closet," Denise said. "Also arranged by style."

Bree made a face at Denise. "Whatever. At least now I know whoever did this rummaged through my clothes as well." She watched the tech flicking the brush across her dresser, leaving a fine layer of dust in his wake. "Although I'd prefer you not dust my clothes."

"No problem. Really hard to get prints off clothing anyway." He returned the canister and brush to his bag, then took pictures of the surface before using large pieces of tape to lift the prints from the dresser. He pulled a portable biometric scanner out of his kit to take Bree and Denise's prints.

"Are you able to access the military system?" Denise asked.

"We can," the tech said, while taking a scan of her prints. "But it's honestly easier to have your prints already handy and not have to waste time searching through the database for them."

"How long will it take to run the prints?" Bree asked.

"A couple of weeks, probably."

"So it's not like on T.V.? You're not going to be able to solve this case in fifty-nine minutes with commercial breaks?" Denise asked.

The tech laughed. "No, unfortunately, it's not that easy. I hate it when I tell people how long it will take and they say, *well, that's not how they do it on CSI*. Crime dramas are the worst thing that ever happened to my job."

Denise and Bree walked the tech out and finished cleaning the living room, vacuuming the floor to make sure all the glass shards were up.

"What do you want me to do with the pictures?" Denise asked.

"Toss 'em." Bree pulled the fridge open. "Do you want a sandwich? I have chicken salad or egg salad."

"Chicken salad."

A knock sounded at the laundry room door as she set the containers on the counter. Jase smiled behind the glass.

"Why did you knock?" Bree asked.

Jase stepped close as he came in and leaned down to kiss her. Open mouthed with just a hint of tongue. Much too brief for her liking.

"I wasn't sure how you'd feel about me just walking into your house," he said.

"We've had sex. I'm think I'm okay with you walking into my house."

He tucked a strand of hair behind her ear. "We've had sex in *my* house and bed. This is your house."

She smiled. She liked the respect he was giving her and her space. He wasn't taking anything for granted, no matter how intimate they had been.

She leaned up and kissed him gently. "You can come in without knocking."

Jase grinned down at her. "Thanks."

"Do you want chicken or egg salad?" Denise hollered from the kitchen.

Bree grabbed his hand and tilted her head toward the kitchen. "Come on, let's eat, then I need to get a new mattress."

~

AT THE FURNITURE STORE, Bree waited for Jase to round the hood and open her door. He slowly lowered her body down against his, giving her a hot, opened-mouth kiss. Bree grinned against his mouth as he kissed her.

He lifted his head. "What's funny?"

Bree ran a hand over the curve of his ass. "I can feel your happiness."

"You can feel more of it later." He pulled her away from the truck and shut her door. He laced his fingers with hers as he led her through the door of the store.

Tucked into the far back corner of the large showroom, a low, half wall separated the bedding section from the rest of the store. Subdued lighting attempted to create a relaxing, boudoir feel in the space.

A salesman approached them as soon as they entered. "Good afternoon, folks. Can I help you find something today?"

"Do you still carry the Sealy Posturepedic Hybrid Elite?" Bree asked.

"We sure do. One of our best sellers. It's right over here." He led them over to the display bed.

"Yeah, that's fine," she said. "Do you have it in stock or does it have to be delivered from the warehouse?"

"I need to check the database, if you don't mind waiting for a few minutes."

Bree sat on the end of the bed after the salesman left and flopped back. Jase joined her, but lay down on his side with his head propped on one hand. He rested his other hand on her stomach, his fingers teasing the bottom of her t-shirt.

"That was quick," he said.

"What?"

"Picking out a mattress."

Bree shifted her gaze from the ceiling to Jase. "I liked my mattress. I don't need a different one, I just need a new one. Why waste time looking for something else when I'm perfectly happy with what I had?"

"Not too many people think that way. They always want bigger and better."

"My grandparents lived frugally, even when they didn't need to. I never knew we had money when I was growing up. Having it makes life comfortable, but I still live well within my means."

He toyed with a lock of her hair spread out over her head. "Did your grandparents raise you?"

"Yeah. My parents died in a car wreck when I was a year and a half."

"Shit. I'm sorry. You don't have any other family?"

She watched Jase twirl the end of her hair around his forefinger. "I have two uncles and an aunt."

"Why didn't you live with them?" He seemed fascinated with the way the end of her hair curled around his finger, then let it fall back to the mattress.

"I asked Gran that one time when I was around ten or so. She said, 'You were my Katie's, so that makes you mine.'"

"That's sweet." Jase's fingers brushed her neck as he moved the lock of hair off her neck where it had fallen, sending goose bumps down her chest and pebbling her nipples under the light padding of her bra.

"I know now it was more complicated than that. My mom was

the oldest. None of them were really in a position in their lives to be able to take me in and raise me."

"That couldn't have been easy, though. Losing your parents at such a young age," he said.

She shrugged. "It was all I ever knew. I didn't realize until elementary school that not all kids lived with their grandparents."

"Still. I can't even imagine."

"You and Tim seem pretty close. What about your sister?"

"We were really close growing up. She broke my parents' hearts by marrying an Air Force guy. They live out in Colorado Springs."

She tilted her head. "Why did it break their hearts?"

"Well, it broke my mom's heart because they moved so far away. It broke my dad's heart because she married a zoomie," he said, grinning.

Bree pushed Jase's shoulder, barely budging him. "Whatever."

Jase leaned forward and kissed her quickly. "I saw your pictures at your house. How long were you in the Air Force?"

"Eight years."

"What did you do? Something medical, I'm guessing."

"I was an aerospace medical technician."

"What do they do?"

"We flew with medical evacuation patients. Made sure they were stable flying from one place to another. What about you? Ranger?"

"What makes you think I wasn't a mechanic?"

"Well, I can tell you were Special Forces. You've got that type-A, alpha-male, door-kicker vibe going on."

"Type-A, alpha-male, door-kicker?" His eyes twinkled.

She smirked. "Yeah. You know. Badass with a beard. Plus, I saw pictures of you in uniform in your office, so I saw the tab."

Jase gave her another quick kiss.

"Good news, folks," the salesman said. "We have a queen size in stock. The manager said he would knock an additional five percent off the price if you're able to take it with you."

Bree sat up and looked over her shoulder at Jase. "Do you mind helping me take it back to my place?"

Jase quirked an eyebrow but didn't bother answering her question.

"Right." She looked up at the salesman. "We can take it today."

"THIS WILL BE EASIER if we take the plastic off first," Bree said.

Jase grunted as he tried to get a grip on the protective barrier around the mattress. "If we take the plastic off here, the mattress will get dirty."

"Then at least cut holes where the handles are on the side to make it easier to carry."

"Huh. Yeah. That makes sense."

Bree put her wrist to her forehead and struck a dramatic pose. "Oh, the horror. Common sense has prevailed."

Jase fought against smiling at her theatrics. "Smart ass."

She winked and stepped back to give him room to slit the plastic. "I can't muscle the mattress into the house without some leverage."

He backed his way up the porch steps, carrying the mattress low so Bree wouldn't have to lift it up so far. Maneuvering it down the hall took little effort, and he cut off the plastic before pushing the mattress up onto the box spring. He bundled up the covering and took it to the outside trash.

Bree finished tucking the corner of the sheet under the mattress when he returned. "Can you grab the comforter and pillows from the guest room?"

He pulled her onto the bed once she had everything made to her satisfaction. "Did you text Denise my address?"

"Yes. I told her around five o'clock. What time did you tell Tim?"

"Between five and five-thirty."

Bree glanced at the clock on her nightstand. Four-fifteen. "So we have about fifteen minutes to fool around," she said.

A slow grin spread across his face. "I can work with fifteen minutes."

CHAPTER 12

Denise wielded the chopping knife with expert dexterity, dicing the tomatoes into perfect bite-size pieces. "How exactly did the women folk end up in the kitchen?"

"Tale as old as time," Bree replied.

Denise turned from her salad preparation. "Did you just quote Beauty and the Beast to me?"

Bree grinned. "It seemed appropriate." She opened the refrigerator and gathered cabbage and carrots for coleslaw.

"You're awfully comfortable here." She hacked into the bunch of lettuce.

"It's a kitchen. How uncomfortable should it be?"

She threw the chopped lettuce into a large bowl. "It's the kitchen of a guy you met a week ago, and you know where he keeps all his cutlery."

Bree looked down at the knife she held. She'd known right were to find it. Cutlery drawer to the right of the stove. She might have to hunt for specialty items, but she knew exactly where to find the essentials. She could tell Denise where to find just about anything she needed.

She raised her gaze to Denise. "This is going really fast," she whispered.

"Shit, honey. I didn't mean to freak you out."

"It was coming whether you said something or not. I haven't thought about how fast this was going." She cleared her throat and turned back to the vegetables. "I think maybe I should back off some."

"Why?"

She set down the knife and picked up the grater, intent on demolishing the carrots. "What do you mean 'why'?"

"Bree, look at me."

She set down the grater and turned to face Denise. She leaned a hip against the counter and crossed her arms over her chest.

"Why do you think you need to back off?" Denise asked.

"It's too fast. I've known him for a week and I'm as comfortable in his kitchen as I am in yours." Bree swept an arm out.

"Who says it's too fast?"

"Me. You. Anyone who hears how we met."

"Whoa, I never said it was too fast."

"You said I looked really comfortable in his kitchen."

"Right. And you do. It's not a bad thing. Bree, you need to go as fast or slow as you need to go. And to be honest with you, Jase doesn't seem like the kind of guy to let you back off, even if that's what you really wanted to do."

Bree snorted and folded her arms over her chest. "Yeah. I called him an alpha-male door-kicker today."

Denise laughed. "It's an apt description. What did he say?"

"Nothing, he just smiled."

Denise paused before confessing, "I never liked Chad."

"I know," Bree said with a rueful smile.

"He never got you. He was never in the military. Never understood what you went through or why you chose to do what you do now. Jase..." Denise took a breath and gazed toward the back of the house. She looked back at Bree before continuing. "Jase gets it. You can see it in his eyes. The way he carries himself. He'll never ask you stupid questions that make you want to throat punch him."

Bree snorted, her eyes stinging.

"He'll protect you in a way Chad never could."

"I know," Bree whispered.

"You need to grab on to that and hold on tight."

Bree's head dropped as she brushed a stray tear off her cheek. "I'm scared."

"Of what?"

"Of everything." Bree looked up at her best friend. "I'm feeling way more in a week than I've felt in a long time. He makes me feel things that…that I don't actually remember ever feeling before."

"And?"

"And a lot has been going on. What if, when it all settles down, it's not so great? What if it goes to shit?"

"What if it does?" Denise asked.

She ran the heel of her hand across her forehead. "I'm not sure I could walk away as easily from Jase as I did from Chad."

"So don't walk away. If you decide it's something worth fighting for, fight for it."

"It's not that easy."

"Of course it isn't."

Bree held Denise's gaze. "Say it. Whatever it is you're holding back.

Denise swept her hair up in a bun on the back of her head. "Brutal honesty?"

"Always."

"Chad was a safe bet. There was never any chance of you actually falling in love with him. You said so yourself it was easier to stay with him than to break it off. Jase is a risk. You're going to feel things. There's a chance you could get hurt. That's what's scaring you."

Bree nodded and looked out the window. "Yeah."

"Yeah."

Sometimes it sucked having a best friend who knew you so well. Everything Denise said was true. It was a chance. A risk. Her heart could end up torn into pieces, something she hadn't risked in so long.

Bree blew out a breath and shook her head. "We're not going to figure out my love life in the next fifteen minutes, and I need time to stop looking like I've been crying."

"Well, if your skin wasn't translucent, you'd be a prettier crier," Denise said.

Bree picked up a carrot. "Bite me."

"Only if you ask nicely." She wet a paper towel and wrung it out before handing it to Bree.

Bree pressed the cool cloth over her eyes.

"So when are you going to ask her to move in with you?" Tim asked.

Jase looked up from the grill. "What are you talking about?"

"Really? This is the first girl you've been serious about since— Have you ever been serious about a girl?"

Jase flipped a steak over. "I don't know. Sarah?"

"That was high school."

Jase shrugged. "So?"

"So, this is the first girl you've introduced me to. You've known her, what? A couple of weeks?" He took a sip of his beer.

He lifted another steak and checked the underside. "'Bout that."

"So, what is it?"

Jase closed the top of the grill and picked up his beer. *What is it?* What was it about Bree that made Jase chase after her? What is it about her that made him want to protect her but still fuck her until she screamed his name?

"I don't know." He shook his head. "It's like she sees me. She understands without having to ask the question." He took a pull of his beer. "She hasn't once asked me about what I did in the Army. She knows I was a Ranger, but it's like she doesn't care. She's not some SOF groupie looking for a little danger."

"She serve?" Tim asked.

"Air Force. Aerospace med tech."

"What's that?"

Jase sighed. "You remember when I came home for a few weeks, middle of my last tour 'cause I was escorting a guy in my unit back?"

"Yeah, is that what she did?"

"No. I was a non-medical escort. Just someone to help the guy out in Germany. Get him to appointments, that kind of thing."

"What did she do?"

"The plane we took back was a C-17, configured for medical patients. The aerospace med techs take care of the patients onboard the plane."

Tim raised an eyebrow. "Like a flying nurse?"

"Kind of. But they have those, too."

"So she's probably seen some pretty serious shit."

Jase pulled from his beer. "Probably. We haven't talked about deployments or anything."

"But she's probably gone through some stuff too, even if she wasn't kicking in doors."

Jase laughed. "She called me a door-kicker today."

"Well, you were." He looked at the bottle in his hand and swirled the dredges. "Where do you see it going?"

"Honestly? Long term. Bree's the first person to make me want things since Tony killed himself."

"It's good to hear that. You had Mom worried for a while. Hell, you had us all worried. You went kind of wild when you first got back. Mom thought you were going to self-destruct. Then, after Tony... Even though you started V.E.T. Adventures, you still weren't really all there. I think that scared Mom even more. Happy looks good on you. Good to have my kid brother back."

Shit, is that what it was? Happy? He felt like something had been lifted from his shoulders. Even before Tony killed himself, he didn't really engage with people. It took too much energy to answer the questions, ignore the looks when people found out he was part of an elite team of U.S. soldiers. Bree saw…him.

But that wasn't something he was going to articulate to his pain-in-the-ass brother. "We gonna hug? Do I need to go get you some tissue so you can dab your eyes?"

"And there's the little shit I know and love." Tim toasted him with his beer before taking a sip.

Jase lifted the cover of the grill to check on the steaks as Bree and Denise came out carrying a salad and other sides. They set everything down on patio table.

"Do you guys need a refill?" Bree asked.

"Sure," Jase said.

Tim drained the last of his beer. "I can do another. Thanks."

The patio door closed behind the girls and Tim asked, "So what's Denise's story?"

"Not sure. I know she and Bree are really close. I got the feeling they met while in the service. Ask 'em over dinner."

Bree and Denise returned with plates, silverware, napkins and beers for everyone.

"How much longer?" Bree asked.

"Depends on how you take your steak," Jase said.

"Medium rare."

"Same here," Denise said.

"Then probably about five minutes," Jase told them.

"So how long have you two known each other?" Tim asked.

"About ten years, I guess," Bree replied, looking to Denise for confirmation.

"Wow, it has been that long."

Tim grabbed foil-wrapped baked potatoes from the top rack of the grill. "How did you meet?"

"We were trailer-mates in Iraq for, what? Nine months, give or take?" Denise took the platter from Tim and set it on the table.

"Give or take." Bree sat at the table. "You got there a few months after I did, and I left a month before you did."

"Where were you deployed?" Tim asked.

"We were at Camp Victory," Bree explained. "I was assigned to the CASH unit there and Denise was working for a Joint Task Force."

"What's a cash unit?" Tim asked.

"Combat Army Surgical Hospital."

"I thought you were Air Force."

"I was, but we were back filling the Army positions because they couldn't fill them. Something about the Army sucking," Bree said, winking at Jase.

Jase smiled and shook his head at her. "Which JTF?"

"High-Value Individuals. We were tracking al-Qaida insurgency leaders."

"That's sounds interesting." Tim said. "What all did that entail?"

"I can't really talk about it," Denise said.

"Or you'll have to kill me?" Tim suggested.

"Nah. We don't kill people anymore, just stick them in secret prisons."

"Was that the only time you guys were deployed together?" Jase asked as he removed the steaks from the grill.

"No, actually. We were both part of a CST in Kandahar."

Jase paused, tongs suspended in mid-air and turned around. "Wow. Really?"

"What's a CST?" Tim asked. "Quit talking in alphabet soup."

"Sorry. It's a Cultural Support Team," Jase explained. He removed the last steak from the grill and set the plate on the table. "All-female team that's trained to go out with Special Ops guys.

They engage with the women and kids on target. They get trained on language and culture and go through five or six weeks of intensive training." He flipped off the knobs of the grill and closed the lid. "It's a really hard course to get through, from what I hear."

"We had four or five guys decide to go through the training with us because they didn't think it could be that hard. You know, 'cause we're women," Denise said. "A couple of Rangers, a SEAL, and a Green Beret, I think. All but two dropped out, and by the end of it they had both injured themselves." She stabbed a steak on the platter and moved it to her plate. "They finished out of sheer stubbornness more than anything else. Needless to say, we didn't get any shit about how easy the training was after that."

The corner of Jase's mouth lifted and he looked at Bree. "So you were a door-kicker too." No wonder she didn't ask him any questions. She was a bad-ass. He took her in. Really looked at her physique and not just her body. She wasn't muscular to the point you would think she lived at the gym, but she was lean and strong. That explained her taking him down at her house. His gaze drifted back up to find an amused smile on her face.

"I didn't do the door kicking. I just walked in after it was already off its hinges," she said.

"You should go out on the trip with Jase next weekend," Tim said, passing the coleslaw to Bree. "You can probably teach some of the guys a thing or two."

"I can't do it next weekend. I'm scheduled through the end of the month, but if you let me know ahead of time, I'd love to go," she said. "My availability for next month is due next Friday. I just need to know dates so I can block them off."

"What about you?" Tim asked Denise.

She shrugged. "I'll go. I just have to know when so I can schedule a couple of extra people for the weekend."

Jase cut into his steak. "I have a trip lined up next month that's a bunch of guys who try to go together a couple times a year. It's more relaxed than the regular trips."

"What do you have to schedule people for?" Tim asked Denise.

"I run a doggie daycare and rescue." Denise took a bite of steak.

"She also does training for service dogs and companions," Bree bragged.

"What's the name of the rescue?" Jase asked.

"Wiggle Butt Rescue," Bree and Denise answered in unison.

Tim put his fork down with a clunk. "You just picked up a contract with the county K-9 unit."

Jase smiled as a flush creeped up Denise's cheeks. "To do what?" he asked.

Denise cleared her throat. "We've been contracted to supply potential candidates to the unit."

"Where do you get the candidates from?" Tim asked around a bite of food.

"We get pregnant surrenders all the time. We assess the puppies and do some preliminary training for the first twelve weeks. Any pups we think would make good K-9s, we'll turn over to their trainers for further assessment."

Bree scooped up a fork of coleslaw. "We also have an agility course on site they're going to use for some of their training. The county's is in pretty bad shape and they haven't been able to get the funding to refurbish it."

"If they don't have the money to refurbish their course, how do they have money for the puppies and training?" Jase asked.

"We're doing a lot of it as a donation. They'll pay for the pups they take for training. The ones they don't take we'll train to be companion animals. Those people pay for the training and upkeep until the dogs are ready to go to their new person."

"We?" Tim asked.

Bree lifted her beer from the table. "I'm a silent partner."

"Bree is the owner," Denise said. "She put up the money for the entire operation and makes sure everyone gets paid."

Bree blushed. "What? I'm passionate about rescue. Sue me. And it's a non-profit, so everything gets written off."

She's passionate about a lot of things, Jase thought. Wounded Warriors. Wounded dogs. Damn, she kept getting better the more he discovered about her. She put her money where her mouth was—literally and figuratively. She took action and got her hands dirty. He smiled, remembering how passionate she'd been that morning. How passionate he was going to make her later on.

"That mama isn't doing so well now that her pups have been weaned," Denise said. Jase shifted his attention to Denise. *What mama?*

"Bring her by tomorrow night. We'll see if she'll settle down out of the kennel with fewer dogs around."

"You know that's going to be a fail if you take her, right?" Denise asked.

Bree shrugged. "Meh."

Denise smiled and shook her head. "You're a nut."

Bree grinned at her friend and took a bite of salad.

"Fail?" Tim asked.

"Foster fail," Denise explained. "Most of our rescues go to foster families. People who can do some basic obedience training and see how the dogs react in a home environment. When a family can't let the dog go, we call it a foster fail. It's actually not a bad thing."

Watching Bree and Denise, Jase felt a pang of jealousy. He missed the easy familiarity that came from having a history with someone. Tim was right. He'd checked out after Tony died. It'd been easier to avoid people than to care. He'd been wrong. How much had he missed out on in the last few years because he wouldn't let people close?

They carried their empty plates back into the house. Bree and Denise cleaned up in the kitchen while Tim and Jase finished cleaning up outside.

Denise wiped her hands on a dish towel and hung it over the bar on the stove. "I'm out. Thanks for dinner."

Jase closed the fridge. "Any time."

Her mouth quirked and she hugged Bree. "I'll call you tomorrow to work out when to drop the dog off."

"Sounds good," Bree said.

Denise waved a hand over her shoulder as she opened the door. "Tell Tim I said 'bye."

"Will do," Jase said.

The kitchen door closed as Tim walked around the corner. "'Bout time to call it a night. Early morning tomorrow."

"Denise left, too," Bree said.

Tim pulled Jase in for a bear hug, lifting him up onto his toes. "Good to have you back."

Jase groaned as Tim squeezed him tight. "Ugh. Put me down, jackass." His heels hit the floor when Tim released him, and he took a deep breath. Shit, he felt like a rib cracked.

Tim kissed Bree on the cheek. "I look forward to seeing a lot more of you, Bree."

Her eyebrows raised and she smiled. "You too, Tim."

"'Night, guys," he said.

Jase watched as Bree closed the door to the dishwasher and started it. He pulled her close and brushed her hair away from her face as she wrapped her arms loosely around her waist.

"You look beat," he noted.

"It's been a long day."

"It has, now that you mention it. What time do you have to be at work tomorrow?"

"Seven-thirty. My first appointment is at eight."

Jase leaned down and placed a soft kiss on her lips. "Why don't you head up? I'll let the dogs out one last time and lock up."

"You sure?"

"Yeah, I got it."

"Okay." She went up on her toes and returned his kiss before heading to the stairs.

Jase let the dogs out onto the back patio and stayed out there while they did their business.

This was easy. It'd been a day, and it felt like a routine they did every night. He scratched the dogs on the head as they trotted back to his side. He locked the door behind him while the dogs settled onto their beds by the fireplace. After walking through the house and turning off lights, he climbed the stairs. Only the top of Bree's head peeked out of the covers, her hair spread across the pillow.

He stripped out of his clothes and climbed into bed. Leaning up on an elbow, he pulled the edge of the comforter away from her face. Her light lashes rested against the pale skin of her cheek, a smattering of freckles sprinkled across her nose and cheek. The corner of her mouth pulled down so she appeared to frown in her sleep. He brushed a finger across her cheek. Shit, she was beautiful. He shifted close to her back and pulled her close. He buried his nose in the nape of her neck and inhaled the light fragrance she used. He smiled and closed his eyes, an unfamiliar sense of contentment settled over him.

BREE WOKE SLOWLY, blinking against the early morning light. Pressed against the length of Jase's body, she flexed her fingers, and released them against his abs. One arm across his torso, a leg thrown over his, her knee nestled against the junction of his thighs. Her head was tucked into the pocket of his shoulder. She glanced at the clock on the nightstand as she calculated how much time she needed to get ready and make it to work on time. Bree smiled. Time to get creative.

She raised her head from his shoulder and lifted her arm and leg off his body, watching him closely for any sign he might wake up. She grabbed a condom off the nightstand. Pulling the sheet down, she revealed his six-pack abs and impressive morning erection. She bit the corner of her mouth. Sweet baby Jesus.

She glanced at his face still relaxed, mouth slightly down-turned and his short but thick, dark eyelashes resting against the soft skin under his eyes. She rose up on her knees and straddled the smorgasbord of maleness before her.

Running her fingertips down his abs, she stopped at the sculpted 'V' and couldn't help but think of a meme a friend had sent her. It was a picture of a male model with chiseled abs and an arrow pointing to the 'V' with the caption, *I don't know what these are called but they make girls stupid.* Bree knew what they were called and they still made her stupid.

Unable to resist the urge, Bree ran her tongue along the valley created by those defined muscles. She grasped the base of Jase's cock and swirled her tongue around the head before slowly sliding as much of his length as she could into her mouth. She pulled her mouth up, dragging her tongue along the base of his cock.

Jase groaned before she reached the crown as he ran his fingers through her hair. He clenched his fists in her hair and held her head in place.

"What are you doing, Bree?"

She flicked the tip of her tongue along the slit, tasting the saltiness of his precum. "Getting creative."

Her hand slid up along his length. Her mouth covered his head and followed her hand down to the base of his shaft. There was no way to take him fully in her mouth; he was really too long and she was no porn star, but she would do her damnedest to make it feel that way for him. She worked his cock with her mouth and hand for several minutes. Jase's groans, his fingers massaging and fisting her hair, and his legs shifting under her drove her own arousal.

"Fuck, Bree," Jase moaned. "I want you on my cock. Ride me, darlin'."

Needing no further invitation, Bree kept moving her mouth up and down Jase's cock as her other hand grabbed for the condom she had placed by his hip. Shifting her weight to her knees, Bree ripped open the wrapper while hollowing her cheeks and increasing the suction before she released Jase's cock from her mouth. She pinched the tip of the condom and rolled it quickly down his erection before climbing over him, sliding her wet pussy back and forth over Jase's rigid length, rubbing her clit against him and coating him with her juices.

"Quit teasing, Bree." Jase grabbed her hips and positioned her over the tip of his cock. He brought her down as he drove his hips up, slamming into her in one hard thrust.

Bree's head fell back as Jase used his hands to rock her hips back and forth, setting a steady pace while keeping his cock buried to the hilt. Running her hands up his abs and chest, Bree dropped her head to look at Jase. She shifted her weight and rose over Jase, allowing him to slide partway out of her hot core before sliding back down his length. Jase kept rocking her hips as she rose and fell.

Jase suddenly sat up, breaking their rhythm. One hand delved into Bree's hair, forcing her head back as he ran his mouth up the column of her neck.

"Keep moving, Bree." He nipped her ear lobe.

Bree closed her eyes and tilted her head toward his mouth with a groan. Running her hands up his arms and over his shoulders, she continued to roll her hips.

"I'm close," she told him with a gasp.

He moved his mouth to her chin. "What do you need?"

"Play with my clit."

"Look at me, Bree." He kept his hand in her hair as he tilted her head forward and brought their faces close. "Eyes on me. I want to see you come."

Jase wedged his other hand between their bodies and thumbed her clit.

Bree's breath caught and she watched Jase with hooded eyes. Her blood gathered in her core. An incoherent shout escaped and she ground down on Jase as her orgasm exploded. Throwing her head back, she dug her nails into his shoulders and rode the wave of pleasure crashing through her.

Jase flipped her onto her back and hooked his arms under her knees. He thrust into her four, five times, before throwing his head back with a shout. He fell forward, slowly unhooking his arms from under her knees as he fought to steady his breathing.

She relished the weight of Jase's body, her thoughts scattering in every direction. Jase let out another groan as she licked the space between his neck and shoulder.

"I think you're trying to kill me," he accused her.

She flicked her tongue again, tasting the saltiness of his skin. "I like the way you taste."

Jase lifted his head and rested his forearms on either side of her head, smiling. "Morning."

Bree smiled back. "Morning."

"What brought that on?"

"You said get creative if I woke up before you."

"I did, didn't I?"

Bree just raised and lowered her eyebrows.

"I like how you get creative." He lowered his head and kissed her deeply. "Shower?"

"I need to get to work."

"We should conserve water. Shower together."

Bree laughed and pushed at Jase's shoulders. "That's not going to get me to work on time."

Jase collapsed onto his back. Bree rose up on an elbow and ran a hand across his chest. "Me first." She gave him a quick kiss. She rolled away him.

"I'll let your dogs out and fix coffee while you shower."

"Thank you."

~

BREE MADE her way to the kitchen dressed in her standard uniform of black yoga pants and long sleeve shirt under a scrub shirt. Jase wrapped something in a paper towel and set it next to a to-go cup of coffee.

"What's that?"

"Egg and cheese on an English muffin," he said.

"Wow. Breakfast to go?"

He kissed the side of her neck. "I figured you worked up an appetite this morning."

She grinned and picked up a sandwich. "That I did. What are your plans for today?" She took one of the cups he held out to her.

"I need to run some errands for the trip this weekend and restock some supplies. What about you? What time do you get done with work?"

"My last appointment is at three, so I should be able to leave around four-thirty."

"Your place or mine tonight?"

"Mine. Denise is bringing that mama dog over before she goes to dinner with her cousin."

"I can keep Charlie and Polly again, if you need me to," he told her.

Bree raised her eyebrows slightly. "You don't mind? Did Charlie get in your way on Friday?"

Jase leaned down and gave her a brief kiss on her lips, but didn't pull away when he told her, "I wouldn't offer if I minded." He straightened before continuing. "It was actually nice having him with me for the day. I might have to talk to you about adopting my own."

She smiled big. "Really?"

"Really," he answered with a smile of his own.

Bree stepped closer and rose up on her tiptoes and gave him a hard kiss. Taking control of the kiss, Jase pulled her closer, his tongue delving between Bree's lips to tangle with hers. Desire coiled low in her belly before spreading out, up through her chest and arms and down her legs. She felt languid and energized at the same time — relaxed, but tingly.

Before Bree could drop her coffee to the floor and have her way with Jase right there in his kitchen, he pulled away slightly with deep inhale. "You need to go before I make you call in sick and drag you back upstairs."

"Yeah," she whispered. "Probably a good idea."

"Dragging you upstairs or you going to work?"

With a quick peck, Bree pulled out of his arms. "Going to work."

One calloused finger tucked an errant strand of hair behind her ear. "I'll see you tonight."

Bree grabbed a sandwich off the counter. She glanced over her shoulder as she opened the kitchen door and smiled at Jase. "See you later."

CHAPTER 13

That smile stayed with her the rest of the day. It was infectious, and she passed it on to everyone. The only person who seemed not to respond was her assistant, Cindy.

Bree took advantage of a lull between patients. "Cindy, I'm going to grab a coffee. Do you want to go?"

Cindy looked up from the computer on her desk. "No thank you, Dr. Marks. I need to input all these patient notes into the system."

Bree leaned against the door jamb to the shared office. Cindy was the only assistant in there at the moment, the three other medical assistants busy checking in patients.

"Is everything okay?" Bree asked. "You seem kind of down today."

Cindy looked down at the keyboard and shrugged. "It was just a long weekend."

"Is there anything I can help with?"

Cindy rubbed her cheek against her shoulder and glanced at Bree. "No," she said quietly. "There's nothing wrong. I just didn't sleep well this weekend. A lot of stuff going through my mind."

"Well, I'm here if you need to talk to someone."

Cindy just nodded and started typing again. Bree stood away from the door jamb to leave.

"Dr. Marks?"

"Yes?

"I'm really glad things seem to have worked out for you," Cindy said.

Bree cocked her head slightly, trying to judge the look and quiet tone. That was an odd thing to say. Cindy was normally quiet, but this was more. She seemed upset about something.

"Are you sure there isn't something you want to talk about? If not with me, someone else?"

Cindy shook her head. "No. Thank you for being concerned, though." She returned to her work, dismissing Bree.

Bree stared another moment before heading out. A fellow physical therapist was walking out ahead of her in the same direction. "Hey, Janet. Where're you headed?"

Janet paused, letting Bree catch up with her. "Caffeine. I need a top off."

"I'm headed that way myself."

"You seem to be in a really good mood today." Janet pushed the button at the elevator bank and a door opened immediately. "Did you get you a little somthin'-somthin'?" She did a sexy shoulder shrug.

They stepped into the elevator, and Bree tried to stop the grin from spreading across her face.

"Yeah you did!" Janet bumped Bree with her shoulder. "Spill the details. Did you and Chad have wild, make-up monkey sex?"

"Oh hell no! Chad is gone. G-O-N-E."

"So you got a new guy?"

Bree felt warmth spread across the top of her cheeks. "I might have." Leaving the elevator one floor down, they continued to the coffee stand.

"Who is he? Where did you meet him? How did you hook someone new so soon?" They joined the end of the line. "I've been single for months without even a nibble. And let me tell you, I need to be nibbled."

Bree let out a bark of laughter. A young sergeant in line ahead of them turned and Janet winked at him.

"Stop." Bree slapped Janet's arm. They placed their orders, and Bree gave Janet an abbreviated version of her weekend with Jase while they waited for their coffee.

"No wonder you've been all smiles today," Janet said.

She grinned. "It's like I have no control over my face."

Janet sipped her coffee. They stepped to the side to allow a patient in a wheelchair to pass. "There are worse problems to have."

Cindy's response came to mind. "Have you noticed anything going on with Cindy?"

"That girl is kind of weird," Janet said.

"No she's not, she's just quiet."

"Those are the ones you have to worry about."

She pushed the up button to call the elevator. "She's sweet."

"I'm not saying she's not sweet. I don't have anything against her personally. She's just a little odd."

"Okay, I'll give you that. I think she's been very sheltered."

"That's one way to put it." They joined three other people in the elevator cab, the button for their floor already lit.

"Be nice. She seems a little down today."

"Okay. Yes, I have noticed she's more withdrawn today than usual. She's perfectly polite to the patients, but that's about all the effort she's putting into it."

"Do you think I should be worried? I asked her if everything was okay and she just said she had some stuff going on."

They exited the elevator on their floor. "Everyone has off days."

"True. I'll give her a couple of days and see how she is then." She glanced at her watch. "I need to hurry; my next appointment should be here soon."

"Mine too. I'll catch up with you again later." Janet waved as they went their separate ways.

~

SHE DROPPED her bag on the bench in the mudroom and hung her keys on the hook by the door. The house was quiet. Too quiet.

Panic coursed through her and she froze. Shit. Where were Charlie and Polly? With Jase.

Relief flooded her, replacing the panic, and she smiled for the thousandth time that day. She kicked off her shoes and padded through the house to her bedroom. Changing into shorts and a t-shirt, she threw her scrubs into the laundry hamper. Going to the foyer, she hesitated briefly before unlocking the front door so Jase wouldn't have to knock, no matter which door he came through. In the living room, she put together another kennel for the foster dog arriving later. Tuning her satellite radio to a hard rock station, she danced around her kitchen as she prepared dinner.

She called out when she heard the front door open and close. "I'm in the kitchen."

The smile on her face died quickly when Chad came around the corner from the foyer.

"What the hell are you doing here?" Her heart began to pound as her anger spread through her. "What part of *it's over* do you not understand?"

"Brianna, I need you to listen for a minute," Chad started as he stood on the other side of the eat-at counter.

"Listen to what, exactly? How you didn't mean to cheat on me? How none of the women you cheated with meant anything to you? What do you think you can say to make any of this better?" She circled her hand in the air.

"It's not like you've been celibate, Brianna." He pointed toward the front door. "You sure didn't have any problem moving some guy in as soon as you kicked me out."

Bree sucked in a breath, astonished at Chad's gall. "Are you kidding me?" Her voice was low and controlled. "At least I had the decency to break things off before I found someone else. I wasn't fucking around the whole time we were together. I wasn't more interested in your money than you."

"Of course you weren't. You didn't have to be more interested in my money because you've always had money."

Blood rushed in her ears and her vision narrowed, focusing on the threat before her. Muscle memory had her shifting her grip on the knife she held, turning it so she held it in a reverse grip, edge out. She needed to keep her anger in check.

"That's always been the issue, hasn't it?" she asked. "You changed when you found out I had money. Got more attentive. Started pushing things. It was what? A couple of months after that you asked me to marry you?"

"If you'd just agreed to set a date, none of this would have happened." Chad jabbed his finger at her.

"Yes, it would have. If you think I would've actually married you, you're delusional. I'd decided to break it off before I even caught you."

"Damn it, Brianna! You ruined everything!"

"What the fuck did I ruin, exactly?"

"I owe a lot of people a lot of money. You have no idea what you've done," he continued to shout.

"Not my problem. Maybe you shouldn't have been a stupid shit and gambled all that money."

"Fuck you, Bree." Spittle flew from his mouth as he lost any facade of calm or cajoling.

She watched a drop of spit hit the counter. *Well, that's disgusting. Note to self: sanitize counter.*

"It's so fucking easy for you. You stupid fucking rich bitch."

And that was her limit. "Get. The fuck. Out."

"I need money." His words seethed through his clenched teeth and he gripped the back of the stool. "If you had just set a date and married me, none of this would have happened." He wasn't even looking at her any more.

"Are you kidding me? You think having access to my money would have made everything better? It would have just made it worse." She shook her head. "I'm done. Leave now or I'm calling the cops."

"You're so fucking selfish!" He shook the stool. "It's not like you use the fucking money! You give it all away to your stupid fucking dogs and your stupid crippled soldiers!"

She sucked in a breath and gripped the knife harder.

"What the fuck is going on?" Jase stormed in behind Chad. Charlie and Polly followed close behind, growling low in their throats. The anger on Jase's face was palpable. It was fascinating to watch him advance across the room.

Chad pointed at Jase. "It's none of your fucking business."

Bree's eyes widened as Jase connected a right hook to Chad's jaw and knocked him to the ground. "The fuck it's not."

He grabbed Chad by the scruff of his collared shirt with one hand as he used the other to bend one of Chad's arms behind his back. Charlie barked and ran around them both as Jase shuffled him toward the front door.

"You have two minutes to get in your car and leave before I call the cops and have you arrested," Jase yelled.

Tension flowed out of Bree when the door slammed. The grip she had on the knife loosened, and it rested on the cutting board as she released it.

Jase stalked back into the kitchen and around the bar. He didn't stop and Bree backed up into the door of the pantry. Jase braced his hands on either side of her head and leaned close. He closed his eyes and took a breath.

Was he counting to ten? Anger etched on his face, visible in the careful way he controlled his movements. Chad had been in a rage. It hadn't scared her, but she'd taken a defensive posture at the possible threat he posed.

He opened his eyes, his gaze intense. "Care to tell me what the fuck he was doing here?" His voice was measured, the tension in each carefully-voiced word palpable. His hazel eyes were shot through with gold.

"Screaming about how I ruined his life because I wouldn't marry him," she said.

"Why did you let him in?" The strain in his voice was still leaking through.

Bree wondered what would happen if he didn't hold himself in check. Why wasn't she afraid? He'd backed her into another wall — her defenses should be on high alert, especially with everything that had happened a few minutes ago, but she felt no fear that he would hurt her. "I didn't let him in; he walked in."

The small muscle under his right eye twitched. He stared, searching her face before closing his eyes and dropping his head. He straightened up and away from her and placed his hands on his hips as he took a step back.

"How did he walk right in?" His eyes remained closed, his head still down.

"It wasn't locked. I'm assuming he turned the knob like anyone else would do."

"Why the fuck was the door unlocked, Bree?"

She pushed away from the wall. Enough was enough. She was tired of men yelling at her and expecting her to take it. "Because I was expecting *you* to walk in the door and I left it unlocked as a courtesy. Won't fucking happen again. In fact, I'll be sure to lock it behind you after you leave," she shouted.

"I'll knock on the damn door if I need you to let me in. You don't leave the fucking thing open," Jase shouted back. He ignored her not-so-subtle suggestion to leave.

She took a step toward him. "I was trying to be nice!"

"I don't want you to be nice; I want you to be safe!"

"I think I proved I can take care of myself quite effectively when I punched you in the balls."

"What is going on in here?" Denise asked as she came around the corner.

"Maybe you can talk some sense into her," Jase said, throwing his hands up in the air. He walked over to the back door and let the dogs out.

"What is he talking about?" Denise asked.

Bree grunted and opened the refrigerator to get a beer. She twisted off the top and threw the cap in sink. She took a long pull from the bottle. "Chad decided to stop by for a visit."

"What did that shithead want?"

"To scream at me about ruining his life."

Denise's lip curled up. "What a douche-canoe."

"Pretty much."

"That's it?" Jase asked.

Denise looked at Jase over her shoulder. "What do you mean *that's it?*"

"That's all you're going to say to her? She left her door wide open. Anyone could have walked in."

Denise looked back at Bree. "Lock your doors."

Bree saluted her with the beer. "Yes, ma'am."

Denise looked at Jase again. "Okay? Okay. Now, on to more important things. I brought the mama dog over."

Bree clapped her hands and jumped up and down. "Squee! Where is she?"

Denise smiled, shaking her head. "She's in the hall bath. I didn't want to bring her in with all the shouting going on." Denise stared at Jase.

Bree got a hot dog out of the refrigerator and skipped around the counter. She cracked the bath door open and peeked in. The small tan-and-white dog cowered in the corner. Kneeling down, Bree broke off a piece of hot dog and held it out to the trembling dog. The dog stretched her nose forward, sniffing at the piece of meat. Softly, she took it from Bree's fingers. Scooting back a few inches, Bree held out another piece, coaxing the dog out of the corner.

"Hey there, sweet girl. That's not so bad, is it?" Bit by hotdog bit, she brought the dog out of the bathroom and led her over to the kennel she had set up earlier and closed the door.

She walked back into the kitchen. "Poor thing."

"She should be fine after she settles down." Denise took a sip of her water. "She got agitated if there were a lot of other dogs around, but she seemed fine with one or two."

Bree tore off a sheet of foil and wrapped it over the top of the large pan. "I'll keep her in the kennel tonight and tomorrow to give her a chance to get used to Charlie and Polly."

"That'll work."

"Dinner with Sarah tonight?" Bree placed the baking pan into the oven and set the timer.

"Yeah."

"How's the treatment going?"

Denise inhaled deeply before answering. "Not good."

Bree walked around the counter and hugged Denise. "You want to bring the kids over this weekend?"

"Let's see how Sarah's feeling." Denise gave her a small squeeze. "Maybe we can meet at the kennel and let them run around with the dogs."

Bree rubbed her hands over Denise's back before she let her go. "Sounds good." She hooked her arm through Denise's and walked her to the door. Jase lounged against the counter, arms and legs crossed. Bree stopped a few feet away from him and waited.

"What's for dinner?" he asked.

Bree blinked. *That's it?* "Spinach manicotti."

"How long does it have to bake?"

"About twenty-five minutes."

Jase uncrossed his legs and arms and closed the distance. Without breaking eye contact, he picked her up and carried out of the kitchen, over to the couch. He sat in the center, forcing Bree to straddle his lap. He moved his hands into her hair and pulled her head close to his.

"I need you to be safe," he said softly. "Even if you don't think Chad is a threat, fine. But someone's leaving notes on bodies addressed to you. We have no idea who they are or what they want."

Bree looked closely at Jase. She saw beyond his anger and stress and found the concern etched on his face. She leaned forward and kissed the corner of his mouth, trying to ease the tension.

"I'm sorry you were worried. I wasn't thinking about anyone but you or Denise walking in." She moved her mouth to the other side of his face and repeated her motions. "I promise to be more careful."

He turned his head and took control of her mouth. Bree ran her hands through his short beard and grabbed the back of his neck. She rocked her hips, creating friction along the seam of her shorts. Jase groaned into her mouth and wound his arms around her back, pulling her impossibly close. Bree's nipples pebbled upon contact with his chest and a moan slipped out. He moved his mouth to her neck. Bree's head dropped back and she closed her eyes in bliss when his teeth scraped her sensitive flesh.

The sensations threatened to overwhelm her, and she remembered her conversation with Denise. *Too fast.* She'd never felt like this. Sexually or emotionally. She thought about the worry she had seen in Jase's eyes. How could someone feel that strongly so quickly? How could *she* feel this strongly so quickly?

"Jase?"

"Yeah, baby."

"This is going really fast."

Jase stopped kissing her neck and pulled back slightly. "This or us?"

"Us," she whispered.

"You scared?"

She swallowed. Lie and play it off or tell the truth and trust him not to crush her heart?

"Yes."

"Good." He brushed her hair away from her face. "If you weren't scared, it wouldn't be real. I don't want this to be casual. There's something about you. From the moment you walked into The Deck, laughing at whatever you and Denise were talking about, I couldn't take my eyes off you. I was pissed when you took off the next morning."

"I got that. Why?"

"I don't know why, I just was. Sometimes you just know."

"What do you know?"

"It's real. It's important. You don't waste time over analyzing it or wondering why. You just go where the ride takes you."

"Scary ride."

Jase smiled. "Best rides usually are."

"What happens when you want to get off?"

Jase's smile turned sensual and he rocked his hips, rubbing against the juncture of Bree's legs.

"That's not the kind of getting off I'm talking about." She slapped his chest.

"Bree, this is the first ride I've wanted to be on in a long time. I don't see myself getting off any time soon. And if it ever gets to that point, I'm going to get right back in line to ride it again."

She bit at her bottom lip. "I'm not sure how I feel about this analogy anymore."

He pulled Bree back against him. "You wanna quit talking metaphorically and get on board?" His grin was lascivious. He dropped his hands to her hips and rocked her against his erection straining the zipper of his jeans.

Bree moved her hands from his shoulders to the button of his jeans. Just as she slipped her fingers into the waistband, the timer on the stove went off.

"We interrupt this program to bring you the following breaking news story…" She pulled her hand out of his pants. "Dinner's ready."

"You're funny."

"I know, right?"

~

HER FINGERS FOUND the snooze button of her alarm clock faintly playing the chorus of Scars by Papa Roach before reaching for Jase. Her eyes flew open when her hand moved across the cool, empty sheets.

"Jase," she called out softly. Why was she the only one who had to get creative? She turned off her alarm before it could go off again. She snagged her sleep shorts from the floor where Jase had thrown them the previous night. The camisole had landed on the dresser. She grabbed it and pulled it over her head as she walked down the hall.

She smiled, sure her heart squeezed a little at the sight before her. Jase lay stretched out on the longest part of her sectional, Charlie and Polly sprawled out on the floor beside him, and the new foster pup wedged between him and the back of the couch. His eyes opened as she drew close. She stepped over Charlie and Polly and braced her hands on the couch.

"Hey," she whispered.

"Hey."

"Whatcha doin'?"

"I got up to go to the bathroom and the dogs apparently had the same thought. I let Charlie and Polly out and then came back for her." He tilted his head to indicate the dog curled against him. "She was trembling and cowering so I thought maybe this would calm her down and help her relax."

A slow smile spread across Bree's face as she leaned even closer.

"Fail." She kissed Jase softly, barely sweeping her lips against his, before raising her head back up.

Jase smiled back and scratched the dog behind the ears. "What's your schedule like today? Got time to work in lunch?"

"I have appointments all day until three o'clock."

"Wanna swing by on your way home?"

"Sure. I need to get ready for work. Want to hang out until I leave or do you need to go now?"

"I'll hang out."

"'Kay." Bree brushed another soft kiss against Jase's lips. "Want coffee?"

"Sure."

Jase was asleep again when Bree walked back in the living room. She got the small travel alarm from the guest room and set it for seven-thirty. Placing it next to his untouched coffee, she scribbled a note asking him to put the new dog in the kennel before he left.

CHAPTER 14

Bree dropped her head back and rested it on the back of the chair. Seven hours of back-to-back appointments was killer. She was exhausted. Sighing, she checked her calendar for tomorrow. At least she'd have time for a proper lunch rather than eating on the run. She logged off and grabbed her bag out from under her desk.

"Dr. Marks…" Cindy called out as Bree passed the front desk.

"Yes?" Bree turned back.

"I was wondering if you wanted to get dinner tonight."

"Thank you, Cindy, but I have plans tonight," she said. "I'm free this weekend if you'd like to do something then."

"Oh. Um, sure." She looked down and tucked a strand of hair behind her ear. "We can talk about it tomorrow. I don't want to keep you."

"Sounds good. I'll see you tomorrow."

CAROL'S BEAMING smile greeted Bree when she walked through the doors of V.E.T. Adventures. "Hi, honey! I was hoping I would see you again. I had a pretty good feeling when Jase brought Ruby in with him."

"Ruby?" Bree asked.

"The little dog he said you're fostering. She's under my desk right now, as a matter of fact." She leaned back and to the side, peeking under her desk. "Just curled right up at my feet and hasn't made a peep all day." She straightened in her chair. "I wanted to talk to you about what I need to do to adopt her. I've been thinking about getting a dog for a while and she is just the sweetest thing ever."

Bree blinked a couple of times. "Jase brought the dog into the office?"

"Of course. Said he didn't want to put her in the kennel by herself while the other two dogs were roaming around."

"Oh." Bree tried to wrap her head around everything Carol had said. "Uh, you'll need to fill out an adoption application. She needs to be spayed and brought up-to-date on her shots."

Carol's eyebrows rose and she looked hopeful. "Is there a way I can keep her until she's officially ready to be adopted?"

Bree smiled. "I think we can probably arrange something. Is he busy?" She tilted her head toward Jase's office.

"Nope. Let me buzz him and tell him you're here." Carol picked up the phone and pushed a couple of buttons. "Jase, someone here to see you."

Less than ten seconds later, Jase opened the door to his office and strode toward Bree. He grabbed her close and bent her over the arm he banded around her upper back. The kiss was hard and open-mouthed. She forgot they had an audience. She sank into the kiss, oblivious to everything. He finally pulled away. "Hi."

"Hi."

He stood her up and grabbed her hand. "Thanks, Ms. Carol." Bree smiled and waved over her shoulder as Jase dragged her into his office.

"You brought the foster with you."

He closed the door behind her and backed her up against the wall. "She was whining when I put her in the cage. It broke my heart so I brought her into the office. Charlie and Polly were curled up on their beds when I left."

"Softy."

"Sue me. You left me asleep on your couch."

"You were sleeping hard. I didn't want to wake you. You haven't been getting much sleep the last few days."

"What did I say about waking me up?"

Bree rolled her eyes. "I didn't have time to get creative on my way out the door."

Jase shook his head at her. "Wake me up before you leave. For whatever reason you're leaving."

"Bossy."

"Yup." He didn't even try to deny it.

Bree rolled her eyes again and changed the subject. "Why do you call her Ms. Carol?"

Jase stared for several heartbeats before placing a kiss on the sensitive skin just below her ear. He pushed away from the wall and sat behind this desk.

"I've always called her Ms. Carol. Ever since I was five."

"You've known her that long?" She inhaled sharply, connecting the dots. "She's Tony's mom."

Jase looked up from his computer. "Yeah. When I started V.E.T. Adventures, I needed help. She was retired and offered to help me get started."

"And never left."

"I don't think I could get her to re-retire even if I wanted to. I need to finish up some emails before I'm ready to leave. You good with waiting?"

"I don't have anywhere else to be. I was going to go let *Ruby* out, but that's been taken care of."

"Yeah. I don't think you're getting that dog back."

"I'm good with that." Bree wandered around Jase's office. The large L-shaped desk took up the far corner. The computer sat on the long side of the L, leaving the short end, facing two tan arm chairs, open. Pictures and ubiquitous military plaques hung on the walls. One picture was of the ribbon-cutting for V.E.T. Adventures. "Are you a 501c?"

"Yes. One of those things Carol helped with."

"How do you get your funding?"

"Donations mostly. We charge a small fee, but we try to cover most of the costs ourselves. Unfortunately, I think we're going to have to cut down on the number of trips this year. We've haven't gotten as many donors this year."

"Put in a grant application with the foundation," she said.

Jase swiveled in his chair to face her. "So that would mean you would give me money?"

"No." She was confused by the bite in his voice. "It means you submit an application and the board votes whether to approve and fund it."

"But if you push it, it gets approved, right?"

"Actually no, I have no say in the matter. It's a requirement that if a board member knows an applicant, they have to abstain from voting. Members can actually be kicked out of the discussion if it becomes necessary."

Jase crossed his arms and leaned back in his chair. "So you'll have no say in whether I get approved if I apply for funding?"

"More than likely, I won't even see the application."

"And I suppose you won't give me any advice on what to say on the application, either."

Bree cocked her head. "No. What are you trying to say?"

"I don't want your money, Bree," Jase told her.

"Okay. I didn't offer you any money. I told you to apply for a grant from a foundation my grandfather established."

"Which basically means your money."

"Jase." She set her hands on her hips and fought her annoyance. "I have no more say in where the foundation gives grants than the other twelve people on the board. If I wanted to give you money, I'd make an anonymous donation. Why are you getting upset?"

"I don't want you—" He leaned forward and rested his forearms against the edge of the desk. "I don't want you to think…"

"That you want my money? I wouldn't be here if I thought that. Not for a minute. I'm not offering you money and I'm not trying to give you a handout. I'm telling you about an opportunity you can take advantage of, if you choose to."

Jase ran his hands through his hair. "Thank you."

She strolled over to the chairs facing his desk. "Don't thank me yet. You haven't seen the application. If Carol got you your 501c approval, you might want to give it to her."

Jase grinned. "Duly noted." He turned his attention back to his computer. He clicked the mouse several times in a row. "Damn it."

"Computer freeze up?"

"No. One of the volunteer guides uses the campsite to go hunting on his off days. He sent an email saying there's pretty bad damage from the storms a couple of days ago. I'm going to have to go up tomorrow to clear the site instead of on Thursday like I had planned."

"When will you be back?"

"Late Sunday."

"Okay," she said with a nod.

"That's it? Okay?"

"Um, have fun?"

He raised an eyebrow. "You're not going to disappear again, are you?"

"Kind of hard to disappear when you know where I live."

"Do me a favor? Check in with Tim while I'm gone? I won't have cell service while I'm on the trip. I don't like that the cops don't know what's going on. I'd feel better if you let him know you're okay."

It was an easy enough thing to do. She'd feel better with someone knowing she was okay. She wasn't going to admit that to

Jase, though. Totally ruin her image. Denise would check on her, but she'd also charge over guns blazing and there was no telling how that might turn out.

"Sure."

He crossed his arms over his chest. "That's it? No argument?"

"Not when it's something to my benefit."

Jase nodded. A few key strokes on his computer and he turned off the monitor. "Dinner tonight?"

"I can't tonight. Taco Tuesday. Standing date with Denise."

"So I won't see you until Sunday."

"Nope."

"So we should make the most of the time we have this afternoon." Jase round his desk and braced his hands on the armrests of her chair.

"What, here?" she asked, surprised.

"Think you can be quiet?" Jase raised his eyebrows in a salacious gesture.

She returned his grin. "I guess we'll see, won't we?"

Jase bent and picked her up. She wrapped her legs around his hips as he spun them around.

"You pick me up a lot." She stared at his mouth.

"It gets you where I want you to be." He sat her on his desk and leaned forward, forcing her to lie against the cool wood.

She ran her hands under the sleeves of his t-shirt, tracing the definition of his muscles. "What if I don't want to be where you put me?"

"Then I put you where you want to be." He brushed a strand of hair away from her neck. "Where do you want to be?"

"Right here," Bree said against his lips

"Then here it is."

CHAPTER 15

Bree sprayed down one of the outdoor kennels. Jase was due back that night. Why had this seemed like the longest five days of her life? Would Jase call her or wait until tomorrow? Should she call him? No. Maybe she should text him and ask how his trip went.

Why was she pining? She was not a woman who pined for a man. When did he start consuming all her thoughts?

A cold spray of water hit her legs. She flinched from the spray. "What the hell?"

"You're thinking about him again, aren't you?" Denise redirected the hose.

"Who? What? No."

Denise gave her the *you're so full of shit, I can smell you from here* look. "Uh huh. That's why you haven't heard a word I've said for the last ten minutes."

"I heard you."

"What was I saying then?" Denise threatened to spray her again.

What had she been talking about? Bree wracked her brain, but came up blank. "Fine, I was spacing. What were you talking about?"

"I asked how dinner went with Cindy on Friday.

"Oh. It was good, actually. She's a lot more easy-going one-on-one. I might try to do lunch with her every now and then to get her out of the office." She moved over to the next outdoor kennel and aimed the hose nozzle at the floor. "What else were you yapping at me about?"

Denise shot another spray of water at her. "The new litter of puppies."

Bree jumped to avoid the spray. "There's a new litter of puppies? Who had puppies?"

Denise threw her free hand up in disgust. "Why do I bother?" She released the trigger on her sprayer, dropped her hose, and led the way into the barn. The eight stalls had been converted into smaller kennels and gave dogs plenty of room to move around. Each kennel had a dog door cut into the back that led to a fenced outdoor pen. Denise walked down to the farthest kennel.

"She's new. What breed?" Bree asked as she came to the edge of the kennel.

"Some kind of shepherd mix."

"The K-9 unit interested in any of them?"

"They want three if we think there are any viable candidates," Denise said.

"Really?" Bree raised her eyebrows.

"Yup. Drug dogs, apparently."

"Cool."

"Yes, which is what I've been trying to tell you for fifteen minutes."

"Sorry." Bree hung her head in mock shame.

"Uh huh. You've got it bad, sister. I've never seen you like this. Not even when we got tasked to that SEAL team for two months in Jalabad."

Bree stared off into space. "Mmm…that was good times."

"My point is you're completely distracted by Jase."

"I know." Bree folded her arms on the stall door and rested her chin on them. "He's only been gone a few days. It's ridiculous. I *feel* ridiculous and I don't know what to do. I'm being all… what's the word for it?"

"Girly."

"Girly!" Bree snapped her fingers and pointed at Denise like she had just solved the world's energy crisis. "How do I quit being all girly and emotional?"

"Don't look at me. I haven't done girly since I went through puberty. I'm void of emotions."

"You do emotions," Bree said.

Denise lifted the latch on the half door and entered the stall. The dog's tail thumped on the ground as Denise knelt next to her head. "I do some emotions, none of which are girly emotions. My emotions usually involve fireballs and razing insurgent strongholds to the ground." Denise patted the dog on the head and checked the water and food bowls.

Bree quirked her mouth. "Valid point. Either way, I need to figure out how to quit doing them."

"Why?" Denise asked.

"Why?" She opened the door for Denise. "Because I don't want to be girly. I don't want to moon over some guy and lose who I am in the process."

"Who says you have to lose yourself?" She swung the door closed and checked the latch. "Why can't you figure out a way to be who you are and still fall in love with Jase?"

"Um, first, no one said anything about being in love."

Denise gave her that look again.

"Fuck." Bree drew the word out as she groaned. She hated it when Denise called her on her bullshit. It was easy to avoid the truth without her around. "I can't. It's way too soon."

"Not according to Gran it's not," Denise pointed out.

"Okay, Gran lived a fairy tale. We know that's not how life really works."

"Says whom?"

"Says everyone except Gran. Hell, even Elsa said you can't fall in love with someone you just met."

"You're referencing animated characters again."

"Hello? Fairy tale?"

"You're ridiculous."

"Whatever. You love my face."

"At the moment, I want to high-five your face," Denise told her.

Bree stuck her tongue out. Denise returned the gesture before leading the way back out of the barn.

"Kimber! Kaden! Be careful with the dogs," Denise yelled. Her young cousins laughed and ran around the large pen with three of the rescue dogs.

"Okay, Aunt Denise!" Kimber shouted.

Bree smiled at their antics. "So, this is different than your usual advice."

Denise continued to watch the kids run around with the dogs. "What is?"

"This sudden *give love a chance* mindset. Not your usual stance on the subject."

Denise shrugged. "I just don't think you should talk yourself out of something that might be worth giving a shot."

Bree knew her best friend better than that. She was avoiding. For all of Denise's light-hearted banter and teasing, something was bothering her. An edge, a rawness, lying just below the surface. One that worried Bree.

"Denise. What's going on?"

Denise crossed her arms and looked at her feet as she leaned against the barn. "Sarah isn't going to make it," she whispered.

"Oh honey, I'm sorry." Bree copied Denise's stance, but rested her head on Denise's shoulder. "How long?" she asked.

Denise's swallow was audible. Her breath caught as she inhaled. "Three months. Six at most if she continues treatment, but she doesn't want to. She's done with it. She wants to spend time with Kimber and Kaden. Enjoy it as much as possible, rather than spend days in bed or throwing up." She shook her head, staving off her tears.

"I'm here, you know that, right?"

Denise nudged Bree's head up off her shoulder and gave her a small smile. "You have enough going on right now."

"Never enough when you need me."

"Thanks."

Kaden tripped and rolled. He laughed as two of the dogs licked his face. Pushing them away from his face, he jumped up and ran across the grass. "When do you need to take them home?"

"I told Sarah I'd have them back before six."

"You wanna come over after you drop them off? Chinese take-out and a movie?"

"Sounds good."

"You know these are emotions, right?" Bree teased.

"That probably explains why I feel the urge to carpet bomb an insurgent camp."

THE INTRO for Boogey Shoes sounded from the side of her purse. Dancing in place, Bree pulled it out and smiled at Jase's name on the caller ID. She stepped out of the line to answer.

"Hey, are you back?"

"We're about an hour out. I need to drop Chris off. Do you have plans for dinner?"

"I'm in line to get Chinese if you and Chris want to come over to the house. Denise and I were going to veg and watch a movie."

"We still need to shower. We're pretty ripe."

"You can shower at the house if you don't need to get a change of clothes." Bree cringed as soon as she made the offer. Could she sound more desperate? Could she rescind the offer without sounding even more ridiculous? As she wracked her brain for an exit strategy, she heard Jase talking to Chris, asking if he had some clean clothes. Maybe she didn't come across as desperate as she thought she did.

"Yeah, we're good with that if you are."

"Um, yeah. I'm good with that." More cringing. Why was this conversation so awkward? "What kind of Chinese do you like?"

"Beef and vegetables for me. Chris wants General Tsao's chicken. Extra spicy."

"Okay, I'll see you in a little bit."

"'Bye."

"'Bye." She hung up before she turned it into a cheesy you-hang-up-first ordeal. Tapping her phone against her forehead, she replayed the conversation over in her mind. He had called her before he even got home to take a shower. Maybe he was just as moony as she was. Taking a deep breath, she got back in line.

Receipt in hand, she called Denise while she waited for the order. "Are you sure you don't mind? It was just supposed to be us."

"No, I don't mind." Denise laughed. "We've done plenty of girl time. We should probably branch out a bit. Think they'd be okay with watching *Magic Mike*?"

Bree smiled. "I'm going to go with *no* on that one."

"Hmm. I might have to make sure it's on when they walk in just to mess with them a little bit."

Bree laughed at that thought of Jase and Chris's reaction to having to sit through *Magic Mike*. "I'm totally okay with screwing with their heads."

"Sweet! See you soon."

~

THE DOORBELL RANG as Bree pulled the last container of food from the to-go bag. Why did Denise ring the doorbell? She looked through the peephole to be greeted with a close-up of Denise's nose pressed up against the viewer. That explains that.

She threw the bolt and swung the door open. "That's hot." Denise's dog shuffled in with her and greeted Bree's dogs.

"I know. Right? How am I still single?" Denise kicked off her shoes by the door and followed Bree into the kitchen. "That's a lot of food."

Bree set the containers on a baking sheet and put them in the warmer. "Two guys are coming for dinner who just spent a week camping, probably getting most of their calories from beer."

"I see your point." She got a glass out of the cabinet. "I'm going to go cue up *Magic Mike* to Channing Tatum's solo so I can press play right before you open the door for them." She poured tea from a pitcher and returned it to the fridge.

"I think you're enjoying this just a little too much," Bree said.

"Maybe, but I'm not getting my kicks anywhere else, so I'll take what I can get."

"I'm going to put towels and soap in the hall bath." She poured a glass of water and joined Denise in the living room.

"What time are they going to be here?" Denise asked.

Bree curled her legs under her and leaned against the armrest of the couch. "Jase said an hour when he called, so should be soon. We're watching *The Expendables*, right?"

"Absolutely."

"Just checking."

"On to more important things. Are there any suspects in your neighbor's murder?" Denise asked.

"Not that I know of. Tim hasn't said anything."

"Would he, if he knew anything?"

"I'm not sure. I'd hope so, but probably not unless they had a suspect."

Denise spread out on the couch. "That kind of sucks. You'd

think having a letter left on a body addressed to you would give you some sort of insider connection."

"I'm pretty sure that happens only in the movies."

"Did they figure out who broke into your house?"

"Nope. Tim said they haven't gotten a hit back on the prints. Guess it really isn't as fast as it is on *CSI*. More's the pity," Bree said.

"No kidding. Talk about building up expectations."

The doorbell pealed from the foyer. Bree got up to answer the door while Denise scrambled to grab the remote.

"Wait! Wait! Wait! Okay, I'm ready," she called out.

Bree shook her head as she opened the door to let in Jase and Chris, dressed almost identically in camo cargo pants and long-sleeved t-shirts.

"Ah, so you're Chris." The guy on the couch. Even though he sported a few days' worth of dark stubble, she recognized his steel-blue eyes.

"Told you not to run." He winked at her as he stepped into the foyer.

Jase gave Bree a quick, hard kiss. "What's that about?"

"Nothing." Bree closed the door and led them into the house. "Do you want to shower first or watch the movie? Denise picked it." Denise had cued it up right to the part where Channing Tatum was grinding, semi-naked, on the stage.

Jase and Chris stepped into the living room and froze, jaws agape, a look of absolute horror on their faces at the sight of Channing Tatum grinding, semi-naked, on the large screen.

Chris dropped his bag and shouted, "Let it rain!" He undulated his hips in a way that put Channing Tatum to shame. Bree and Denise laughed and whooped when Chris turned and shook his butt at them.

"Okay, okay. We're kidding," Denise said, wiping tears from her eyes. "We're actually watching *The Expendables*, but good to know you'd be all right with half-naked guys dancing around on stage."

"Chris has a somewhat questionable past," Jase said.

Denise turned off the movie. "Nothing wrong with that."

Chris raised his eyebrows.

Well now, Denise might get her kicks somewhere else after all. Bree led Chris and Jase down the hall and showed Chris the guest bath. When she tried to go back to the kitchen, Jase grabbed her hand and pulled her along behind him.

"Jase."

Tugging on her hand, he led the way into her bedroom and shut the door behind them.

"I'm not having sex with you while our best friends are in the house waiting on us!"

"I want a better kiss."

She smirked. "Better, huh?"

"Way better." His hands delved into her hair and tilted her head to the side. His mouth was hot and urgent. His arms wrapped tight around her and pulled her against him, forcing her up on her toes.

He smelled like woodsmoke, outdoors, and sweaty man. As hot as the kiss was, Bree couldn't help but think he really needed a shower. She pulled back slightly and created a hair's breadth of space between their lips.

"Would you take it the wrong way if I asked you to take a shower?"

"Manly man-smell doesn't turn you on?"

"Normally, yes, but five days' of manly man-smell is a little much."

He grinned before kissing her quickly. "I can fix that for you."

"Thanks. Dinner'll be ready to go when you get out." She pulled out of his arms and slipped through the bedroom door.

Denise pulled the food out of the warmer and had already set plates on the table.

"We're eating in the dining room?" Bree asked.

"Sure. Why not?" Denise shrugged.

Bree grabbed silverware out of the drawer. "When was the last time we ate at the table?"

"A couple of Thanksgivings ago?"

"Oh, yeah. Wasn't that the one where your date—"

"Let's not go there again."

A deep male chuckle came from the direction of the hall as Chris joined them. "Glad to hear I'm not the only one that has awkward holiday dinners. Is it okay if I leave my bag in the foyer?"

"Sure. Make yourself at home," Bree said. He rejoined them and sat at the kitchen counter.

"Beer? Water? Tea?" Denise asked.

"I'll take a beer, thanks."

Denise took a bottle out of the fridge and popped the top, setting the bottle on the counter. "Bottle good, or do you want a glass?"

"Bottle's good."

"How do you and Jase know each other?" Bree asked.

"We were in the same platoon. How do you two know each other?"

She poured the rice into a large serving bowl. "Pretty much the same way. We were deployed together a couple of times."

"Army?"

"She was." Bree tilted her head toward Denise. "I made better life decisions and joined the Air Force."

Denise waved a serving spoon at her. "And yet you still ended up serving with the Army."

"*With* the Army, not *in* the Army. Big difference."

"I take it this isn't a new argument," Chris said.

"We've had it a few times." Denise smiled and bumped Bree's hip. Bree bumped her back.

Jase came into the kitchen, rubbing his belly. "I'm starving"

Chris ran his hand up and down his beer bottle. "Well, if you hadn't taken the time to rub one out in the shower, we'd be eating already."

Bree's eyes widened. "Oh my god."

"Jackass." Jase tapped the back of Chris's head as he gave him a death glare.

Denise shook her head a few times. "Not an image I needed in my head. Thankfully, I don't have a weak stomach. Let's eat so we can watch hot guys blow shit up."

Bree picked up two bowls to take to the table. "What do you do on the camping trips?"

Jase grabbed another bowl and Bree's glass. "It depends on the season and varies from group to group. Some groups are serious hunters and fishermen. Others just want to sit around, drink beer, and reminisce." He sat next to Bree at the round table. "Most fall somewhere in-between. They'll hunt or fish, but really aren't that serious about it. I try to tailor the trips to the people in the group."

"A lot of guys want to go out with a group that understands where they're coming from without it being a therapy session." Chris took the carton of egg rolls from Denise. "I mean, it kind of is, but it's not forced. If guys want to talk, they talk. If not, no one bugs 'em. No questions. No recriminations. No judgment."

"Do you work for Jase or just volunteer?" Bree blew on a fork full of food.

"I volunteer when I can," Chris said.

"Which is more often than not." Jase took a bite of beef and broccoli. "He helps me run the classes as well."

"Jase said y'all are going on the trip with us next month," Chris said.

"We've both arranged to have the time off," Denise said.

Bree nodded. "I'm looking forward to it. I haven't been camping in a couple of years."

When they finished eating, Jase and Chris offered to clean up the dishes while the girls packed away the few leftovers.

Between Bree's large sectional and lounger, the four of them were able to spread out without touching. Jase pulled Bree down in front of him after he lay down along one side of the L-shaped couch. Charlie jumped up and joined Chris, where he had propped his head up on a couple of pillows.

Bree snapped her fingers. "Charlie, get down."

Chris wrapped an arm around Charlie's big head and rubbed his ears. "Don't worry about it. He's good." The other two dogs took up space near Bree and Denise. Fifteen minutes into the movie, Jase and Chris were asleep.

"I guess camping takes a lot of a guy," Denise said.

"I guess so." Bree shifted her hair away from the nape of her neck where Jase had his nose buried.

Thirty minutes later, Denise stood and stretched her arms out over her head. "I'm falling asleep, so I'm going to head out."

"Okay, let me untangle myself."

"No, stay there. I know where the door is."

"I know, but I'm going to get blankets for them." She lifted Jase's arm from where it lay heavy on her waist and rose from the couch. Charlie raised his head from where it rested on Chris's legs when she stood. He took that as his cue it was time to go outside and jumped off the couch. His hind paw landed square in the middle of Chris's crotch, causing him to curl up in a fetal position and groan.

"Son of a bitch," he ground out.

"Oh, shit. Are you okay?" Denise asked.

"Hell no, I'm not okay. Shit, that burns."

"Do you need some ice?" Denise asked.

"What happened?" Jase sat up and ran his hands through his already sleep-tousled hair.

"Charlie unmanned Chris," Bree bit her lip.

"Seems to be a thing in this house." Jase stood and stretched, exposing the bottom of his toned abs. "You ready to go or do you need a minute to retract your ball sac?"

"Screw you," Chris replied.

"I'll pass, thanks for the offer, though."

"I can drop him off once he's recovered enough to walk," Denise offered.

"You sure?" Jase dropped an arm over Bree's shoulders.

Denise shrugged. "Sure. No reason for you to leave and come back when I'm leaving anyway."

Chris rolled off the couch and landed on his knees and one hand on the floor, the other hand still cradled his manhood. Using the couch to brace himself, he stood up but remained hunched over like an old man.

"Shit, that dog has some pointy paws on him. I can't imagine how dangerous he'd be if he had all his legs."

"Just be glad it wasn't Sprocket," Bree said. The large mastiff raised her head.

Chris looked at the large dog, still sprawled next to the chair Denise had occupied. "Please tell me you have a truck for that dog and I don't have to try to share a seat with it."

"SUV. She sits in the cargo area." Denise told him.

With a small nod, he hobbled his way to the front door, straightening more with each step until he was mostly upright.

"Thanks for dinner, Bree. Later, asshole." He waved at hand in Jase's direction.

"Later, shithead." Jase clapped Chris on the back as he passed.

"It just warms my heart when boys show love and affection for one another." Denise hugged Bree and followed Chris out the door, Sprocket close on her heels.

Bree closed and locked the door. Jase stared at her with an intense but conflicted look.

"What?" Her brow furrowed.

"I'm wiped."

"Okay."

"I also want my hands all over you." His disgruntlement was obvious in the gruff tone of his voice.

"Oh. Okay." Her gaze dropped to his full bottom lip as she bit her own.

"I'm afraid I might fall asleep in the middle of it if I try anything tonight."

Her surprised laughter filled the foyer. "That might prove to be problematic. Go lie down. I need to let the dogs out. I'm good with cuddling. For tonight."

He gathered her close and draped his arms loosely around her waist. "You sure? I can rise to the occasion if I need to."

"Yes, I'm sure. Go lie down." Her kiss was gentle.

His fingers grazed her neck as he tucked a strand of hair behind her ear and kissed her forehead before releasing her. She turned off the TV and lights as she made her way through the house. She opened the French doors and Charlie charged across the yard. "Charlie! Charlie, come back here! What is that damn dog doing?" She stepped onto the porch, barely able to see his white coat in the dark. Whenever she let the dogs out, Charlie took an interest in something along the fence line before she managed to get him to return to the porch.

She made sure the doors were locked and the newly installed bolts engaged. She joined an already sleeping Jase, pressing herself close to his back.

CHAPTER 16

ase woke to Bree's hair tickling his nose and her ass tucked tight against his morning erection. His hand ran from the base of her neck to between her breasts before delving into the soft hair at the junction of her thighs and brushing a finger over her clit. A soft moan escaped as she arched her back, seeking more contact. He crooked the arm under her neck and tweaked her nipples through the thin sheet. Her body shifted as her hands covered his, pressing harder. She rubbed her ass against his hard cock.

Jase shifted his hips and slide his shaft between her slick folds. He nipped and bit his way across her shoulder and up her neck.

"I need to get a condom, darlin'." He raised his head slightly when she stilled. "What's wrong?"

"I was tested." Her soft voice was no more than a whisper. "After I caught... after I found out. Even though we hadn't been together in weeks, I needed to know. I have a clean bill of health. And I'm on the pill."

"You saying you're good with me going bare?" He nuzzled her neck. A barely perceptible nod was the only thing she gave him.

"I need you to tell me you're okay with it, Bree. I get tested annually so I know I'm clean. If you're doing this because you think it's what I want, then we're not going to. You have to want it, too."

She shifted, looking at him over her shoulder. Her hand guided his fingers deeper between her folds, encouraging him to press a finger into her core. Sharp white teeth bit into her bottom lip as he pressed deeper.

"I want you bare. I want to feel your hard, hot skin sinking into me. Sliding—"

Jase covered her mouth with his, cutting off her words. He turned her fully onto her back and wedged his hips between her thighs. Her hands rested on his hips and ran around the underside of his ass.

His hard cock sought her slick entrance and pressed forward with one hard stroke. Jase stilled and lifted his torso. He inhaled sharply and stared down at their intimately connected bodies. Shit, she felt good. He'd never been this close to a woman. Never this intimately. Everything in him clenched and released, like a heartbeat he could feel through his entire body. He looked at Bree. Her eyes hooded as his hips retreated and surged forward again.

"Hottest thing I've ever seen." His elbows bent as he lowered his body. Bree brought her legs high up on his back as she met his thrusts.

"That feels so good," she gasped. "I can feel the ridge of the head of your cock."

Her walls clenched around him and he ground his teeth, trying to hold on to the last shred of his sanity.

"Please be close. You're so fucking tight. Like a fist clenching around my cock."

"Play with my clit." Sharp teeth grazed his neck before her tongue followed the same path.

God, he loved that she wasn't afraid to ask for what she wanted. He shifted his weight to allow room for his hand between them. Jase found her sensitive hood and pressed. His thumb circled in a rhythm that matched his thrusts. Seconds later Bree threw her head back and let out a shout. Her hands flew above her head to use the headboard as leverage, pressing harder against him.

He withdrew his hand from between them and wrapped his hands up and around her shoulders, holding her tight as he continued to surge into Bree's tight core. She clenched around him and he let out a growl. The tingling in his spine right before his sac drew up against his body had him burying his face in the crook of her neck. One of the most intense orgasms he'd ever experienced ripped through him. *Fuck.* His hips continued to softly thrust as he shuddered his release.

A thin sheen of sweat glistened on her skin, and he ran his tongue along her collarbone. He could feel Bree's chest heave as she recovered, and he stopped himself from collapsing on top of her. He rolled them to the side as his soft cock slid from her. Their kiss was languid and gentle as they recovered. He explored her lips, taking his time to taste her, no longer fueled by lust.

He brushed his nose against hers and stared at her for several heartbeats. A flush bloomed on her cheeks and she averted her gaze.

He smiled. "Why are you embarrassed?"

"I don't know. Why are you staring at me like that?"

He brushed her hair away from her face. "You're beautiful."

The heat from her face was perceptible under his palm and he laughed when her blush spread to the tops of her ears and down her neck.

"I can't believe you're laughing at me." She pushed against his chest and tucked her face below his chin, her actions contradicting themselves.

He gathered her close and rested his chin on the top of her head. "I'm laughing with you, I promise."

"Do you see me laughing?"

He pressed a kiss to her forehead. "I think that's the hardest I've come since I lost my virginity," he whispered in her ear. She tucked her face even closer into his chest and he laughed again. Her embarrassment surprised him. She'd demanded he touch her, give her an orgasm, and now she was hiding. Damn, she was adorable.

He held her a bit tighter. More than the lush body pressed close to him, her trust and acceptance meant…hell, he didn't have the words. Couldn't describe what he was feeling.

Grounded. Bree grounded him. As if he had been adrift and she was his port-of-call, a safe zone where he could just be him. Chris and his other military buddies accepted him for who he was, but that was different. They shared history. Knew each other from their time in the Army. Fought the same battles. Carried the same scars. Haunted by the same ghosts, although his were more personal than most.

Bree hadn't given him platitudes when he told her about Tony. No crap about *sorry for your loss*. She'd just listened. Let him talk. No judgment, just compassion. Would she be able to handle it when he finally worked up the courage to tell her the truth?

Tony's suicide was his fault.

The alarm jerked him out of his reverie and Bree's entire body twitched. She must have dozed off while he was lost in his own thoughts. She groaned and told him to hit the snooze button.

"Time to wake up, sleepy head," he stroked her hair.

"Snooze."

"What?"

She forced her way over his body, reaching for the alarm clock. Her fingers pushed the snooze button, then she curled back up in his arms.

"I set the alarm so I can hit snooze a few times before I get up," she mumbled against his chest.

"Why not just set the alarm for when you need to get up?"

"Not a morning person. Need time to face the day."

Jase shook his head. Adorable.

"I'm going to take a shower while you snooze, then."

"Mmkay."

JASE SET down the grant application he was reviewing to answer his cell phone. "Jase Larken."

"Did Bree get a hold of you?" Tim asked.

He smiled at her name, remembering how he'd gotten her off with his hand before sending her out the door to work. "Not since I talked to her this morning, why?"

"Shit. I thought she'd call you."

"About what? What's going on?"

"There's been another murder. The Chief asked her to come in for questioning."

He pushed back his chair and grabbed his keys from his desk. "Questioning for what? Do they think she's a suspect?"

"No, but we're concerned. The note left on the body was addressed to her again. We need her to come in and answer some questions for the record."

"Are you with her? Of course you're not with her, you wouldn't be calling me. Does she have a lawyer?"

"I don't know, man."

"I'm on my way. Don't let her leave before I get there. Hog tie her if you have to." Jase pocketed his phone and stormed out of his office. "Ms. Carol, I'm out for the rest of the day. I'll be on my cell if you need to reach me." He marched out the door and all but ran to his truck.

His mind raced. Why hadn't Bree called him? Maybe it wasn't allowed. Had she forgotten her phone at work? Was she scared? Visions of interrogation scenes from *Law and Order* filled his head on the short drive. By the time he arrived at the police station, he had convinced himself Bree had already been arrested and charged with murder.

The desk sergeant recognized Jase and waved him through. Jase stormed over to his brother's desk. "Where is she?"

Tim held up a hand as he finished his phone call. "She's still being interviewed," he said after he hung up. "She has a lawyer, and her grandmother is here as well."

Jase glanced around, looking for an elderly lady. "Is her grandmother in the restroom?"

"No, she's in with Bree," Tim explained. "You didn't tell me her grandmother is Vivianne Coffee."

Jase started. The Coffee family was the closest thing Haven Springs had to royalty. They'd donated several million dollars over the years to the schools, revitalizing downtown, and to the police department. "I had no idea. She told me her grandfather left her some money, but she never referred to her grandparents by name. Hell, her last name is Marks."

"That answers whether you were keeping that from me."

"First I heard of it. What happened?"

"Same as last time. Body. Note. I don't know what this one said exactly, but from what I gather, it's along the same lines as the first."

A door across the large, open office opened and Bree walked through, accompanied by two officers, another man Jase didn't recognize, and an older woman. Her silver hair hung in a sleek, shoulder-length bob, and she was dressed in walking shorts and a sleeveless top. Watching her, he'd never have guessed she was in her mid-eighties–nor that she was worth millions. She stood next to Bree with one arm around Bree's waist. Bree's arm was draped loosely across her grandmother's shoulders, but he could see the tension lines on her forehead from where he stood.

She glanced in his direction and some of the tightness left her face. She gave him a small smile and said something to her grandmother, who looked their way. In profile, the resemblance between Bree and her grandmother was evident. They shook hands with the two officers, then with the man Jase assumed to be the lawyer. They crossed the open expanse between the interview room and Tim's desk. It took all his control not to pick her up and carry her out of there, but he crossed his arms across his chest and waited for them to get to him.

"Gran, this is Jase and his brother Tim." Bree indicated to each of them in turn.

Tim stood and walked around his desk, holding his hand out. "Ma'am. I wish we were meeting under better circumstances."

"That's all right. I understand things have to be done a certain way." Her soft voice carried a cultured, southern lilt that made Jase think of formal teas and cotillions. *Had Bree been presented to society? Did they still do that?*

"Ma'am," Jase said, holding out his hand. She turned to him, and he accepted her outstretched fingers and gently shook her hand.

"It's lovely to finally meet you, Jase. Bree has spoken of you quite a bit in the last few days."

"Gran." Bree's cheeks pinked.

"Is that so?" He quirked an eyebrow, feeding her embarrassment. It was the least she deserved after not calling him.

The man in the suit joined them. "Vivienne, I'm going back to the office. I've instructed the investigators that if they need to question Bree again, they are to contact me first." He turned his attention to Bree. "You are not to talk to them without me or one of my associates present."

"I want to help if I can."

"You can help them while you have legal representation. Vivienne, I'll give you a call later."

"I'm going to head home, dear. I'll call you later after I deal with all the gossips at the old folks' home," her grandmother said.

Bree kissed her grandmother on the cheek. "It's not an old

folks' home." She watched Vivienne walk away before turning back to Jase. "What are you doing here?"

He frowned. "What am I doing here? My brother called me and told me you were taken in for questioning about another murder."

"I wasn't taken in. I was asked to come in to help identify the victim and try to figure out why someone is leaving notes addressed to me."

"That's not the point, Bree." His voice rose.

She crossed her arms. "Then what's the point? Why are you getting angry?"

"My point is, I shouldn't have had to hear it from Tim." He pointed in his brother's direction. "Why didn't you call me?"

"It didn't occur to me." She broke eye contact with him and uncrossed her arms.

He took a deep breath. Something in his gut hardened. "It didn't occur to you?"

She threw her hands up. "Cut me some slack, Jase. I called Gran because she knew who to call to get a lawyer. I'm not used to having to inform anyone of every little thing that happens to me."

He leaned close. "I'm only interested in the things that end with someone killing people and leaving notes on the body addressed to you!"

Tim stepped in between them, making a T with his hands. "Can you two please take it outside? You're making a scene."

Jase glanced around to find almost everyone in the office looking at them. "Come on, I'll walk you to your car." He grabbed her hand and pulled her behind him. "Where did you park?"

"Down the block. In front of the old general store."

He turned right out of the police station and walked briskly down the sidewalk. He used the short walk to burn off some of his anger. How could it not occur to her to call him? What did she think was going on? Didn't their conversation last week mean anything? He thought he'd been pretty clear on where he stood.

He had never been in a real relationship with a woman. He'd been a kid when he'd joined the Army. He'd dated and had girl-friends, but never anything serious. When he got out, women were an outlet. Like alcohol. He wasn't proud of how he'd been, but he'd never made anyone any promises. Never let it get to the point where promises were expected. After Tony killed himself, he'd stopped partying. Stopped getting drunk all the time. Started talking to someone at the VA. Started his company and put his focus into making it successful. Now here was Bree, not expecting promises when he was willing to give them. The irony could choke him.

He spied her SUV parked in one of the metered spaces and slowed his pace. He needed to make sure she understood exactly what he wanted from her. He caged her between him and the driver's door. Her blue eyes held his gaze, her unspoken question evident in their depths.

"I know this is new. For both of us. I get the sense your ex didn't treat you the way you should be treated."

"Jase—"

"Let me finish. He was a fuckwit who didn't appreciate what he had. Didn't protect it like he should've. I'm grateful he fucked up because it means I got a shot at you. I know what I have. I see it in everything you do." He took a breath. She needed to under-stand what he saw. "How you get excited about a scared little dog. How you talk about the folks at your gran's retirement commu-nity. When you ask me questions about what I do and I know you're asking because you're trying to figure out which of your patients might be interested." He brushed his thumb across her cheekbone. "More importantly, I know what we can have together. I'm going to do everything I can to protect it. I need to know if you're willing to do the same."

Bree dropped her gaze. She raised her hand and touched the

hollow of his throat before running her fingers up to his jaw. She ran her thumb over his bottom lip as her eyes followed the movements of her hand.

She finally looked up. He could see the shimmer of unshed tears in her eyes and braced himself. "I haven't been serious about a guy in a long time. I'm not counting fuckwit because I never actually intended to get serious with him. The whole time we were together, I was ambivalent. About him. About our relationship. It would never have occurred to me to call him about things, good or bad." She swiped her fingers under her eyes. "I'm scared of everything I'm feeling," she ended on a whisper.

He kissed her forehead. "We talked about this."

"It doesn't change the fact that this is a lot. You and me. Someone leaving bodies addressed to me. I have to compartmentalize things and when I do that—" she took a breath and looked back down at his throat. "—when I do that, some things get left out. I can't help but think I compartmentalized Chad out of my life. I'm worried I might do the same with you."

"That's what your scared of?"

"I'm freaking the fuck out."

He tilted her chin to get her to look at him. "Bree. I will fight for this. I will fight to be in every compartment you create. But I need to know you're going to fight too."

She nodded a few times and sniffed. "I'll try."

"That's all I'm asking." He kissed her. Sweet. Gentle. Undemanding while sealing their promise to each other.

He raised his head and brushed a lock of hair behind her ear. "Your place or mine?"

"Dogs," she said.

"Yours. I'll follow you." He stepped back to give her room to open the door and get in. He knocked on the window and motioned for her to roll it down. "If I'm not right behind you, wait for me before you go in the house."

"Okay."

He stuck his head in the window and kissed her. He jogged around the corner to his truck and started it before he had the door closed. She was still in the parking spot when he drove down the street. She backed out when he stopped a few cars behind. He watched his rear and side view mirrors on the drive to her house, unable to shake the unease that had settled over him when he had left her at her car. He wanted answers. He wanted Bree safe.

Jase parked beside Bree minutes after she turned her car off. She sent Denise a text to let her know she was okay. Denise texted back that she was on her way and Jase could just deal with the company. Bree didn't think Jase would mind. It would also save her from having to tell the story twice.

She'd been with her second-to-last patient when Cindy told her she had an urgent call. One of the techs had finished the treatment for her. She'd surprised when it was Tim on the phone. He'd shared only that the investigators wanted her to go to the station to make an official statement. When she got there and learned there had been another murder, she immediately called her grandmother for the name and number of their lawyer. Not that she had anything to hide, but she'd learned to always have a lawyer present when dealing with any official business. Up to this point, that had applied only to issues with the foundation.

She hadn't been expecting Gran to show up with the main partner of the top law firm in the area. The detectives had definitely sat up and taken notice. She'd gotten the feeling they were much more solicitous to her because of her grandmother and the lawyer.

She finished her text to Denise and got out of her car. Jase met her at the hood of her car and took her hand. He led her to the side entrance. She unlocked the door and the dogs trotted in to greet them. Jase bent and gave them each a scratch on the head.

"Stay here while I check the house."

"Jase—"

He grabbed her hips. "Please. Stay here."

Bree sighed. After not calling to tell him she was at the station, she was willing to let him have this. "Fine, but I'm letting the dogs out." She followed him into the kitchen. The deadbolt on the patio doors was still locked.

"All clear?" she asked when he came back into the kitchen.

"Yes. What did they ask at the station? Do you know who was killed?"

"Slow down, Perry Mason. Denise is coming over and she's going to have the same questions you do. I'd rather do this once."

"How long until she gets here?" He pulled a glass from the cabinet.

Bree opened the refrigerator and grabbed the pitcher of tea. "Not long enough for us to have sex."

"Why, Dr. Marks. What a dirty mind you have." He wiggled his eyebrows and smirked. "That wasn't what I was asking at all, but now that you bring it up—" he sauntered over "—do we have time to make out?" She walked backward until she hit the counter.

"Maybe." She set the pitcher down. "Depends on your definition of making out."

"How many definitions are there?" He pushed close, resting his hands on the counter behind her. His body pressed against hers from chest down to her knees. He bent his head into the crook of her neck and scraped his teeth along her sensitive flesh.

She ran her hands up his chest. "Well, there's middle school making out."

"What's that?"

"My hands on your shoulders." She rested her hands on his shoulders, the muscles bunching and moving under her fingers. "Your hands on my hips. Mouths closed and just our lips touch."

He licked the spot on her neck. "Nope. Don't like that one at all. What's next?"

"Junior high making out. Arms wrapped around each other. Mouths open, but very little tongue."

"A little better, but not really interested in that." He bit her earlobe before switching to the other side of her neck.

She closed her eyes and a small shudder passed through her.

"What's the pinnacle definition of making out?" he asked.

This was fun. She enjoyed teasing him and the way he teased her back, not holding a grudge from earlier. "Well, I'd have to say the ultimate definition of making out would be strangers in a dark hallway."

He lifted his head from her neck. A sexy smile spread across his face at her reminder of the night they met. "Yeah. I think that one is my favorite."

He cupped her head and kissed her. Hot. Open-mouthed. Tongues intertwining. He wrapped his arms around her and pulled her even closer. Her arms wrapped around his neck. Everything but his warm body enveloping hers faded from her mind. The heady scent of his skin. The desire racing through her as she clung to him. She slowly came to her senses when he ended the kiss and pressed his forehead against hers.

"I think we need to go back to the middle school definition, or I'm going to put you up on the counter and Denise can get bent."

She threw her head back and laughed.

He dropped his head into the crook of her neck. "I love that sound."

She leaned back. "Let me get dinner started. You want something to drink?"

"Sure. Is that iced tea in the pitcher?"

"Sure is." She moved out of his arms and put ice in the glass he'd pulled out earlier.

"Did you have a coming out?" He leaned his hips against the sink, hands beside his hips. His t-shirt strained across his chest.

"A what?" Her brows met in the middle of her forehead.

"You know. Did you come out? As a debutant?"

She looked at him like he was crazy. "Uh, no. Why on earth would you ask that?"

"Because your grandmother is Vivienne Coffee."

"Ah. Gotcha." She poured tea into the glass. "No, I was not a debutant. I did not have a coming out. The summer I turned sixteen, my grandparents took me on a cross-country road trip to Yellowstone. In an RV. For three weeks."

"Not a fun trip, I take it."

She shrugged. "Now that I'm an adult, I realize it was great experience. I'd love to do it again. But I wish I could slap my sixteen-year-old self for not appreciating it more while it was happening."

"But you were still a Coffee."

"No. I'm a Marks. Gran didn't become *Vivienne Coffee—*" she hooked her fingers twice "—until my grandfather was diagnosed with cancer. The hospital here wasn't equipped to treat him, and they were advised to go up to Raleigh." He took the glass she held out. "She didn't want to do that. She wanted them to be here, at home, with family and friends. They could afford in-home hospice care, but it bothered her that other families didn't have that option. So she donated money to the hospital on the stipulation that it be used to build a new cancer treatment center."

She poured another glass of tea and returned the pitcher to the fridge. "Her reputation for philanthropy grew from there. Before my grandfather got sick, they donated money anonymously. Gran wanted the new center named after my grandfather."

"How come you never mentioned it?"

She sighed and leaned against the counter across from him.

"People already look at me funny when they find out I have money, which is why I don't tell a lot of people. When they find out my grandmother is Vivienne Coffee, their entire attitude changes. They either think I'm some stuck-up rich girl and treat me like shit, or they start sucking up to me for who they think I might have connections to. To me she's just Gran, so I don't tell anyone."

He set his tea down and pulled her into a hug. "I already told you I don't want your money. I was surprised when Tim said her name, that's all."

"Thank you." She tucked her face into his neck. Little by little, her muscles relaxed, and tension eased out of her. Her eyes stung and she swallowed hard. The emotions she'd held pent up crashed, threatening to overwhelm her. It'd been so long since someone held her for no other reason than to just hold her.

They stood that way for several minutes, arms wrapped around each other, until Jase's stomach rumbled. "You said something about dinner, right?"

Bree chuckled. "Yes. Is chicken okay?"

"Sure. You want some help?"

"You can chop the onions." She smiled sweetly before moving out of his arms.

"Gee, thanks."

"Don't mention it."

Jase sniffed and slid the onions off the chopping board into the sauté pan. The kitchen door opened, and Sprocket trotted in ahead of Denise. Denise looked in the pan.

"Stuffed chicken?"

"Yes," Bree said.

"Sweet. And there's tea."

She fixed herself a glass of tea and sat at the counter next to the refrigerator. "Spill. What happened at the station?"

Bree began with getting the call at work and then finding out there had been another murder.

"Did you know her?" Denise asked.

"No. I'd never seen her before. I didn't recognize her name either. She was a junior editor at one of the magazines Chad wrote for."

"Shit. Was Chad screwing around with her as well?"

Bree shrugged. "I asked the investigators the same thing. They said he had said no, but I'm willing to go out on a limb that he was probably lying."

"Is it possible Chad killed her?" Jase asked.

"Before all this happened, I would have said no." She mixed frozen spinach in with the onions in the pan. "After the way he was when you kicked him out, I'm not sure any more. But, the police said he has a solid alibi for when this girl was killed. He was in Atlanta covering a game."

"So, not Chad," Denise said.

"Nope." She split the chicken breasts to stuff with the spinach and onion mixture.

"Tim said there was another note," Jase said.

"Yes. This one said, *A woman like you should be treated better.*"

"What does that even mean?" Denise asked. "Don't get me wrong, I completely agree with it."

"Your guess is as good as mine. I told the investigators about Chad. Steven, my old neighbor, Jaelyn's husband? He provided them with all the information the PI got for him. They're looking into this latest girl's life to see if there's a connection to Chad. Right now, they're going on the assumption that someone has fixated on me because of Chad."

"So it's a guy?" Denise asked.

"They don't know. They're leaning that way because both the girls were stabbed, but there was no sexual trauma, so it could also be a woman. Or an impotent man. They don't know. Or they aren't saying."

"What about the prints from your room? Did anything ever come back from that?"

"No. They didn't get any hits. They did ask about my room again. What had been moved. What pieces of clothing had been messed with. I told them everything I could." She turned on the faucet and washed her hands.

"Do they think there's a direct threat to you?" Jase asked.

She put the chicken in the oven before she answered him. "They don't know. They don't think so, but they're going to have a patrol car drive by randomly. It's a dead-end street so it's not exactly going to be random. If someone is creeping around, hopefully it will spook them."

"I don't like it," Jase said, a fierce scowl on his face. "You'd think they'd know whether or not there's a threat to you."

"I agree with Jase," Denise said.

"I'm not all that happy about it either, but there's not much I can do about it. The notes haven't been threatening. They've been…flattering? I don't know." Bree shook her head and crossed her arms over her chest. "I haven't noticed anything that makes me feel uneasy or makes me think someone's watching me, but I haven't been hyper-vigilant either." Polly padded over to her and whined. Bree placed one of her hands on the dog's head and scratched her ear.

Denise walked around the counter and hugged her. "Hey. You got this. We got this."

Bree dropped her head to Denise's shoulder and closed her eyes. "Someone is killing women because of me."

"No." Denise forced Bree's head up. "Do not take that on yourself. Someone is killing women because they're bat-shit crazy. It has *nothing* to do with you."

Bree tilted her head. Her forehead furrowed as she pursed her lips. "It's easy to say that. It's a lot harder to believe that when someone is leaving me notes on their bodies."

"I know. But you need to try."

Bree simply nodded her head.

Jase put his hands on Denise's shoulders and moved her to the side. He took her place and embraced Bree. "Tell me what you're thinking."

She rested her head and stared at Denise. "I know, intellectually, it's not my fault. It doesn't stop me from feeling responsible for those women's deaths." What-ifs ran through her head. What if she'd broken it off with Chad sooner? What if she'd made a scene and turned him down when he proposed? Would any of this be happening?

CHAPTER 18

The alarm beeped, and she groped for the snooze button. Jase leaned over and kissed her shoulder. "How many times are you going to hit snooze?"

She snuggled deeper under the covers. "A couple."

"I'm going to get in the shower then." He dropped another kiss on her shoulder.

Bree rolled over. "Why are you getting up?"

"I'm going to follow you to work."

She watched his tight, naked butt walk toward the bathroom. *Wait. What?* She rose to her elbows. "Why are you following me to work?"

"Because a murderous psychopath is stalking you."

"Jase—"

He stopped in the doorway, turned, and braced his hands against the doorframe. "Don't argue with me about this, Bree. I'm following you as far as the gate."

What was the question? Her strength left her and she dropped down to the bed. The alarm started beeping again, and she turned it off. There would be no snoozing with that full frontal image burned onto her retinas.

He was angry. No…he was afraid. For her. Something unfurled in her chest and she rubbed the heel of her hand over the spot. She looked at the half-closed door, catching a glimpse of his naked back as he turned on the water. The least she could do was thank him for looking out for her.

She grinned and threw back the covers.

Jᴀꜱᴇ ɢʀɪᴘᴘᴇᴅ the top of the car door and pulled it open for her. "You've got your cell?"

"Yes."

"Call me if you see anything suspicious. Or anyone suspicious."

She threw her bag onto the passenger seat and sighed. "Jase, I know you're worried, so I'm trying to see this overprotectiveness as cute rather than annoying and overbearing." She set her hands on her hips. "But I swear to almighty god, if you don't stop talking to me like I'm an idiot, I'm going to punch you in the balls again."

He stepped closer, but kept his hand on the door. "You like my balls."

She tilted her head back to maintain eye contact. "I do. So it would be a shame if I couldn't use them because they had to be surgically extracted."

He rubbed his thumb across her bottom lip. "I don't like that you can't carry your gun on base."

"I promise to be safe. I know how to maintain situational awareness. Okay? I'll check my six."

He grinned and kissed her. "It's hot when you talk tactical. Do me a favor? Text me when you leave work."

Tension left her shoulders. "I can do that."

"Thank you." He kissed her again before stepping back and heading to his truck.

SSPRAWLED on the couch after dinner, Bree was dozing off when Jase's chest rumbled under her ear.

"What?" she asked.

"We should practice combatives."

Her head jerked up. "What?"

"You know…Army combatives. Grappling."

"I know what they are. Why should we do them?"

His hand ran up her back. "In case someone attacks you."

She dropped her forehead to his chest. "Jase…"

"Come on. It'll be good exercise."

He slid out from under her and moved the coffee table out of the way.

Groaning, she sat up. "Fine, but you need to put the dogs out. They aren't going to like this."

"Charlie. Polly." The dogs raised their heads when he called their names. "Outside." They rose from their beds and trotted after him. Charlie stared up at Jase, tongue lolling from his doggy smile. Silly mutt probably thought they were going to play ball.

She stood and twisted at the waist, popping the joints in her back. Jase strolled back into the living room and rolled his neck from side to side. Bracing her legs, she waited, hands loose at her side. He matched her wide-legged stance, but braced his hands on his hips.

She raised her brows. "Well?"

"Come at me."

"No. You come at me. I'm supposed to practicing against an attacker."

He rushed her. At the last moment she stepped to her left and jammed her knee into his stomach. It hit him low because of the height difference.

His breath left him, and he grabbed his stomach. Bree spun and took two steps back, watching him catch his balance. He straightened and turned slowly.

She smirked.

One of his eyebrows raised. "Don't get cocky." His eyes became intense and he stepped to his right, circling her.

Shit. He let her have that one.

He took her down in less than ten seconds.

He straddled her in mount position and held both her hands in one of his. "What are you going to do?"

She stared up at him. None of the ideas she had involved getting him off her. More like getting him further on top. She bucked her hips. He didn't even move. She rolled her hips and licked her lips.

"What're you doing?"

"Let go of my hands and I'll show you."

Instead of letting them go, he raised them above her head, bracing his other hand on the floor by her head. He shifted and moved his legs between hers, forcing her hips wide. Lowering his head, he hovered his mouth over hers. "So your plan is to seduce your attacker?"

"Only if it's you." Her tongue flicked out and licked his bottom lip. His mouth slammed down on hers and his hips rocked against her. She moaned, pulling at his hold. He let her go and she ripped his shirt over his head. Her shirt and bra got shoved up and he pulled her breast into his hot mouth.

She tossed her head as heat pooled in her core. "Fuck. I need you."

He was gone.

Her eyes snapped open. "Wha—?"

He crawled back on his knees away from her. His eyes were dark — almost angry. "Up. Turn around." He pulled her back to his front and palmed her breasts. Her head dropped back onto his shoulder. She reached behind her for his hips and rubbed her ass against his erection. His rough palms skimmed down her stomach, leaving small tremors in their wake.

God, yes. Her whole body shook as his hand delved into the front of her running shorts. He slid two fingers between her folds at the same time he scraped his teeth on her neck.

She panted. Each quick breath released as a gasp.

He removed his hand.

"No!" She grabbed it, trying to push it back in.

He pulled out of her grasp and hooked his thumbs in the sides of her shorts. "Shirt and bra off. Now." Her shorts were shoved down her hips to pool around her knees.

She yanked the shirt over her head and fumbled with the clasp of her bra, throwing it away from her once she freed herself.

Pressure between her shoulder blades forced her forward. "Down. Hands on the ground."

Another shiver wracked her body. *Holy fuck, that's hot.* His control. His demands. Moving her body where he wanted it. She dropped her head and waited.

He rubbed his thick shaft through her slick folds, hitting her clit with each forward stroke. One hand stroked down her back and the other dug into her hips in a punishing grip. She'd have bruises tomorrow and she gave not one single fuck.

"Brace yourself, Bree. I'm not going to be gentle." His voice growled and she felt herself growing even wetter.

"I don't want gentle. I want you to fuck me."

He buried himself to the hilt and stayed deep inside her, not moving. Bree turned her head to look over her shoulder just as he brought his hand down on her ass, causing her to gasp.

"I've been thinking about that since the morning I found you gone." He smacked the other side of her ass before he pulled back slowly and slammed home, hitting her core and speeding her toward her orgasm.

Again. And again. A slow withdrawal, then slamming back in hard. His balls slapped against her with every thrust.

"Shit. Fuck. Jase. I'm gonna come."

"Wait for me. I want to come while you scream my name." Her

arms collapsed and she rested her head on her hands, shaking it back and forth.

The hell with this. She needed Jase to be as uncontrolled as she was. She reached through her legs and grabbed at his sac. Each time he thrust forward, she curled her fingers on the underside of his balls and gave a light squeeze, milking him as he fucked her.

"Fuck," he grunted. His thrusts sped up, became shorter. He pushed her hand out of the way and pinched her clit.

She screamed. Her orgasm exploded through her and she saw stars. Jase buried himself to the hilt and roared. His chest met her back. He bit the base of her neck as he groaned and shoved into her one final time. The combination of pain and pleasure pushed Bree into another orgasm.

Breathing heavily, Jase shifted his weight so his hands were braced on either side of Bree. He licked the spot where he bit her. "You okay, darlin'?"

She nodded, unable to speak.

It was a lie. She was not okay. In that moment, she realized she was falling in love with him.

Please be the endorphins.

He kissed his way down her spine as far as he could reach without separating from her.

She was so screwed.

CHAPTER 19

"I'm going to cancel the trip this weekend."

Bree looked over the top of her book. Her feet rested on Jase's lap, and he was rubbing the balls of her feet while he watched a baseball game. "Why? What happened?"

His thumbs stilled, and he shifted his gaze to her. "You have a stalker who is killing people. That's what happened."

She set her book face down on the back of the sofa and pushed up. "You want to cancel your trip because of me?"

"Yes." He continued rubbing her feet and went back to watching the game.

Bree yanked her foot from his grasp and stood. Grabbing the remote off the coffee table, she turned off the TV and threw the remote back down.

"Absolutely fucking not."

"Bree—"

"No." She glared down at him. "I've put up with you following me to base every morning. I've put up with you losing your shit when I forget to text you when I'm leaving work. But you will *not* cancel your trip because of me."

Polly raised her head from her bed and whined.

Jase stood and matched Bree's angry stance. "Excuse me for wanting to keep you safe."

"This isn't about keeping me safe, Jase. This is about a promise you made to guys who need this trip. You are not going to cancel on them so you can sit here and play mother hen."

"You seriously think that's what I'm doing? Playing mother-fucking-hen?"

She closed her eyes and took a breath. Polly's heat pressed against her leg, and Bree rested a hand on her head. Fighting for calm, she opened her eyes. "I'm exhausted. It's been two weeks and I'm tired of constantly being on alert. I'm tired of looking over my shoulder and staring at everyone who passes me in the street like they're going to pull out a knife and stab me."

When he opened his mouth to answer, she covered it with her hand. Anger still rolled off him in waves, and whatever he wanted to say was going to piss her off even more.

"I'll ask Denise to come stay with me for the weekend. I'll call Tim every afternoon. But you are *not* going to cancel this trip. We are *not* going to put our lives on hold because of this whacko."

He bit her palm. "Ow." She yanked her hand away from his face, shook it, and glared at him. He grabbed her around the waist. Her struggles to get free were pointless. She huffed and folded her arms in front of her.

"You deserved it."

"Like hell." She refused to meet his gaze and stared off to the side.

He nuzzled her neck, tickling her with his beard. "You'll call Tim every day."

Sighing, she gazed up at the ceiling. "Yes."

"Denise will stay with you."

"Yes."

He raised his head and held her chin between his forefinger and thumb. "You're more important to me than my business or five strangers I've never met."

Her anger and annoyance melted. She wrapped her arms around him and rested her cheek on his chest.

"I don't want anything to happen to you, Bree." He rested his chin on top of her head.

"Nothing will."

BREE LEANED back against the arm of the sofa and stared at her phone. No messages or missed calls. "I haven't heard from Jase yet."

"Did he say he was going to call?" Denise asked.

"Yeah. He said he'd call when he was on his way back."

"Maybe his phone died."

"Maybe." It didn't feel right. He would have borrowed someone else's phone.

"Call him. Maybe he hasn't left yet. Or is still out of range."

He answered on the third try. "Hey. Are you back?" she asked.

"Yeah. Got back a few hours ago." His voice was flat, with a slight slur.

"Oh." Pressure built in her chest, squeezing her heart. Something was wrong. "Are you coming over?"

"I'm wiped. I'll see you later."

"Wha—"

"'Night." The call disconnected.

She stared at the screen again, like it was magically going to provide an explanation for what just happened. "What the fuck just happened?"

"What?" Denise asked from the kitchen.

Bree raised her head. "Jase just told me he'd see me later."

"Okay. What's wrong with that?"

"He hasn't left me alone except to go to work for the last two weeks and now it's *I'm wiped; I'll see you later*? What the eff?"

Denise joined her on the couch, holding a plate and glass.

"Maybe he realized you're okay by yourself. Maybe he really is wiped and knew I was going to be here. Maybe he needs to decompress."

"I guess… It just seems like it's a complete one-eighty from how he's been this entire time."

"I know. But we all have our off days." She bit into her sandwich. "This whole thing has been stressing him out. Give him a day and let him relax. You can freak out if you don't hear from him tomorrow."

Bree shook her head. "There was something in his voice. It was…I don't know. It was off."

"Call him tomorrow. If it's still off, then you can unleash unholy fury on his ass."

He didn't reply the next morning when she texted him on her way to work. When she still hadn't heard from him by late afternoon, she stopped by his office on the way home.

"Hi, Ms. Carol. Is Jase in today?"

"Oh no, honey. He never comes in today."

"Monday?"

"No. It's— I thought for sure he would have told you."

Bree frowned and tilted her head. "Told me what?"

"Oh, Bree. Today is the anniversary of Tony's death."

Bree's hand flew to her mouth. "I'm so sorry. I didn't realize. Wait. Why are you here then?"

Carol sighed. "I accepted Tony's death a while ago. Jase…hasn't been able to get past it, I'm afraid."

"Why is he having such a hard time?"

"Tell you what. There's a nice little cafe a few doors down. I was getting ready to lock up anyway. Why don't we go have a cup of coffee and talk?"

Carol locked up and set the alarm before hooking Bree's arm and leading her down to the end of the strip mall.

"Let me explain about Tony and Jase first." Carol opened the door to the cafe and scanned the small bistro. "How about over there?"

"Sure." Bree followed her over to the small corner table.

"Jase's family moved across the street from us when the boys were about four. I'm a few years older than Melissa, Jase's mom, but we became good friends."

The waitress stopped by their table. "Hey, Ms. Carol. The usual?"

"Yes, please."

"And for you?" the waitress asked Bree.

"Coffee with cream, please."

"Okay." She flashed a smile. "Be right back."

"Where was I?" Carol asked.

"Uh, Jase's family moved in across the street."

"Right. Jase's daddy was in the Army and was gone a lot. I was never sure what he did, but I think he was Special Forces. Tim was six, and Shannon, their sister, was a baby. Poor Melissa had her hands full. Tim was a serious little boy. Always watching before joining in on things. Never gave his mama any bit of trouble. Jase, though, was a little hellion. I started taking him in the afternoons to give her a bit of a break. Tony was my youngest and I had him late in life. He was unexpected, if you know what I mean."

The waitress returned with their drinks. "Here you go. Can I get you anything else?"

"No thank you, dear," Carol said. She took a small sip of her coffee before continuing.

"Jase and Tony were like night and day. I think if Tony had been older, he and Tim would have been friends. They're much more alike. Whereas Jase would run hell-bent into anything, Tony would follow cautiously, but he always followed Jase. I thought when they started school, Jase and Tony would find other friends, but neither of them did. They had their own groups and interests, but they remained best friends all the way through high school."

Bree sipped her coffee and listened in rapt fascination as Carol unveiled a part of Jase's life she might not have learned otherwise.

"Jase idolized his daddy. Always said he wanted to be a soldier like him. Wanted to save the world. Melissa convinced him to wait a year after he graduated before enlisting. Jase took some classes at the community college, but he knew it wasn't for him. He did it only because his mama asked. He walked into the recruiter's office as soon as his last class was over. Tony went with him."

Carol contemplated her coffee, as if drawing courage from the tendrils of steam rising from the cup. "Tony was…sensitive. Always bringing home strays. Sticking up for kids at school. He was a very talented artist." She glanced back up at Bree.

"I saw one of his drawings. The one Jase has."

"He drew that one after he got out. The Army offered him a position in the media. What's it called? The news network?"

"Armed Forces Radio and Television Service?"

"Yes. That one. They wanted him to be a graphic artist or something, but he refused. Said he joined with Jase and was going to stay with Jase. Even Jase told him it was a great opportunity and to take it, but he was adamant. I asked him once why he was so hell-bent on staying with Jase. He told me, 'Mama, Jase needs me. He'll lose himself if I'm not there to remind him who he is.' That was Tony. Always looking out for everyone."

Bree sniffed, fighting back her tears. She ached for Carol's loss. For Jase's loss.

"He came back haunted. Physically, he was whole, but that war killed something inside him. I could see it. A huge piece was missing from my boy. He'd go out fishing or camping and come back happier, but it would last only a day or two. I convinced him to get counseling, but he did it only because I pleaded with him. I had hope when he and Jase fixed up that house that things were going to turn around. He was drawing again. But…."

She sipped her coffee, gazing out the window.

Bree bit her lip and swiped at an errant tear.

"I found some of his drawings when I was going through his room…after. Some of them, like the one Jase has, were beautiful. Poignant. But others were horrible. The nightmares he must have suffered to draw those pictures," she whispered.

A tear escaped and she dabbed at her eye with a napkin. "I had no idea the depths of his despair. But it helped me understand why he killed himself. Why he felt that was the only way out. The pain is always there, in the corners of my heart, but I've come to accept it. Jase, though. Jase blames himself."

"Why?" Bree blinked rapidly, trying to prevent her tears from falling.

"He thinks if he hadn't let Tony follow him into the Rangers, he wouldn't have been scarred by the war the way he was. I've tried to make him understand he couldn't have made Tony do anything he didn't want to, but Jase still blames himself. I had hoped, since he started dating you, he'd finally realize there are more important things in life than regret."

Carol reached over and grasped Bree's hand. "I'm glad you came by today. Jase is like a son to me, and I'm going to ask you to do something very difficult."

Bree placed her hand over Carol's. "Whatever you need."

"I need you to go and kick Jase's ass for me."

A surprised laugh escaped Bree. She slapped a hand over her mouth and shook her head. "I'm sorry. I didn't mean to laugh. You just surprised me."

Carol's eyes twinkled and she patted Bree's hand. "That's all right, dear. Laughter is the best medicine. Go get Jase's head out of his ass."

BREE PARKED NEXT to Jase's truck and shut off the engine. Dim light from the kitchen window shone like a beacon in the darkness surrounding her car. She found the kitchen door unlocked and made her way through the quiet house to the family room. A floor lamp threw soft light onto the recliner where Jase sat, staring vacantly at the picture above the mantel. Beer bottles lay scattered on the coffee table and a few more on the floor where they had rolled off.

"Jase."

He started. Lines appeared on his forehead as he stared at her. "What are you doing here?"

"Carol told me what today is," she said softly.

Jase looked away and lifted the bottle of liquor to his lips. Apparently beer wasn't getting the job done.

"Jase?"

"I forgot."

"Forgot what?" She walked farther into the living room, stopping a few feet in front of him.

"Forgot what today was." He looked at her again and her heart clenched. His eyes were vacant. Devoid of emotion. Pain, even anger, she could have handled. But there was nothing in his gaze.

"That's understandable," she said, thinking as time passed, he would begin to forget. Begin to hurt less. In time, the good memories would override the bad. But that wasn't how he took it.

"How is that understandable, Bree? How is forgetting about someone killing themselves because of you *understandable*?"

"Carol told me about Tony. It's not your fault."

"Bullshit. You think because Carol shared a story with you, you understand? You have no idea. You couldn't possibly understand what he went through. What I went through." He took another pull from the bottle in his hand and looked away from her.

His dismissiveness slashed through her heart in a way that nearly brought her to her knees. She gasped at the pain as it radiated outward from her chest. And it infuriated her. He didn't have a monopoly on pain. After everything they'd talked about —

everything that had happened the last few weeks — how dare he dismiss her?

"How dare you?" she seethed.

"Go home, Bree."

"Fuck you. I don't understand? You think I don't know what it's like to be standing at the gas station and hit the ground because you think someone's car backfiring is incoming mortars? You think I don't know what it's like to not want to sleep because of the never-ending nightmares? To not want to see the montage of faces of everyone you lost?" Her hands balled into fists. "To not want to wake up when you finally do sleep because you have to face the world? A world so fucking wrapped up in its own selfish bullshit and oblivious to everything else that's going on?"

Her chest heaved, a sob fighting to escape. "You think I don't know what it's like to be in a crowd of people trying not to have a panic attack because there are too fucking many of them and no one is watching where the hell they are going? Or how about almost crashing your car because the asshole in front of you threw his cigarette butt out his window? Or when it takes everything not to throat punch the motherfucker in front of me complaining about the cashier taking too long?

"Or how about when your best friend calls you and says she can't take it anymore and all you can do is pray you aren't too late?" Tears flowed freely now. She scrubbed the heels of her hand across her cheeks, angry she couldn't stop them. "You think I haven't had days where it was everything I could do to make it through the next five minutes? And the five after that?" She gasped and fought to catch her breath. "Or that I haven't stood in front of my gun safe and thought it would be so easy. One bullet and the pain would end?"

She gritted her teeth and took a step back. "It's a conscious decision every fucking day to wake up and promise the people who love you that you won't leave them. That you won't take the easy way out and leave them with the bottomless well of pain they'll have to live with for the rest of their lives."

"Bree…" The light flickered back into his eyes. It was a painful light, highlighted by the shimmer of tears.

"Fuck you, Jase. This is how you protect this?" She pointed a finger at her chest. "This is how you fight for it? Bullshit." The sob tore through her, compressing her chest with its forcefulness.

"Bree." His voice broke when he spoke her name.

Lost in her pain, she whipped around and blindly stormed back to the kitchen. The pain in her chest throbbed with every heartbeat. She tore through the door as Jase shouted her name.

Fumbling with her keys, she slammed the door to her car. The headlights illuminated Jase as he stumbled out of the kitchen after her. The tires chirped on the concrete as she pressed on the gas pedal, reversing in a wide arc around his truck. Throwing the SUV into drive, she sped down the long dirt road. She sobbed and wiped furiously at her tears as she drove to the one person she knew she could always turn to.

CHAPTER 20

ase tripped on the edge of the concrete where it met the grass. Reflexes dulled by an entire day of drowning his sorrows, he couldn't stop himself from sprawling on the rough surface. The pain radiating from his cheek as it bounced against the concrete was nothing compared to the pain gripping his chest. He pushed himself up to his knees and watched as Bree's taillights faded.

He roared into the night, slamming his fists into the ground. "Fuck! Fuck! Fuck!"

He'd done it a-fucking-gain. He'd lost his best friend to his own goddamned selfishness. Now he might've lost the woman he loved. Her words had seared through his chest and ripped out his heart. The pain in his chest beat in rhythm to where his heart used to be as he admitted the truth to himself.

He dropped his head to the ground, curling in on himself. *Bree*.

He hated this fucking day. He'd forgotten. Actually forgot what day it was. He wouldn't have even remembered if a guy on the trip hadn't made an offhanded remark about the date. He'd hated himself in that moment. Hated that he'd forgotten he was the

209

reason Tony was dead. Hated the happiness he'd been living for the last few weeks when Tony wasn't alive to be happy at all.

Bree hadn't deserved what he'd said. He'd just wanted her to leave. Not see him like that — wallowing in his misery. He was such a fucking asshole.

Her pain had resonated with every word she spoke, ripping through his heart like razor wire tearing through skin. He'd let her down. Broken his promise to take care of her.

He stumbled back into the house and collapsed face down on the couch. Tomorrow. He'd make it up to her. Apologize. Grovel. Anything to erase the agony on her face. Anything to have her back in his arms. To make good on the promise he'd made her.

THE STEADY, painful throb at the base of his skull woke him. Bright sunlight streamed in the windows and he covered his eyes to add a layer of darkness. His cheek was wet and he lifted his head off the puddle of drool.

He wiped his cheek with the heel of his hand and rubbed across the scrape. "Ow! Shit." He rolled onto his back, and his stomach rolled with him.

"Fuck." He bolted for the bathroom, kicking at empty bottles littering the floor. He purged his stomach, then rinsed his mouth. Sinking to the floor, he leaned against the wall next to the door.

He propped his elbows on his knees and fisted his hands in his hair.

Bree.

Fuck.

He banged his head against the wall. His watch showed nine thirty-three. Groaning, he heaved to his feet and went to find his phone.

He scrolled through his contacts until he found her work number. Holding the phone to his ear, he stared at the mess of his living room. The ringing sounded like a firehouse bell vibrating in his ear.

"Physical therapy. May I help you?"

"Yes." He cleared his throat. "Dr. Marks, please."

"I'm sorry, sir, she's out sick today. May I take a message or have you speak with one of the other providers?"

He grabbed at his hair again and paced back and forth behind the couch. "No, thank you. I'll try back tomorrow."

"Fuck." Pulling up his favorites, he called Bree's cell.

"This is Bree. Leave a message."

"Fuck!" Leaning his hands against the back of the couch, he hunched over, dropping his head between his outstretched arms.

He heaved a sigh and stood. Thumbing through his contacts, he stared at the name his thumb hovered over. He pressed the name.

"You're a fucking asshole." Denise hung up. Well, Bree had talked to her. He dialed again.

"Are you shitting me right now?" If phones could click anymore, he was sure she'd have slammed hers down. Inhaling deeply, he dialed again.

"Meat grinder, motherfucker."

One more time. "Denise, let me—"

"Not on your fucking life."

That was a lie. He was going to keep calling until she told him where Bree was.

"Denise, please. She's not answering her phone."

"No shit. Did you really expect her to?"

"Denise, I'm trying to make this right. I was an asshole. I know that. But I can't apologize if I can't talk to her. The clinic said she called in sick. I don't have her grandmother's number and I don't know who else to call."

Silence. *Please, Denise, help me.* More likely, she was planning how to chop up his body. Just in case, he came clean.

"I love her. I fucked up. I need to fix it."

Denise sighed. "She's at her gran's. Haven Springs Village. Villa 42."

"Thank you."

"Don't make me regret this." She ended the call.

He rushed through a shower and brushed his teeth. Sweeping his fingers through his wet locks, he got dressed and grabbed an apple from the counter. He looked up the directions for Haven Springs Village on his phone as he got in his truck.

Jase pulled into a visitor's parking spot a few doors down from Villa 42. After taking a deep breath, he got out and walked down the landscaped path to the small cottage. He opened the screen door, but hesitated before he knocked. Doubt assailed him. How would she react to him being there? Would she see him? Let him apologize? He steeled his courage. It didn't matter. He would make this better. Had to. There was no way he would let her go without a fight.

The door opened before he could bring his knuckles down.

"Hello, Jase. Would you like to come in?" Vivienne Coffee's polite invitation was the last thing he expected.

"Thank you, Mrs. Coffee." He followed her in and closed the door behind him.

"Call me Vivienne, dear. Have a seat. Is iced tea all right?"

"Yes, ma'am." He sat at the small kitchen table and watched her bustle around. He glanced around the well-appointed villa. Across the open floor plan, he spotted Bree's service picture on the mantle in the living room and went to take a closer look. A younger Bree stared out from the silver picture frame. Her hair cut just below her ears. Her face serious, as all basic training pictures tended to be. He studied the other pictures on the mantle. Bree as a child and a teenager. A picture of a man in a World War II-era uniform. Her grandfather.

On the center of the mantle, in a place of prominence, sat a framed Bronze Star medal with a Valor device. Next to it, the citation. He picked it up, stunned to see Bree's name on it.

CITATION TO ACCOMPANY THE AWARD OF THE BRONZE STAR WITH V DEVICE FOR HEROISM IN ACTION AGAINST AN ARMED ENEMY, WHILE SERVING AS A CULTURAL SUPPORT TEAM MEMBER DURING OPERATION ENDURING FREEDOM.

"She's an extraordinary woman." Vivienne interrupted him before he could finish reading the citation. "But then, you know that already."

"Yes, ma'am, I do." He set the frame back on the mantle. Damn, he owed her a huge apology. He'd been a self-righteous ass.

He joined Vivienne at the kitchen table and accepted the glass she offered him.

"She's sleeping right now. I checked on her when I heard your truck drive by."

He nodded, not sure where she was going to take the conversation.

"I'll be honest. I'm hesitant to let you see her. She hasn't been this withdrawn since she came back from Afghanistan — after that happened." She pointed toward the citation on the mantle. "The fact that you're here speaks volumes, so I'm willing to give you the benefit of the doubt."

"Thank you. I don't know what she told you about last night, but I messed up." He looked down at the glass in his hand.

"She hasn't told me anything. She showed up last night with Polly and Charlie, so I knew things were bad. She came out this morning for breakfast and went right back to bed."

"I'm guessing she wouldn't want to leave her dogs by themselves with everything that's been going on."

Vivienne cocked her head and considered him for a moment. "Jase, dear, Polly is a therapy dog. Bree got her when she was diagnosed with PTSD. She helps Bree cope when her emotions overwhelm her. Or when she retreats into herself."

Jase rocked back in the chair. He'd had no idea. How many times had he watched Polly lean against Bree. His brow narrowed.

Each time Polly had stuck to Bree, she'd been upset or stressed. "I didn't know. She just seemed like a sweet dog."

"Oh, she is. Bree doesn't rely on her as much as she used to. She hasn't had to."

Jase raked his hands through his hair. Guilt and regret crashed against him like storm waves against a rocky coast. At least this time he could do something about it. "Can I talk to her?"

"Down the hall, on the left."

"Thank you."

"Don't thank me yet," she warned him. "You still have to talk to Bree."

He nodded and walked down the short hall. He paused outside the bedroom door and took a deep breath. Easing the door open, he entered the darkened room, barely able to make out Bree's form curled up on the bed. Charlie stood from his position on the floor at the end of the bed. He brushed past Jase and left the room. Polly lifted her head from where it rested on the crook of Bree's knees and thumped her tail against the bed. Jase closed the door and walked over to her. Polly rose from her spot next to Bree and hopped off the bed.

He gathered Bree in his arms and fit his body close. Her breath shuddered, evidence that she had been crying. He cringed. Shit, he had screwed up.

Her head shifted on the pillow. She stiffened, and he tightened his arms around her. Her silence pained him. He kissed her shoulder.

"I'm sorry for what I said last night. I'd like to explain." She remained silent and he took it as permission.

"I always knew I wanted to be in the Army. I never expected Tony to follow me. Selfishly, I was glad he did. We went through basic training together. Infantry and Pathfinder school. Finally, Ranger school. I was so proud of Tony. I didn't think he'd make it through, but he surprised me. Hell, he even pulled me through at times. We both got orders to Savannah with First Battalion. Back-to-back rotations to Iraq, then Afghanistan. We were done. Couldn't take it anymore.

"We both had PTSD. *Have*," he corrected. "For me, *have*. We dealt with it differently, though. Tony pretty much became a recluse. He'd barely leave the house to go to the store. I bought my house because of the land it sits on. It gave us space. There's a pond a half mile from the house. We stocked it so we'd have a place to fish without having to go anywhere. He'd go fishing, and when he came back, it was almost like I had my best friend back. It didn't last long." He drew in a deep breath, dreading what he had to tell her next.

"I dealt with things the exact opposite. I'd go out every night and get drunk. Bring home a different girl every other night."

She stiffened again.

"I'm not proud of how I dealt with things. Or didn't deal with them. I wanted an escape. A way to drown the anger and the bitterness. I started to resent Tony." He whispered his horrible admission in her neck. "He always wanted me to hang out with him. Talk about what'd happened. I didn't. I wanted to forget. Bury it so far down it'd never see the light of day. I started avoiding him. Ignoring his calls."

He took a deep breath. Moment of truth. He had to get the worst out. The shame. The guilt. She'd hate him when she knew, although she couldn't possibly hate him more than he hated himself. "The night he killed himself, he called me. I ignored him. I turned my phone off and kept partying. Went home with some chick I couldn't even pick out of a lineup. I found him the next day. An empty bottle of whiskey and pills next to him. He didn't leave a note. Just that drawing that's above my mantle."

Bree's breath heaved through her again as her fingers dug into his forearms. She turned her face into his arm and tried to muffle her sob. Tears slid from her face to the skin of his arm. He placed another kiss on her shoulder. Polly climbed back onto the bed in front of Bree and low-crawled over to them. She rested her head on their entwined arms and whined. Jase placed a hand on Polly's head and rubbed his thumb over the spot above her eye.

"Jase…" Bree said, his name coming out on a broken sob.

"Not yet. Let me finish."

She nodded. He took another breath and moved his hand back to her arm. "It tore me apart when I realized he'd been calling me at the worst moment of his life and I ignored him. I quit drinking. Quit partying. Started seeing a counselor at the VA and went to group therapy. During one of the sessions, a few of us made plans to go on a camping trip. It was great. One of the first times any of us had really relaxed. Six months later, I started V.E.T. Adventures. I talked to Ms. Carol about it and she helped me get it off the ground.

"I was…okay with my life. I had a routine. Some close friends. I'd go out every now and then to blow off steam, but nothing too crazy. I dated a couple times, but nothing serious." He held her tighter. "Until that night you walked into The Deck. You laughed, and it fixed something. Like sewing a wound back together. That was the best night I could remember in a long time. When you were gone the next morning, that piece of me ripped apart again. You made me want to be whole again. But you also made me forget."

She stilled, and he rushed on. "It's not a bad thing. Or, it shouldn't be a bad thing. But my guilt wouldn't let me see that. I saw it as a betrayal to Tony that I didn't remember. That I was so happy I'd forget for even a moment he wasn't here to be happy, too. I knew if you stayed last night, I'd forget again, so I lashed out.

"Watching you walk out was a thousand times worse than finding Tony. The thought of not having you in my life shredded me. It ripped apart all the pieces you'd stitched back together without even knowing it. I love you, Bree. I can't lose you too. It would destroy my world."

Her body rocked with the force of her sobs. "Bree, shh. Please don't cry. Darlin', you're killing me."

She turned suddenly and dislodged Polly. She buried her face below his chin and fisted her hands in his shirt. It took only seconds for her tears to soak his shirt. His hands rubbed her back and hair as he tried to calm her. He peppered small kisses along her forehead and cheek. She turned her head and his mouth found hers. He tasted the saltiness of her tears on her lips and pulled back to look at her. Brushing her hair away from her face, he looked into her swollen blue eyes and hated himself just a little bit more.

"I'm sorry," she whispered.

"Don't. You have nothing to apologize for."

"I'm sorry you lost your best friend."

"Me too. He would have liked you."

"I'm sorry you went through that."

"Me too. I miss him. I hate myself for not being there for him."

More tears welled in her eyes. One fist unclenched and she rested it on his face, fingers brushing the raw spot on his cheek. Her eyes searched his. "I love you. I'm still scared shitless. You have unimaginable power to hurt me."

"I promise, Bree. I promise I will do everything I can to never make you feel this way again."

She nodded and took a deep breath. He kissed her softly. Her mouth opened and her tongue flicked at his bottom lip. He parted his lips and her tongue swept in. He kept the kiss gentle. Languid. A balm for them both. She pulled back, her expression unreadable.

"What is it?" he asked.

"I need to blow my nose."

He smiled and unwrapped his arms.

CHAPTER 21

Ugh, that's gross.

She threw the wad of tissues in the trash and blew her nose again before splashing water on her face. There was no hiding her puffy eyes and splotchy face. She just wasn't one of those women who was a pretty crier. Leaving the bathroom, she heard Jase's voice in the living room. And Denise's.

Oh, jeez.

The thick carpet was soft as she walked down the short hall. Denise leaned against the kitchen counter, arms crossed, and stared down Jase who sat at the kitchen table with Gran. She met Bree at the island and hugged her hard.

"I brought a shovel," she said, loud enough for Jase to hear.

Bree laughed into Denise's shoulder, riding that fine line of emotional hysteria. She didn't know if she could take anymore today. She was just too raw after being numb for so long.

"You good?" Denise asked.

"Yeah." *No.*

The wall she'd so carefully constructed around herself lay in rubble. Jase had crashed through it with the force of a bulldozer.

219

Her heart ached. For Jase and Ms. Carol. For Tony. For everything she'd had to feel in the last day.

"You lying?"

"A little bit. But I'll be okay."

"I figured that out when I didn't see any blood stains on the carpet."

She huffed. "Like Gran would let me get blood on the carpet."

"I have a large tarp in the shed," Gran said.

Bree broke the hug. Jase was a little wide-eyed, finding himself in a room of women calmly discussing the disposal of his body. "You're fine," she told him. "They're kidding. Kind of."

She looked at Denise. "How long have you been here?"

"Not long. About fifteen minutes or so."

In a low voice, Bree asked, "Can I get you to leave again so we can finish talking?"

"Denise, why don't you walk down to the coffee shop with me?" Gran must have heard her. Or knew her well enough to understand she needed a few more minutes.

"Sure. I could use some caffeine." Denise rubbed her hand over Bree's arm before following Gran out the door.

Jase stood and gathered Bree close. She wrapped her arms around his waist, her head rested on his chest while the steady beat of his heart thumped under her ear.

"Are we okay?" His voice rumbled in his chest, sending shivers through her.

"We will be. I just need some time."

"Bree. Don't compartmentalize me."

She held herself still, unblinking. That was exactly what she would end up doing. Dealing with the pain meant tucking it away in places she didn't have to visit. It was the only way she knew how to deal with the emotions raging through her. "I need a day or two to process everything I'm feeling right now."

One of Jase's hands left her back and rested on the side of her face. He tipped her head back, forcing her to look at him.

"Go out with me."

"What?" Her brow furrowed.

"On a date. I'll give you your day, but you have to go to dinner with me tomorrow."

"You're asking me out on a date? Isn't that kind of backward?"

He grinned. "We didn't really do this the normal way. And I want to see you in a dress."

Could they do normal? It felt like a step back. They'd said they loved each other, and now he was asking her out.

"Don't overthink it. It's my way of giving you space without giving you a chance to shut me out."

She dropped her gaze to his chest. He was being his usual overbearing self, but he was also right. Left to her own devices, she would find a way to distance herself in an effort to manage everything she was feeling. Still gazing at his chest, she nodded. "Okay."

"Okay?"

She met his gaze and smiled. "Okay, I'll go out with you."

His smile was wide and unreserved. He framed her face with his hands and kissed her. Closed mouth, sweet, and chaste. Yet carnal desire still raced through her veins. She parted her lips to deepen the kiss, but he pulled away.

His thumb brushed over the arch of her eyebrows. "If I kiss you like I want to, I won't leave, and it might be a little awkward when your gran and Denise come back."

That should have banked her desire like a bucket of water on a fire, but it didn't. Even with the turmoil storming in her heart and mind, her body wanted him. Her physical response contradicted her earlier words.

"Stop looking at me like that while I'm trying to do the right thing," he said. "Six-thirty tomorrow work for you?"

"It should. I'm not sure when my last appointment of the day is. If it's later in the afternoon, I'll let you know."

"Call me tonight before you go to sleep." He kissed her forehead, then the corner of her eye. The soft and tender way he held her saved him from being told he was bossy.

"Okay."

"Okay." Another chaste kiss. He stepped away from her and strode across the room. Opening the door, he looked back over his shoulder and winked.

❧

BREE PULLED a glass from the cabinet and poured water from the filter pitcher on the counter. The water soothed her throat, swollen from crying. *I need a beer.* A couple of shots wouldn't hurt, but Gran kept only wine in the house. Gran and Denise returned, carrying to-go cups of coffee.

"Where's Jase?" Gran asked.

"He left." Bree took the cup Denise held out to her.

"He what?" Anger laced Denise's voice. "I though you said everything was all right."

"It is. I told him I needed a little bit of time."

"And he agreed?" Denise's eyes narrowed.

"Kind of. He said he'd give me a day, but only if I'd go out with him."

"What? Like, on a date, go out?"

Bree let out a small laugh. "Yeah, like on a date."

"Huh." Denise crossed the small kitchen and flopped down onto one of the recliners in the living room. "Told you he wouldn't let you go very far."

Bree rolled her eyes at Denise. Gran took her shoulders in gentle hands. She searched Bree's face, and a soft hand tucked a stray strand of hair behind her ear. "Do you want to talk about what happened?"

Bree swallowed hard. She'd never been comfortable talking to Gran about her lingering issues. She didn't want to burden her with the pain, the nightmares, or the guilt. But if she was going to stop compartmentalizing things, maybe she should start with the person who loved her most.

"Let's sit." Bree sat on the end of the couch and curled her legs under her. She took a sip of the coffee, flicking at a drop of foam on the lid. Polly climbed on the couch and curled up next to Bree.

"Jase's best friend, Tony, committed suicide a few years ago. Jase blames himself."

"Why?" Gran asked.

"The night Tony killed himself, he had called Jase, and Jase ignored the call. Jase found Tony the next day." She glanced at Denise, who averted her gaze.

"Well now I wish I had given him a hug," Gran said. "He must feel so guilty."

"He does. This year was really bad."

"Why?" Denise asked.

"He forgot. Because of me."

"What the fuck?"

"Denise. Language," Gran admonished. "Why does he blame you, dear?"

"He doesn't really blame me. He's happy. Because of me. But that makes him feel even guiltier."

"What happened last night?" Denise asked.

She rubbed Polly's ear, who licked the inside of Bree's upper arm. "Quit licking." She pushed Polly's muzzle down and wiped her arm against her shirt. "I went by his house after talking to Ms. Carol."

"Who's Ms. Carol?" Gran asked.

"Tony's mom. She's also Jase's receptionist."

Gran nodded.

"I went by his house, and he was drunk. Said I wouldn't understand what he was going through and told me to leave."

"What did you do?" Denise asked.

Bree gave her a baleful stare. "I lost my shit. Then I came here." Gran let that one go.

Denise assessed her. "How're you really doing?"

"I'm raw." Bree shrugged. "More emotional than I like to be."

Gran rose from her chair and sat on the other side of Polly. Bree put her feet on the ground and Gran leaned in as close as she could, clasping Bree's hands between hers. She stared at their hands before looking at Bree. "You remind me so much of your grandfather. When he came back from the war, he was different. Back then it was called *shell-shocked*. He'd retreat to his office for days, working on ideas. I worried for years. In much the same way, I worry about you."

Bree dropped her head on her Gran's shoulder, tears welling up in her eyes again. Polly licked at the underside of her chin. Gran's simple, unfailing love washed over her. "You don't need to worry about me, Gran."

Gran's cool hand, smelling faintly of her citrus lotion, rested on Bree's cheek. "I will always worry about you, my darling girl. No matter what." She kissed her forehead and rose from the couch. "Just promise me you're talking to someone." She looked between Bree and Denise.

"I am. I promise."

"Denise?"

"Yes, ma'am."

She nodded. "I'm going to Bingo. They're giving away an e-reader tonight. Are you girls staying for dinner?"

"I'm going over to Sarah's," Denise said.

Bree tilted her head back. "I'm going home."

"All right. Make time next week to come for dinner. Bring Sarah and the kids." Gran leaned down and kissed Denise on the cheek. A few, short steps took her to Bree, and she repeated the gesture. "I love you girls. Lock up behind you."

"Love you too, Gran," Bree said. She and Denise stared at each other for a few beats.

"The truth?" Denise asked after Gran had closed the door behind her.

"I've had better days."

Denise inhaled deeply. "You going to call Dr. Tailor?"

"I called this morning. She had an opening next week. You?"

Denise nodded. "Tomorrow. With everything going on with Sarah, I need to talk to her." She stood and scratched Polly behind the ears. "I'm going to head out. Are we still on for this weekend?"

"As far as I know. I'll check tonight when I talk to Jase."

"Let me know."

"Will do."

～

"Good morning, Dr. Marks."

"Morning, Cindy." Bree set her bag on the floor by her desk and sat down.

"Are you feeling better? You don't call in sick very often."

Bree finished logging on to her computer and swiveled her chair to face Cindy who was standing just inside the door of her office.

"I am, thank you. I think it was one of those twenty-four hour bugs." She didn't feel great about lying but *I needed to recover from an emotional breakdown* probably wasn't the best reason to call in sick. "Were you able to reschedule everyone from yesterday?"

"I was able to fit most of them in next week, but I had to add a couple of time slots to your schedule."

"Morning or afternoon?"

"Both." Cindy's face twisted in apology.

Bree clicked through her schedule and noted where Cindy had added the appointments. She was going to have some long days next week. The only other option was to cancel her day off on Friday and skip the camping trip. Not an option. Jase had been relieved she still wanted to go, and she didn't want to disappoint him by cancelling now.

She turned back to Cindy. "That's fine. Can you keep a list handy of everyone you had to reschedule? If someone calls to cancel, go down the list and offer the spot to them first."

"I already made the list."

"You're the best, thank you."

"Of course. Are you sure you're feeling better? You don't really look a hundred percent."

Nothing like being told she looked like crap. "I'm fine. I promise."

The doorbell rang just as she reached for the shower knob.

Of course.

She wrapped her well-worn flannel robe around her and tied the belt tight. The peephole revealed a young man holding an arrangement of flowers.

She unlocked the bolt and cracked the door. "Can I help you?"

"Hi." He checked the form on the clipboard he held. "Brianna Marks?"

"Yes."

"These are for you." He raised and lowered the vase, an abundant bouquet spilling over with white and yellow day-lilies, interspersed with large red and pink stargazer lilies.

Surprised, she opened the door fully. She'd never had flowers delivered before. "Thank you."

"Can I get you to sign the form?"

"Of course." She took the clipboard and pen, scrawling her signature where he indicated.

He took the clipboard and handed her the vase of flowers. "Have a good day."

"Thanks. You too." She closed the door and turned the deadbolt while she searched for a card. The small white envelope sat tucked under a large red petal.

Blank. *Huh.*

The waxy petals were smooth under her fingers. Flowers. Just because. Her cheeks hurt from the wide smile she couldn't hold back. After centering the vase on the dining room table, she danced down the hall to her room. She had a date to get ready for.

CHAPTER 22

The doorbell chimed, and a dog barked on the other side of the door. Charlie, probably. He'd noticed Polly wasn't much of a barker.

Jase smoothed his hand down the front of his tie, trying to settle the nervousness trembling under his skin. The last time he could remember being nervous about picking up a woman for a date had been his high school senior prom. Adrenaline made him restless, and he slid his hands in his pants pockets.

Bree's heels on the wood floor signaled her approach. He should have braced before she opened the door. His breath left him in a rush.

A small, light blue stone rested in the hollow of her throat. His gaze fell to the deep V of her blue sleeveless dress, exposing the gentle curve of her cleavage. Long auburn hair spilled over her shoulder in soft waves, the ends curling around the swell of her breasts. His gaze travelled down the short, flared skirt to her toned legs and sexy heels. A vision of her strappy black heels wrapped around his hips almost broke his resolve. Christ, she had to be trying to torture him. He swallowed hard and shifted his stance, trying to make room for the hard-on pressing against his zipper.

He dragged his gaze back up her body and met her sapphire blue eyes. A few shades lighter than her dress, they sparkled with amusement, and a smile tugged at the corners of her berry-stained lips. A faint hint of jasmine teased his nose.

"Hi," she said.

"Hi."

They stared at each other. Her heels brought her up several inches so they were almost eye-to-eye.

"Are we still going?" she asked.

"What?"

"To dinner. On a date. Are we still going?"

His body jerked as he broke out of his daze. "Yes," he said, a tad too loud. "Yes, we're still going." He took her hand in his and led the way to his truck. Opening the door, he waited to help her in, unsure whether she could manage in her skirt.

"You look good, too." She winked and boosted herself into the truck, flashing a lot of thigh.

Jesus. He scrubbed a hand over his mouth and closed the door on her laughter. She totally had his number. He grinned and walked around the hood. After buckling his seatbelt he turned, one hand on the steering wheel. "You're beautiful."

"Thank you." She leaned toward him and he met her over the center console. Her lips were soft and pliant. He growled low in his throat as erotic images of her lips tracing over his body flashed through his mind.

She created a small space between them. "Is everything all right?"

"It's taking everything in me not to drag you back inside, strip you naked, and bury my cock in you while you dig those sexy heels into my ass."

A small gasp escaped her parted lips and a flush bloomed high on her cheeks. "Do you, uh..." She licked her lips. "Want me to encourage or discourage those thoughts?" Her chest rose and fell with her quicker breath.

He forced himself to say the right thing. He wasn't going to fuck this up again. She'd asked for space; she was going to get it until she told him she didn't need it anymore. No matter what their bodies wanted.

"I need you to discourage me."

"Oh." Her disappointment evident, she bit at the corner of her mouth. He was ready to take his words back, but she pulled away and leaned against her door. "Where are we going to dinner?"

Her words sounded nonchalant, but her fingers clenched in her lap gave her away. He turned the key in the ignition, thankful one of them had the strength. "Catch 22."

"Wow. Really? How did you get reservations? I had to call four months in advance to take Gran there for her birthday."

"I called in a favor. The owner's a buddy."

"Yay for favors."

He stole a peek at her cleavage. Then another. His fingers itched to trace the smattering of freckles on her delicate skin. He needed something mundane to take his mind off her body. Something innocuous. "How'd work go?"

"Good. My assistant was able to reschedule all my appointments from yesterday."

"Shit." He hadn't even though about that. "I'm sorry." He glanced at her as he pulled onto the highway toward Raleigh.

"Don't." She rested her hand on his arm. "It's not a big deal. It's not the first time I've ever called in sick."

He grabbed her hand and laced his finger through hers. Raising it, he kissed her knuckles, earning a gentle smile. Resting their hands on the console, he held her hand until he was forced to downshift getting off the highway.

Outside the restaurant, the valet took his key in exchange for a ticket, and Jase jogged around the front of the truck. "I got her." He patted the second valet on the shoulder and edged him out of the way. Bree had both her feet in front of her, prepared to hop down. He set her gently on the ground and watched as she smoothed the back of her skirt.

"Ready?"

"Yes," she said.

The decor was rustic. Roughhewn wood pillars broke up the large space, creating the illusion of smaller rooms. Low lighting and candles added to the sense of intimacy.

"Welcome to Catch 22," the hostess said.

"Hi. I have a reservation."

"Jase!"

He turned at the sound of his name. "Scott. Hey, man." He released Bree's hand to embrace his friend and exchange one-arm hugs. Releasing his hand, he pulled Bree close to his side.

"Scott, this is Bree. Bree, Scott. Creator of the gourmet MRE."

Laughing, Scott said, "I haven't cooked MREs in almost ten years. It's nice to meet you, Bree."

"It's nice to meet you too, Scott. I love your restaurant."

"You've been here before?"

"A couple of times, for special occasions."

"You're in for a treat," Scott told them. "You're my special guests tonight. Jenny, can you take them to the chef's table?"

Jase and Bree stepped to the side as the hostess joined them. "If you'd like to follow me?"

Scott clapped Jase on the shoulder. "Enjoy your dinner. I'll check on you in a few."

"Thanks, man." Jase and Bree followed the hostess to a small table tucked behind the hustle and bustle of the kitchen.

"Wow, you really did call in a favor," Bree whispered, laying the cloth napkin across her lap.

"I wasn't expecting this. I just asked him if he could fit us in."

～

THE SILVER FORK slid between Bree's lips, and she closed her eyes and hummed. Her pink tongue darted out. She licked at the corner of her mouth, catching a tiny dot of sauce that had been left behind.

Fuck, she was trying to kill him. He was pretty sure Scott was in on the plan. The last hour had been sheer torture. Scott spared nothing, going above and beyond by serving them a full chef's tasting. They were on their seventh course. He hadn't tasted any of it.

"Oh my god. This is so good," she moaned.

The erotic images playing in his head had nothing to do with food.

"I swear each plate is better than the one before."

Jase glanced at his nearly untouched food. He'd have to take her word for it.

"How is it?" Scott asked from the side of their table.

"This is probably the best meal I've ever had." Bree licked her lips. "Everything is so delicious."

"Jase, everything good?"

"Yup." Fucker smirked at him.

"For dessert, the pastry chef has created a stacked vanilla bean cake with lavender-infused white chocolate ganache and a rum buttercream frosting."

"Holy cow," Bree said. "Yes, please."

Jase's cock throbbed. He wasn't going to survive.

"Great, I'll have that brought right out." Scott grinned at him before going back into his domain.

Jase jolted when Bree laid her hand on his thigh. Just a few inches higher, and her slender fingers would brush against his hard-on. Pure fucking torture.

"You hardly ate anything." Her fingers rubbed back and forth on the inside of his thigh.

He clamped his hand over hers and threw his other arm around the back of her chair. Leaning close, he brushed his mouth against the soft skin under her ear. She tilted her head toward him and her breath blew gently across his cheek.

He spoke low her ear. "I've been watching your mouth all night. Every time you took a bite, licked your lips, moaned around the food in your mouth, I imagined you doing that to my cock. Better than any porn I've ever watched. I'm so fucking hard right now I don't think I'm going to be able to walk out of here without help."

Her breath rushed hard against his cheek and she shifted to meet his gaze. Dark-blue desire-heavy eyes met his.

"Dessert." Scott set the plate in front of them with a flourish.

Bree tore her gaze away. "Can we get that to go?"

Scott laughed. "Sure thing."

"And the check," Jase said.

"Nope. No check. My treat."

"Scott."

"Jase. I'm not taking your money."

Jase stood and helped Bree push back her chair. He held his hand out to Scott. "Thanks." He pulled him in for a one-armed bro hug and slapped him on the back. "You're an asshole. You know that, right?"

Scott threw his head back and laughed. "Yeah. I know. Food is passion. Have Bree walk in front of you on the way out so you don't scandalize my patrons." He turned to Bree and took one of her hands between both of his. "It was great to meet you. Anytime you want to come back, give me a call."

"Thank you. It was all wonderful."

"Enjoy the rest of your evening.

Jase's hand on the small of her back burned through the thin material of her dress. He walked close to her side and slightly behind her. A pulse of desire coursed through her as his hand slid to her hip. It was all she could do to control her breathing while the valet went to get Jase's truck. He ran his hand slowly, back and forth, from her hip to her back until she couldn't take it anymore. She took a step to her left, just out of his reach.

"What's wrong?"

"I need you to stop touching me," she said, facing him. It did nothing to cool her desire.

"Why?" A crease appeared between his eyebrows.

She spared a glance for the valet before glaring at Jase.

He slipped his hands in his pockets and rocked back on his heels, a self-satisfied grin spreading across his face. Pure sex appeal. The perfect fit of his suit accentuated the width of his shoulders and trim waist. His pale lavender shirt and dark purple tie had been a surprise; she'd expected something more plain. She squeezed her thighs together as her eyes traveled down his body.

"Why, Bree?" She could hear the amusement in his voice.

He took a step forward. She matched it with a step back.

"You know why, Jase."

"It's only fair, you know. My zipper's probably imprinted on my dick by now."

The valet made a choking sound and began coughing.

Heat spread across her cheeks. "I can't believe you said that."

He wiggled his eyebrows, never losing his grin. His truck pulled up before he could embarrass her further. He tipped the valet and opened her door, then thwarted her attempt to edge around him when he gripped her waist and boosted her into his truck.

"I'm not taking any chances of you accidentally flashing anyone," he said. He smoothed his hand up the outside of her calf, branding her skin. "Legs in."

She shifted her legs in front of her and settled in the seat. He closed her door and moved around to the driver's side.

She stared at the center console separating the passenger and driver's seat. It wasn't moveable, and there was no way she could lean over it without her ass sticking up in the air. Guess giving Jase head on the way home was a no-go.

He climbed into the driver's seat and graced her with a lascivious grin. She glanced at his lap and reconsidered hanging her ass out for the world to see. *Think of something else.*

"I forgot to thank you for the flowers," she said.

His look turned quizzical as the truck turned out of the parking lot. "What flowers?"

"The ones you sent earlier today."

"I didn't send you flowers." He still looked confused.

"Oh." She blinked a few times. If he didn't send them, who did?

"Was there a card?" He continued to dart glances at her while watching the road ahead of them.

"Yes, but it was blank." She shrugged. "I just figured they were from you."

"Who delivered them?"

"Local florist. I think it's the one on Main Street in town."

"Do you think it was Chad?

"Probably not. I haven't heard from him since you tossed him out."

He rubbed his bottom lip with two of his fingers. "I'll give Tim a call. See if he can find out who sent the flowers."

Her eyebrows lifted and a corner of her mouth curled up. "Why don't I call the florist first? See if they can tell me who sent them before you assume they're from some nefarious person? For all I know, Gran sent them and didn't think to sign the card."

"I guess that probably makes sense." His smile was sheepish.

"A tad."

He reached over and took her hand, kissing her knuckles like he had earlier. "Are you disappointed?"

It was her turn to be confused. "About what?"

"That I didn't send them."

"A little bit."

He held her knuckles against his mouth for a moment before

rubbing his lips against the back of her hand and settling their hands on the console. "I'm sorry I didn't think about it."

"It's okay."

"You were excited when you got them, weren't you?"

"Yeah. It's nice to get flowers for no reason."

He released her hand to downshift as he pulled into her neighborhood. He was silent as he navigated to her house and eased into her drive. Setting the parking brake, he shut off the engine and faced her. His look was serious in the dim light of the cab.

"I'll find no reason to send you flowers." His voice was heavy with promise.

She ran her hand along his jaw, his trim beard tickling her palm. Pressing her lips to his, she accepted his promise. "Let's go inside."

She waited for him to come around and open her door, happy when he took advantage of "helping" her down by pulling her close and sliding her down his front. He took her hand as they strolled up the walkway.

"What time do you get off tomorrow?" he asked.

"I should be home around five-thirty."

"I'd like to take you out again." He stopped at the bottom of the porch. She stood on the first step, putting them eye-to-eye.

"Okay."

"Wear jeans. Hiking boots, if you have them." He took advantage of their equal height and pressed his mouth to hers.

His lips were soft. She wrapped her arms around his neck, pulling herself closer to his hard body. A hint of the wine they'd had with dinner still lingered on his tongue. The sweetness of his taste, combined the scent of the fresh soap on his skin, threatened to overwhelm her senses.

She wanted this man. Wanted to wrap him around her. To feel safe. Cherished. His promise of "no reason" echoed in her mind and her heart ached from the possibilities stretching out before them.

I promise, too.

She led him up the steps, onto the porch. He took her keys from her and unlocked the door. Pushing it open, he waited for her to enter, but didn't follow.

"You aren't coming in?"

"No. Not tonight." He stepped back and put his hands in his pockets.

"What—? I— Why not?" *What the hell?* They'd been having foreplay for the last few hours and he wasn't coming in?

"Told myself, no matter what, I was going to this right. Romance you. Pick you up and drop you off." He grinned. "Close your mouth, darlin', before something flies in it."

She snapped her mouth shut and glared at him. Bastard didn't lose his grin.

"I'll pick you up tomorrow before six." He turned and jogged down the steps.

She closed the door and tossed her purse on the foyer table. "What the hell just happened?" Polly walked toward her, tail wagging. Bree leaned down and rubbed Polly's head between her hands. "What guy does that? Does Charlie do that? Of course not, he doesn't have any balls."

Knock, knock, knock.

She whirled and snatched open her door. "Oh, thank—"

Jase's mouth was open and hot. His tongue invaded, possessing her.

Yes.

She dug her hands into the material of his coat. He thrust a leg between hers and pulled her up his thigh. One hand dove under her skirt, his fingers digging into the fleshy part of her ass; the other spread across her lower back, holding her in place. She wrapped a leg around his hips, seeking closer contact.

More. She wanted him naked. Wanted him pounding into her. Wanted—

He pushed her away suddenly and she teetered on her heels. His eyes shone with lust. And determination.

"I needed one more for the road." He stepped back out the door and pulled it shut, never breaking eye contact until he had to. "Lock your door." His voice reached her from the other side.

She flipped the deadbolt with a low, frustrated scream. Hands on her hips, she glared at the offending barrier. The sound of his engine pulling out of her drive reached her and she looked at Polly.

"What the fuck? You think if I cut off his balls, he'd still do that?"

Polly's doggy grin held no answers.

CHAPTER 23

Jase's mood was very different than the previous night. He seemed almost somber. Reserved.

What the hell happened?

Doubt assailed her. Why did he want her to bring Polly and Charlie? Was he having second thoughts about "romancing" her? Was he having second thoughts about *them*? Did he suggest bringing the dogs because he was worried about her having a breakdown? Would he take her somewhere to break up with her? Her thoughts raced, keeping pace with the scenery flashing by.

She had to get a grip; her emotions were running wild, making her imagine the worst-case scenario. Making her act like some silly school girl.

He pulled her hand out of her lap and kissed her knuckles. It soothed her nerves. Would he always do that when they were in the car?

"You're quiet," he said.

"*You're* quiet. What's wrong?"

He glanced at her. "I'm second guessing where I'm taking you."

"Where are you taking me?"

His Adam's apple bobbed up and down. He released her hand

to shift gears. Easing to a stop at an intersection, he fiddled with the gearshift.

"I want to introduce you to Tony." His voice was low, threaded with hesitation.

Tears welled up in her eyes, spilling down her cheeks.

"Shit, Bree." He set the brake. Grasping the back of her neck, he leaned over the console and rested his forehead against hers. "We don't have to go. It was just a thought."

She shook her head and mirrored his gesture by grabbing the back of his neck. "It's just stupid girl emotions." She kissed him, wetting his mouth with her tears. "I'd like you to introduce me to Tony."

He pulled away and brushed his thumb over her eyebrow. "It doesn't have to be tonight."

Her gaze was soft. "I don't have anywhere else to be."

He released her, then the brake, and eased onto the road. She wiped a hand under her eyes. They rode in silence until he pulled onto a dirt road.

"Where are we?"

"The backside of my property."

They bumped down the road, the setting sun creating long shadows in the woods on either side of the road. Two deer, startled by the truck, bounded away into the thick underbrush, and Charlie chuffed in the backseat. Jase pulled off into a small clearing and shut off the engine. Orange light glimmered on a body of water a few yards ahead of where they stopped.

She looked around as she got out of the truck and let the dogs out of the back. Birds sang high in the trees. A splash from the water could be heard from where they parked. She wouldn't have guessed they were only a few miles away from town. Charlie and Polly trotted off, sniffing around their new surroundings.

"It's beautiful here," she said. "Is that a lake?"

"A big pond." He rounded the bed of his truck, carrying a cooler and a blanket. "You can walk around the entire thing in about thirty minutes." He tilted his head to the dogs. "Will they go far?"

"No, they'll stay close to me. Let me help." She took the blanket from him and tucked it under her arm. He took her other hand and led them toward the water.

They skirted the edge of the pond for several minutes, the dogs exploring close by. The sun painted the sky in shades of red and orange, sending silver shafts of light reflecting off the surface of the water. Twigs and leaves crunched under the soles of her hiking boots. Jase drifted away from the water, leading her under the canopy of a large oak tree. Spanish moss hung in layers, fluttering in the slight breeze. He stopped on the far side of the trunk so they faced the breathtaking vista of the pond. She looked up at Jase, then followed his gaze to the base of the tree.

A lone, light-colored headstone sat low to the ground.

"This is Tony. We got permission from the county to bury him here."

She stepped closer to Jase and they stood in silence for several minutes. She could feel the tension in his body. After their talk the other night, she didn't think his thoughts were in a good place. Tears stung her eyes and she clenched her teeth in an effort to keep them from falling.

"What's your favorite memory?"

His body jerked next to her. "What?"

"What's one of your favorite memories of Tony?"

He stared up into the branches of the tree. His chest heaved and she worried, until a chuckled escaped. He looked at her and a smile played at his mouth.

"We were about eight or nine and we had built this fort with Legos. We decided we needed more guards for our fort because we didn't have enough G.I. Joes. So we took my sister's Barbies, cut all their hair off so they had buzz cuts, and camouflaged them with brown and green marker." His shoulders shook as he laughed.

"Shannon screamed so loud when she found us, my mom said later she thought someone was trying to kidnap her. Tony said it was his idea, even though it was mine. He knew his whoopin' wouldn't be anywhere near as bad. My dad still laid into me, but mostly for scaring my mom. We both had to give up our allowance for a month to buy Shannon new Barbies. We got to keep the ones we conscripted." He flashed a smile. "They ended up being promoted to general."

He set the cooler down and pulled her into his arms, resting his chin on top of her head. She dropped the blanket on the ground as he continued.

"Another time, our parents went out together and hired a babysitter to watch all of us. Some teenage girl who had her boyfriend come over not too long after our parents left. Tony's house had an overhang on the back of the house, and you could climb out the window from Tony's room and walk on it. We were always getting in trouble for doing it. The girl took her boyfriend up into the spare bedroom, which was next to Tony's." Jase rubbed his hands up and down Bree's back and she wrapped her arms tighter around his waist.

"Tony had a strong sense of right and wrong, even then. He didn't like that our babysitter wasn't watching us like she was supposed to. He got Ms. Carol's face lotion and we slathered it on our faces real thick, climbed out his window and walked along the roof to the other bedroom. We stared in the window, thinking they'd see us and think we were ghosts, but they were too busy, if you know what I mean. So we scratched at the glass to get their attention. When she saw us at the window, she shrieked loud enough to give Shannon a run for her money, pushed her boyfriend off her and ran out of the room." His body started shaking again.

"She'd shoved the boyfriend so hard he rolled off the bed. Hit his head on the table and knocked himself out. Tim called 9-1-1 'cause the guy was bleeding. Our parents came home to a cop car and an ambulance in the drive." His chuckle echoed in his chest. "Needless to say, she never babysat us again."

"Did you get a whoopin' that time?"

"Not that time," he said. "A stern talkin' to about safety and appropriate behavior, but our parents agreed she shouldn't've had her boyfriend over. They just didn't agree with our methods."

"You got a lot of spankings, didn't you?"

His chest rumbled again. "Yeah. Eventually our parents figured out the best punishment was to not let us see each other, so any time we got in trouble, we weren't allowed to play together for a few days."

She tilted her head back and rested her chin on his chest. "It sounds like you have a lot of good memories."

He framed her face with his hands. "I do. Thank you for reminding me." His kiss was gentle. "You hungry?"

She grinned. "For food?"

"What else do you think I have in the cooler?"

"Just checking."

"Let me take you to my favorite fishing spot."

He picked up the cooler and Bree gathered the blanket. Taking her hand, he led her a few yards away, closer to the pond.

They spread out the blanket and sat, digging into the cooler. Fried chicken, coleslaw, and a mixed salad ended up spread out between them. Charlie and Polly took up positions close by, panting and happy to be outdoors.

"Did you make all this?"

"Uh, no. I grabbed it at the store on the way to pick you up. I didn't have time to make anything to bring with me. I thought about bringing some poles so we could fish, but didn't want to chance not having dinner if the fish weren't biting."

"Good call. I'm hungry." She winked at him and opened the container of salad.

"So, how did you get into physical therapy?" He took a bite of chicken.

She finished chewing her salad. "Whenever we'd med-evac guys out of country, I always wondered what happened to them. Did they make it? Did they recover? There were a couple of guys, kids really — probably couldn't even buy a drink back home — who lost everything."

She looked at her salad and pushed it around with her fork. "How do you get past that? How do you go forward when everything you know has been shattered?" She continued poking at her food. "I knew I wanted to work with veterans after I got out. I thought about going into psychology, but I wanted to help heal their bodies. So I decided on physical therapy. It's not as long as medical school, and I get to work directly with 'em."

She looked back at Jase. "I had re-upped during that deployment, so I got as many prereqs out of the way as I could on Uncle Sam's dime. Used my G.I. Bill for the rest of it when I got out." She took a bite of salad, chewing without tasting it.

"You like it?"

"I love it. Nothing I'd rather be doing."

He shifted so he was facing her, his legs spread wide, arms resting on his knees. "Can I ask you something else? About something you said that night." His gaze was hesitant.

Shit. She didn't remember half the things she'd said to him, but she swallowed hard and nodded. Polly whined, rose, and lay back down on the blanket next to Bree.

Jase reached over and scratched Polly's ear. "I'd pretty much come to my senses right after you started, but something you said was like a punch in the gut."

Her heart stuttered. "Jase—"

"It's not bad," he interrupted. "I needed it." He took a breath and looked at Polly. "You said something about getting a call from your best friend in the middle of the night. Was that Denise?"

She looked down and nodded.

"What happened?"

She shook her head, unable to give him an answer. "It's not my story to tell," she said gently. "What I can tell you is this: if someone wants to commit suicide, they're going to."

"I just can't help but think if I had picked up the phone that night…" He looked back toward Tony's marker.

She set her salad aside and scooted closer so she could touch his face, turning him to look at her. "Don't do that to yourself. You can't blame yourself for what happened. Did he leave a message that night?"

He shook his head.

"So you don't know why he was calling you. You don't know what ultimately made him choose that path. If it wasn't that night, it could very well have been the next. Or the next week. You have to remember that he was—*is*—more than his suicide."

He gripped her hand, pressing it more firmly against his jaw. "Did you ever think about it?"

"I'd be lying if I said I didn't. Not in the sense of 'everything would be better if I were dead.' It was more…flashes. Seeing myself doing it in my mind. Not really having a conscious thought of killing myself. But it scared me."

"What did you do?"

"I went to therapy. Talked to a couple of counselors until I found one I liked. She set me up with the program that gave me Polly."

"I wonder if Tony would have gotten better if he'd had that kind of help."

"I don't know. But that's one of the reasons I helped Denise start Wiggle Butt Rescue. Sprocket's a therapy dog as well."

Jase's eyes widened. "That horse?"

"They come in all shapes and sizes." She smiled. "So, how long do you plan on romancing me?"

He traced her bottom lip with his thumb, his hazel eyes serious. "Until you trust me again. Emotionally, with your heart."

She opened her mouth to argue, but he continued. "You were right when you said we were going fast. I didn't have a plan.

Figured we'd ride the ride and see how it played out. I got stupid. Did something to almost jump us off the tracks. I'm not going to make that mistake again."

"You understand I wouldn't have shared everything I did if I didn't trust you, right? I love you."

He moved fast, catching her off guard. His mouth was heavy, almost brutal in his possession. He took her down to the blanket and pulled her underneath him.

He lifted his head and stared down at her. "I love you, Bree."

She lifted her head and found his mouth again. Tasting him. Branding him. Possessing him as much as he possessed her. The ringing of his cell phone startled her, and she pulled away with a gasp.

"I'm ignoring it. It's just us right now."

The phone stopped ringing, only to start again immediately.

"Maybe you should answer it," she said.

"Damn it." He raised up onto his elbow and pulled his phone out of his back pocket. He glanced at it before swiping his thumb across the screen.

"What?" His tone angry, impatient. "What?" Worry crept onto his face. "Yeah. She's right here. Hold on." He held the phone out to her. "It's Tim."

She took the phone. "Hello?"

"You weren't answering your phone. Figured I'd try Jase," Tim said.

"It's in Jase's truck. What's wrong?"

"There's been another attack."

She put her other hand over her eyes. *Oh god, not again.*

"Wait." She dropped her hand to Jase's upper arm. "You said attack, not murder."

"The girl's roommate came home early and found her. EMS was able to stabilize her and get her to the trauma center."

"There was another note?"

"Yes."

"For me?"

"Yes."

She tried to swallow around the lump in her throat. Jase's fingers threaded into her hair, brushing it away from her temple. She took strength from the calming, repetitious movement. Polly whined low next to her.

"Bree, can you come in again? The investigators would like to ask you some more questions."

"We're supposed to go camping tomorrow."

"You can come tonight. Or first thing in the morning before you leave," Tim said.

"I'll call my lawyer. See if he can meet me tonight."

"Okay." He paused. "Bree."

"Yeah?"

"Be careful."

"I will," she whispered.

She gave the phone back to Jase. She curled into him and felt his chest rumble as he talked to Tim. Polly took up position next to her.

"Yeah… It's late. I'm going to tell her to set it up for the morning… We aren't leaving until around noon… I'll let her know… She's staying with me tonight."

She nodded her head against his chest.

"See you then." She heard the phone thump against the blanket. He wrapped his arms around her and rubbed her back, the gentle strokes soothing her. Tension slowly eased from her neck and shoulders.

"We can go back to your house so you can get your stuff, or we can just go in the morning," he said.

"I need to get the dogs' food."

"Tonight, then." He continued to rub her back. "We'll figure this out."

She wanted to believe him; she did. But it was hard to imagine someone killing anyone for her. Because of her.

CHAPTER 24

Bree picked at the skin around her nail, pacing in the small conference room. She knew enough to look for the small camera in the corner, close to the ceiling, when they'd been escorted in. No stereotypical one-way mirror, but they didn't need it when whoever was watching had live video.

The door opened, and Detective Johnson entered. "Thank you for coming in again, Brianna. We just have a few questions." He sat on the far side of the table.

"I'm not sure why my client needed to be here again. She's as much a victim in these killings as the women being attacked," her lawyer said.

Bree pulled out the chair next to him. "Mr. Dell, please don't compare a few notes to these women being murdered. It's inappropriate."

Mr. Dell tried for a stern look. "Bree—"

"Don't. I'm here to help and answer any questions I can. This has to stop," she said. She looked at the detective. "What do you need to know?"

"Do you know this woman?" He slid a photo across the table.

Using a finger, she slid it closer. She shook her head. "No. She doesn't seem familiar at all." She slid the photo back across the table. "How is she doing?"

"She made it through surgery. She's in ICU. The doctors said if she makes it through the next couple of days, she should recover."

Bree nodded and looked at her lawyer. "You'll make sure everything is taken care of."

"Bree—"

"Make sure she's taken care of." She tapped her finger on top of the table.

Her lawyer exhaled a heavy sigh.

"That's very generous of you," the detective said.

She gave him her attention. "No. It's not. These women are being attacked — being killed — due in some part to me. So making sure this girl and her family don't have to worry about anything while she recovers is not generous."

She held Detective Johnson's gaze. He had to understand. No one else could die because some whack-a-doodle had fixated on her. "What else do you need from me?"

"When was the last time you had contact with Chad?"

"A few weeks ago. He came to my house and we got into an argument."

He wrote some notes on the pad in front of him. "What was the argument about?"

"He accused me of ruining his life because I wouldn't marry him." She rubbed the middle of her forehead with two fingers. God, she was tired.

"How did the argument end?"

She braced her elbows on the table and gripped the back of her neck with both hands. "Jase threw him out."

"Jase is Jason Larken? Officer Larken's brother?"

"Yes."

"How long have you known Mr. Larken?" he asked.

"Five or six weeks, I guess." She sat back in the hard-backed chair.

He nodded and wrote more notes. "When did you meet?"

"The night I caught Chad cheating on me."

"How did you meet?"

"At The Deck."

"Was that the first time you met Mr. Larken?"

"Yes." Bree tilted her head and squinted her eyes a little. "Why are you asking me about Jase?"

He raised his pen from his pad and looked her in the eye. "We're just exploring every possible angle."

Bree laughed and shook her head. "I'm sorry, I know I shouldn't laugh, but Jase has nothing to do with this."

"You seem very sure of that."

She gave him a patient look. "I am. Jase had no idea who I was when we met. We had a one-night stand and I took off. It wasn't until I went unknowingly to his office that he learned my full name and where I worked. Not only that, we were together the night the first woman was killed."

"So you don't think there's any way Jase could be involved in these killings?" he asked.

Bree leaned forward again and folded her hands on the table. "Detective, the kind of man Jase is, if he was going to kill anyone because of me — for me — it wouldn't be these women. It would be Chad." She gripped her fingers tightly and pressed her hands into the table. "I don't know why these women are being killed, but I guarantee I want it to stop more than you do. If I thought for even one minute Jase had anything to do with these murders, I would tell you."

Detective Johnson leaned back in his chair, threw his pen on the pad, and sighed. "We're at a loss." His tone changed. Less courteous. More honest. "The only connection we can find between you and the victims is Chad, but he can account for his whereabouts for all the murders." His stare was steady. "We thought you looked good for it, initially."

The corner of her mouth quirked. "I was surprised you didn't explore that more than you did."

Bree turned her head to her right, following his pointed glance at her lawyer, who was allowing the conversation to flow. She looked back at the detective. "No lawyer in the world would have stopped you from arresting me if you thought I was guilty."

He smirked. "Maybe. The letters left with the victims are…nice."

"They're creepy. I'd rather they said, 'Die, bitch, die.' At least then I'd know what the hell this person wanted from me."

"They're almost like love notes," he said.

"Like the flowers." Bree looked at the table, her gaze unfocused.

Detective Johnson leaned forward again. "What flowers?"

She blinked a few times. "I got flowers the other day. Jase said he didn't send them. I forgot to call the florist to see if they could tell me who they were from."

"They were delivered by the florist? Not left by the door?" He picked up his pen again, taking more notes.

"Yes. The one on Main Street. Uh…Love in Bloom, I think?"

"Detective," Mr. Dell said. "Bree has plans to go out of town this weekend. Do you have any more questions?"

He finished writing. "Not right now. We're hoping the latest victim will be able to tell us more when she regains consciousness. Let me know if you receive any more deliveries or gifts." He handed her a business card. "My cell is on the back, if you need to reach me for anything."

"Thank you. I appreciate that," she said. They shook hands, and Mr. Dell ushered her out of the conference room.

Jase paced in the hall. As soon as she cleared the door, he grasped her face between his hands and searched her eyes. His thumbs traced the edges of her brow. "We're good?"

She wrapped her hands around his wrists. "Yeah."

He closed his eyes and dropped his forehead to hers. She reassured him with a kiss, leaning up into him and tightening her grip. Pulling away, she ran a thumb along his cheekbone, tracing the line of his beard. "We're good."

He smiled at her and released his grasp on her face. They turned as a door opened down the hall. Chad stepped out with the other detective. He glanced down the hall toward them. His skin was pallid and his eyes were red, making the bags under them more prominent. His dirty blonde hair stood up on end like he had been running his hands through it. It was the first time she'd seen him look so unkempt. He broke eye contact and walked toward the entrance.

Bree squeezed Jase's hand and gave him a small smile. "Let's go camping."

CHAPTER 25

"I'm worried about her," Jase squatted down next to Denise. He watched Bree laugh at something Chris said. The tightness around her eyes and stiffness in her shoulders belied her carefree response.

Denise set the last tent peg in the ground and stood. "She's good."

Jase rose from his squat. "Why'd you guys leave the dogs at the rescue?"

"There's too much going on out here for them." She crossed her arms over her chest. "We've brought them hiking before. But with so many people, and since we're staying out here a couple of nights, it was better to leave them at the kennel."

"What if she needs Polly while she's out here?"

"Polly helps Bree because she senses her moods. She touches her to provide her comfort. To bring her back to the moment."

"Okay. And?" What was she getting at?

She raised her eyebrows and gave him a small smile. "Jase, you do the same thing."

"What?"

"Jeez. You're telling me you're worried about her? That's

257

sensing her mood. You touch her all the time. Bree is a touchy-feely kind of person. She leans into your touch and takes comfort from it."

He pushed his hands into the pockets of his jeans. "I didn't realize that's what I was doing."

She smirked. "That's probably not why you were touching her, but that's what she takes from it. Most of the time, anyway."

He rocked back on his heels. "Thanks."

"She's family." She shrugged. "But I'll still feed you to my dogs if you fuck up again."

"Not gonna happen."

"I figured." She turned and looked back at the group of people. "So is there a plan or are we just going to sit around and drink all weekend?"

"Just tonight. Probably tomorrow."

"So, all weekend then?"

He grinned. "Yeah, pretty much. There's fishing and hiking tomorrow, if people want."

"Cool. Let's get to it then."

They joined the group standing off to the side of the small fire burning in a good size circle of stones.

"Denise, this is Paul Coleman. We call him Cole." He pointed to each guy in turn. "Jordan Grant. You know Chris. Matt Baldwin. Patrick Shaw. Guys, this is Denise Reynolds."

"Why *Cole* for you, but everyone else goes by their first names?" Denise asked.

"We had six Pauls in our unit. It was either that, or number us," Cole explained in his thick Texan drawl.

Jase pulled Bree close to his side and lay his hand on her hip as they talked with Patrick and Matt. She leaned her weight against him and rested her head in the crook of his shoulder. He smiled. Denise was right.

He used every opportunity to touch Bree. The small of her back. Holding her hand. Every time she smiled at him. Returned his touch in some way. He never realized the power of something so small. Not to arouse lust or slack desire, but to reassure and comfort.

"We doin' a beer hunt?" Matt rolled the bottle in his hand, sloshing the little bit of liquid in the bottom.

"We're hunting bear?" Bree asked.

"Bear's not in season for another five months." Denise said over her shoulder.

"Wow," Paul said. "I'm impressed you know that."

"I still go out with my dad every year."

"In any case, he said beer, not bear," Patrick said.

"What's a beer hunt?" Denise asked. "And why are we hunting beer instead of drinking it?"

"It's a friendly competition we do when we come out," Jase said. "We stage beer at designated points and record the coordinates. Divide into two-man teams. Try to find as many of the locations as possible."

"What's the winner get?" Bree asked. Her hand rubbed in a small arc across the middle of his back. He wasn't even sure she knew she was doing it.

"Lots of beer," Chris said.

"What's the loser get?" Denise asked.

Chris grinned. "Less beer."

"Did you set out the beer?" Denise asked.

"I did. Wasn't sure you girls were going to be up for it, so I brought extra in the truck," Chris said.

"I hear a challenge." Denise faced Bree, hands on her hips. "Did you hear a challenge?"

Bree dropped her arm from his back and stood up straight. "I did, in fact, hear a challenge."

"Y'all think you can beat us?" Cole asked.

Bree and Denise shared a look. A twinge pulled deep in Jase's chest. He and Tony used to do that — know what the other was thinking with just a look. Fondness rode behind the ache instead of the guilt that usually followed. He kissed the top of Bree's head. Without her, he may never have gotten to this point. The pain might never go away, but maybe that was okay.

He jerked at Denise's loud clap. "All right," she said. "Let's do this. What are the rules?"

"Chris, you got everything in your truck?" Jase asked.

"Yeah. Give me a sec." He set off in a jog to the edge of the clearing where everyone's cars were parked.

"Each team gets a map, a compass, and a list of coordinates." Jase handed out the maps, lists, and V.E.T. Adventures backpacks to carry the beer in. "You get an hour to find as many points and beer as you can."

Bree pulled her hair back in a ponytail. "What happens to the beer that isn't found?"

"We get it tomorrow." Matt shrugged. "There are usually a few bottles left out there."

"Cool. Let me get my hat," Bree said to Denise. She came back from their tent, her hair pulled through a faded blue ball cap.

"You sure you don't want to join up with a couple of the guys?" Chris asked.

If looks could kill, he would have keeled over instantly from the glare Bree and Denise shot him. Jase chuckled. This was going to be interesting. He wasn't sure Chris or the other guys knew about their CST experience. *They're going to hand the guys their asses.*

Denise folded her arms across her chest, her stance a challenge on its own. "I'll bet you ten bucks we come back with more beer than the guys."

Chris matched her stance and smirked at her. "I'll take that bet."

Jase looked at Bree, who tried to hide her smile, without success. She shook her head slightly and pursed her lips, clearly used to this side of Denise.

"Yo! We doin' this or what?" Cole asked.

Chris and Denise continued their stare down for several more seconds. "Ten minutes to plot your points," Chris said, never breaking eye contact.

Denise grinned and threw him a saucy wink before she pivoted and joined Bree, already marking the map.

"You and Denise have something going on?" Jase asked him in a low voice.

"Just having a little fun," Chris said.

"You know she's got an industrial meat grinder, right?"

Chris stared at him a moment.

"Mind out of the gutter, ass. She grinds her own meat for dog food."

A slow grin spread across his friend's face. "Yeah. Not what I was picturing at all."

"Asshole." Jase shook his head.

"Ready," Patrick said.

"Ready," Jordan said.

"Ladies?" Cole asked.

"What?" Bree asked, distracted from her whispered conversation with Denise. "Oh. Yeah. We're ready."

Jase checked his watch. "Okay. I've got sixteen-oh-four. I'll give you 'till seventeen-oh-five."

"Aww, man. That's so generous, that extra minute," Cole said.

"Ready?" Jase asked.

"Wait," Bree said. "Are the locations marked with anything?"

"Orange tape," Chris said.

Bree nodded and leaned close to Denise to whisper something.

"Go!" Chris called.

"Bree." Jase flipped her ponytail over her shoulder. "Be careful."

She winked and tweaked the brim of her hat like she was Humphrey Bogart in a fedora. She jogged after Denise, and they headed off into the woods.

"Fuck." Jordan stopped cold in his tracks, staring slack-jawed as Bree jogged after Denise.

What the fuck? Jase looked at Jordan's ashen face.

"Jordan. You comin'?" Patrick called out as he hurried off.

"What was that about?" Chris asked.

"I have no idea," said Jase.

"You know the girls headed off in the wrong direction, right?"

Jase grinned and clapped Chris on the back. "Don't count your ten bucks just yet."

"Why's that?"

"They're heading to the last point first."

"What?" Chris looked in the direction the girls had taken.

"Think about it. We usually run out of time before we hit all the points. If we do get to the last point, we're dragging on the way back. Hit the last point first and work back. Better chance of hitting all the points, and shorter distance to run back."

"Son of a—"

"Smarter, not harder."

"I think I got played," Chris grumbled.

Jase threw his head back and laughed.

THE GIRLS CAME BACK with six more beers than either of the other teams.

"I still say Chris gave them an advantage." Patrick set a foil pan full of burgers and dogs on the large picnic table.

Chris dropped another pan full of foil-wrapped potatoes next to the meat. "Dude. I lost ten bucks."

Denise laughed. "If it makes you feel better, sure. We had an advantage."

Patrick pointed the tongs at Denise, then Bree. "I knew it. What was it? Jase plot the route? Put more beer at the points?"

Bree smirked and shook her head. "We used our superior intellect."

A chorus of groans rang out.

Matt picked up a plate and dug into the bag of hamburger buns. "I've got to go with Patrick on this one. The Army didn't issue you smarts, so you don't get to use 'em."

"Good thing Bree was Air Force, then." Denise took a sip of her beer. "Ahhh. Refreshing."

"Don't be mean." Bree picked up her beer. "Their fragile egos are already bruised from getting their asses handed to them by women."

"You're right. I'll be nice and share my honestly-gotten gains."

Jase pulled on Bree's ponytail, forcing her head back. He leaned over her so he was looking at her upside down. "You're enjoying this, aren't you?"

She grinned. "Yup."

He shook his head at her and gave her a quick kiss. Letting go of her ponytail, he sat next to her at the table and pulled her closer. His heat enveloped her side where they pressed close to each other. She relaxed into his embrace.

Laughter flowed as freely as the beer while the sun set. The guys continued to accuse them of cheating. She smirked at Denise every time one of them tried to find a reason for their victory.

"Do either of you two-step?" Cole asked.

"She does." Denise pointed at Bree.

She glared at Denise, then looked at Cole. "So does she. She just doesn't like to admit it."

"All right then. Matt!" He smacked his hand on the table. "Turn on some music." Cole unfolded his legs from under the table and rounded it. "Jase. Out of the way. You can paw her later."

Jase's look was questioning. She kissed him. "You can paw me later." She threw a leg over the bench and Cole reached for her hand to help her up.

"No slow songs," Jase said.

Cole smirked at Jase. "I make no promises." He led Bree to the other side of the fire and took both her hands in his.

A high-tempo country song played on the radio Matt had

turned on. Cole pulled her close, then pushed her away. He crossed his arm over her head so her back was to him before pushing her out and spinning her away — right into Denise and Matt. She threw her head back and laughed. It had been a while since she'd danced with anyone. She fell back into the rhythm of the steps. Cole was a good lead and easy to follow. They danced for two songs before Patrick cut in.

I need a break.

A slow song came on and Jase stepped in. "My turn." He pulled her close, tucking her right arm in, close to his chest. She wrapped her other arm around his back. Firelight glinted in his eyes, giving him an otherworldly look.

"Having fun?" he asked.

"I am."

"Good."

She laid her head on his chest and listened to the beat of his heart. Wasn't there a new country song about this very situation? Her lips curled up, and she closed her eyes. His thumb brushed back and forth across her fingers, keeping time with the music. Everything else ceased to exist. It was just the two of them wrapped in firelight and darkness. She sighed when the song ended, switching back to a higher tempo song.

"I need a drink," she said. He walked her over to the folding camp chairs set up around the fire.

"Tampax."

Bree's head snapped up and the bottom dropped out of her stomach. She hated that damn call sign.

Jordan stared right at her. "I thought it was you, but I wasn't sure. Not until you did that thing with your hat. You always did it with your booney hat down range. You're her."

Bree swallowed hard. "Yeah." She'd recognized him when they'd arrived. He hadn't said anything, but he'd been quiet since they came back from the woods. She'd caught him watching her, studying her, like he was trying to figure out where he knew her from. So much for hoping he wouldn't remember until after the weekend.

"What? What's her?" Cole asked.

"She was a CST," Jordan said. "Imbedded with our team. On a mission, riding in a convoy. It wasn't that far–fifty or so miles, but like most fucking routes, only one way to go. Three-quarters of the way there, we get hit. Coordinated attack. IEDs, RPGs, small arms fire. Insurgents were just waiting for their chance."

Jordan took a pull of his beer as he stared into the fire. The other guys were quiet. Waiting for him to continue.

Bree closed her eyes and swallowed hard. *Please, god, don't.* She didn't want to see the looks on everyone's faces. The assessment. Or the judgment. She opened her eyes, trying to stave off the tears.

"Lead vehicle made it through. Second and third Humvees got caught in the center of the ambush. Ten guys. All of them took hits. Tore 'em up." He locked eyes with Bree. "We were in the second-to-last vehicle. I turned around to tell her to stay put and her crazy ass has her door open. You looked down to check the road. I remember thinking *at least she knows enough to do that.* Then you were out and running to the third vehicle."

Bree's lip trembled and she sucked in a breath. The screams echoed in her head. Could smell the burning metal and flesh. She flinched when hands rested on her shoulders. *Jase.*

"You managed to pull the door open. Had to put your boot on the side of the vehicle to get enough leverage. Pulled your cutter out. Got Dantes out of his seat belt and dragged him out of the back. Pulled him down onto the road, back to our vehicle, out of the line of fire. Must have been thirty, forty yards. I didn't think you'd be able to do it, but you did. Did it five more times." He took another pull of his beer and looked away.

"We were laying down cover fire, fighting off the ambush, and she just kept dragging guys out of the wreckage."

Tears rolled down her cheeks. Denise reached over and grabbed her hand. Bree clutched it like it was her last lifeline.

"Fucking angels watching over you." Jordan looked back at Bree. "Didn't get hit once."

"No," Bree whispered. She'd come close. Some small pieces of shrapnel, but that was it.

"We finally got some air support. Attack's over. Twelve of us took hits. Four guys dead. Sawyer took a round to the leg. Nicked a vein. Dark red blood bubbling out of his skin like lava flowing over the top of a volcano. Couldn't get it under control. We're all thinking he's going to bleed out." He took a pull from his beer, then let out a short laugh. "This crazy bitch pushes through, kneels down next to him, and pulls out a tampon. We're all like *what the hell is she going to do with that*, right? She pushes it into his leg and plugs the hole." He rubbed his free hand through his hair, making it stand up on end. "Damn things are designed to expand. Put pressure on the wound from the inside." Jordan let out a small snort and looked back at Bree. "Damndest thing I ever saw. Medic trick. Saved his life. He got to go home to his wife and kids."

Her chest compressed as she tried to keep the sobs from escaping. "Yeah."

Jordan started laughing. A little drunk and a little crazy. "We all gave him shit about having a tampon stuck in his leg, but we sure as hell hit up the exchange when we got back to base and stocked up." His laughter died off. "Bronze star with valor, right?"

"Yeah."

"Should've been a fucking medal of honor." Jordan finished his beer and threw it in the trash before heading in the direction of his tent.

Matt pushed up from his camp chair. "I'll check on him." He paused and stopped in front of Bree. He reached down, setting his beefy hand on the back of her neck before kissing her on the forehead. He put his head against hers. "Sawyer's youngest is my goddaughter. Thank you."

Bree closed her eyes and swallowed hard. Matt let go and headed after Jordan.

Jase lifted his hands from her shoulders and came around to her front. He scooped her up in her arms. "Night guys." She wrapped her arms around his shoulders and buried her face in his neck.

A chorus of *good nights* followed them as Jase carried Bree to their tent.

"You okay?" he asked.

Bree nodded against his neck.

"No, you're not."

Bree gave a small shake of her head.

His hold tightened, and Bree pushed her head farther under his chin, claiming as much contact as she could get. He set her down in front of their tent and unzipped the flap. She looked back toward the fire. Chris stood in front of Denise, as if trying to stop her from following Bree and Jase.

"Chris." Bree waved her arm, telling him to let Denise by. Denise glared at Chris as she passed.

She hugged Bree tight. "Sorry, babe. I know you were hoping he wouldn't remember."

"Yeah. Shit happens."

Denise looked Jase. "Take care of her." She looked back at Bree. "Talk to him."

Bree nodded. "I know."

"See you in the morning." She hugged Bree one more time before heading back to the fire.

"You wanna hit the sack?" Jase squatted in front of the tent.

She nodded and sat in the opening to remove her hiking boots. She scooted back onto the air mattress. Her bra came off without taking off her t-shirt. Laying down on the mattress, she shucked her jeans and set them to the side. She lay there, staring up at the peak of the tent, her hands resting on her stomach. Jase lay down next to her and took off his clothes except for his boxers. He turned off the electric lantern hanging from a D-ring, then pulled her close to his side. She tucked her face into his chest and inhaled deeply. A hint of woodsmoke lingered on his skin. "I dream about them. The guys I couldn't get to. Even the guys I did get to."

His fingers traced up and down her spine. "What do you dream?"

"They talk to me. Beg me to help them. When I see them, I freeze in place. Or I can't stop the blood. They all die because I can't get to them in time."

"How often do you have those dreams?"

"Used to be every time I closed my eyes. Even when I took something to help me sleep." She traced his collarbone with her fingers. "That was even worse 'cause I couldn't wake myself up."

"What about now?" The gentle baritone of his voice as soothing as his hands brushing along her skin.

"I've had a couple in the last few weeks. My doc said it's normal, given what's going on with the murders. My subconscious trying to process the new danger by relating to a danger it's familiar with." She rubbed her forehead against his collarbone. "I wish it'd find something different."

"You gonna have trouble sleeping tonight?" His hand continued its motion. Calming her. Soothing her. She took a shuddering breath.

"I don't know."

"I've got you."

"I know."

THE MUG WARMED her fingers as she stood on the edge of the bluff. The valley spread out below, blanketed in a wispy layer of mist in the early morning light. A breeze shifted through the branches of the trees, creating eddies of fog between the muted green branches, giving the illusion of ghosts walking amongst the trees. She drew a deep breath, trying to find peace in the stillness of morning. She smiled as she took a sip of her coffee, imagining what Jase would say when he woke and found she'd left him asleep again.

The crunch of boots behind her broke the silence. She looked to her right, surprised to see Jordan standing next to her. His hands in his pockets, he stared out over the valley. She looked down into her mug and took another sip, allowing the silence to stretch out.

"Did you recognize me?" he asked.

She glanced at him, but he was still looking forward. "Yes, but I didn't remember from where until we were out on the beer hunt."

"I'm sorry about last night."

"It's all right."

She felt him shift and met his gaze. "It's not. I shouldn't have put you in that position." He stared back out over the valley. "Of all the shit I experienced, over all the deployments, that day is the one I remember the most. Because of you."

She raised an eyebrow. "Because I'm a woman?"

He snorted. "No. Because without you, a lot more guys would have died. Including Sawyer."

"Oh." She looked back out over the valley.

He sighed. "I'm going back."

Her head snapped back to look at him, her eyes wide. "What? When?"

"Month or so." He looked down and kicked a rock.

"Shit. That sucks." There wasn't much more she could say. No use asking if he could get out of it. He wouldn't, even if there was a way he could.

"Yeah."

They stood there for several more minutes.

"Anyway," he said. "I wanted to say sorry. And thanks." He pivoted and walked back toward the camp.

"Jordan?"

He stopped and turned back.

"Be careful."

He nodded and walked away. She watched him approach the fire. Jase broke away and headed toward her, a scowl on his face. Yeah, he was annoyed she'd left him sleeping. She turned to hide her smile.

CHAPTER 26

*B*oth dogs raised their heads and looked in the direction of the front door before the bell even rang. Bree dropped her head on the back of the couch. *I should ignore it.*

This was the first weekend she'd had all to herself since the camping trip two weeks prior. Jase was on a trip until the next afternoon, and Denise was spending the day with her cousin. After all the drama over the last couple of months, a quiet afternoon on the couch was in order. The bell rang a second time. She sighed and kicked off the light blue chenille throw covering her legs.

She scratched Charlie's head. "They'd better be selling something good."

Dread settled over her when she checked the peephole. She dropped her head against the door frame. So much for a drama-free day. She unlocked the deadbolt and braced herself before she opened the door.

"Chad."

"Hi. I know I'm probably the last person you want to see, but I was hoping we could talk for a few minutes."

What could he possibly have to talk about at this point? Hadn't they both said enough? She stared at him for a heartbeat. Dressed in his usual khakis and button-down, something was different. He seemed more reserved. Less flashy. She rubbed the spot between her eyebrows, sighed, and swung the door open. "Sure. Just a few minutes."

She stepped back and allowed him to walk through. He waited for her to close and the lock the door. "Is the kitchen okay?" he asked.

"Yeah, that's fine. Would you like some tea or water?"

"Uh, tea would be great. Thank you." He sat at the small table in the kitchen while she poured two glasses of sweet tea. She set one glass in front of him before sitting on the opposite side of the table.

"What did you want to talk about?"

Chad took a large, audible gulp of his tea and cleared his throat. "I came to apologize." He glanced at her before looking at his glass. "I realize I asked you to marry me for all the wrong reasons. It was really selfish of me."

Bree raised her eyebrows. Of all the things she had expected him to say, that wasn't at the top of the list. Where was this coming from? Was it some new angle? What was he hoping to gain?

"I know you don't have any reason to believe me. I've been in denial for a long time. When the cops questioned me about Jaelyn, I thought there was no way it was because of me. But then Patty was killed. I, uh…it made me realize how badly I was screwing up my life."

"You had an affair with her as well?"

"Yeah. We…uh…yeah, I did."

"What about the girl who was attacked?

"Her name is Rachel. I wasn't involved with her while we were together. I'd only met her a week or two before she was attacked." He ran his hands through his hair. "I don't understand it."

"Why did you ask me to marry you?" She knew the answer, but wanted to hear it from him.

"When I met you, I was already gambling pretty frequently. I didn't have nearly as much debt as I do now, but I was in pretty heavy. There were a couple of games, though, that I lost big on. And a couple more after that. I kept thinking I could make just one good bet and cover all my losses." He gave a small laugh. "I just kept digging a deeper hole.

"Then I found out who your grandmother is and it seemed like the answer to my problems. Here you were with a big inheritance you didn't even use. If we were married, I'd have access to it, and everything would be okay." He shook his head a couple of times. "I know it's stupid. I know it wasn't fair to you, but I was in a panic. I knew if I asked at your grandmother's party, you wouldn't say no. To be honest, I never saw us together long-term."

He twisted his glass on the table, running his fingers through the condensation. "You're a lot. You've traveled the world. You've been to war. You have millions, but you work and lead a really low-key life. You intimidate me. I was surprised you let the engagement go for a week, much more a month."

One corner of her mouth rose. "I decided the next day to tell you I wasn't going to marry you, but you went out of town, and there just didn't seem to be a right time. I didn't want to be a bitch and do it over text."

He glanced at her quickly, a small smile on his face. "You should have. Maybe I would have gotten my shit together earlier."

"Why are you apologizing now?"

He took a deep breath and blew it out. "I don't like that guy–the guy I became. My behavior, my lifestyle, it was all out of whack. Everything just kind of blew up on me all at once. I lost a couple of freelance contracts when it came out I was gambling on the games I was covering. A couple of my editors agreed to keep me on, but only if I got help. It was hard to admit–hard to face–

but I realized I have a problem. So, I joined Gamblers Anonymous."

"Good for you."

"Yeah. It has been. It works on a twelve-step program like other anonymous groups, and one of the steps is apologizing to the people you've hurt. So, I'm...well...you know."

"Apologizing?" A small smile played at her lips.

"Yeah." His own smile answered hers.

"Isn't it kind of early in the process? I thought apologizing was one of the later steps."

"It is, but I talked to my sponsor about everything that's happened. We agreed it would be good for me to do it now."

Bree nodded, still unsure what he wanted to get from all this. She needed to let it go. Move on and get Chad out of her life. "It wasn't exactly fair of me, either. I shouldn't have said yes when you asked, and I shouldn't have let things drag on for a day, never mind a month."

"I knew you didn't want to marry me. Hell, I knew you were planning on breaking up with me. But I was an asshole. So caught up in the gambling and trying to break even; you were like my Hail Mary. I can't help but think if I had been a better person, Jaelyn and Patty would still be alive."

"The killer is the only person to blame."

"Intellectually, I know you're right, but it's still hard to accept they died because they were with me."

"You need to try."

He nodded and took another sip of his tea. "There's something else I need to tell you."

"Okay..."

"I'm seeing someone. Well, someone I want to see, but she won't go out with me unless I come clean with you."

Bree's eyebrows raised again. "Uh, who?"

"It's Katherine."

"Who's Katherine?"

"She was the one you caught me with. She cut me off after you found us." He scratched the back of his neck. "A few weeks ago, I ran into her at a coffee shop near where I attend meetings, and I apologized. We started talking. She turned me down the first couple of times I asked her out. I almost didn't ask her again, but something told me I should give it one more shot. She agreed, but on the condition that I tell you and you're okay with it."

Her eyebrows raised. "She told you you had to get my blessing?"

"Basically, yeah."

Really? It was hard to reconcile the image of the woman she had caught with Chad with a woman who would demand her blessing. But hell, why not? "I don't think I really have a say one way or the other about whom either of you date, but if it's important to you — to her, then you have it."

"Thank you. She said with the way things went down before, she needed to know you'd be okay with it."

"I can understand that."

"So what about you? What's the deal with this new guy?"

"I love him." She grinned. "He loves me."

"I'm glad. You deserve to be happy."

"Thank you."

He leaned back in his chair. "Katherine would like to have dinner with you one night. Not anytime soon. But maybe after a little time has passed."

Forgiveness was one thing–she didn't think she was up for dinner. Not even coffee. "Uh...let's hold off on that."

"Sure." He nodded. "I'm going to head out."

She walked Chad to the door. He turned on the threshold. "Thank you, for being so understanding. For hearing me out."

"Of course."

He raised his arms to hug her, but hesitated. Bree stepped forward and embraced him. "Take care of yourself, Chad."

He squeezed her gently and let her go. "You too, Bree."

CHAPTER 27

"Private Morris, do you know if Cindy called in today?"

The young man rose from the front desk and stood at parade rest. "No, ma'am."

She waved her hand down. "Sit, please. If she calls in, can you please let me know?"

"Yes, ma'am." He remained standing.

"Thank you." She left the desk with a sigh. When did she become a ma'am? She couldn't figure out if they were getting younger or if she was getting older. Both, but it just made the new ones seem that much younger.

No messages on her work phone or cell. She called Cindy's number again. Straight to voicemail. "Cindy, it's Dr. Marks again. It's about ten-twenty. I'm getting really worried. Please call me when you get this."

She left her office and walked two doors down to Janet's. Bree lucked out and Janet wasn't with a patient. She knocked on the open door to get her attention. "Hey. What's the process for a staff no-show?"

Janet looked up from the record she was annotating. "Military or civilian?"

"Civilian." She leaned against the door jamb and crossed her arms.

"Not much, unfortunately." She set her pen down. "You can call the local police and ask them to do a health and welfare check, but that's it really. Unless there's a reason."

Bree chewed her lip, not sure she wanted to go that far.

"Who is it?"

"Cindy."

Janet's forehead wrinkled. "She didn't call in?"

"No."

"That's not like her."

"I know. That's why I'm worried. Her phone's going straight to voicemail."

"You can always go by her house."

"I don't know if I want to wait that long, but I have patients and I'm going to be backed up as it is."

Janet rose from her desk. "I'll make a couple of calls. Go take care of your patients."

Bree pushed away from the door frame. "What about your patients?"

"My next appointment cancelled. I have a few minutes."

"Thank you. I appreciate it."

Janet rubbed her upper arm. "I'll let you know what I find out."

"Thanks." Bree hurried back to her office and her next appointment.

An hour later, Janet tapped on the exam room door and popped her head in. "Hey. Sorry to interrupt. Come by when you get a chance."

Bree glanced at the wall clock. "Give me about fifteen?"

"Sounds good." The door eased close behind her.

"We can finish up now if you need to go," her patient said.

Bree grinned. "Nice try, Mr. Hanson. You're not getting out of it that easily."

SHE TAPPED on Janet's open door. "What's the verdict?"

Janet swiveled in her chair. "The police did a drive-by. No one answered the door when they knocked. Without a reason, they couldn't go in."

"Crap. I figured."

"Do you know anyone who might have a spare key?"

"No idea."

"What do you want to do?"

Bree brushed a hand over her ponytail. "I'll keep calling. If she's not in tomorrow, it should be enough time for the cops to go into her house, right?"

Janet looked at her with wide eyes. "I don't have a clue."

BREE SAT in her car and let the air conditioner cool down the interior. Screw it. She pulled the office employee roster from her purse and tapped Cindy's address into her GPS. The directions led her to a well-maintained apartment complex north of the base. Cindy's car wasn't in any of the spaces close to her apartment, and no one answered when Bree knocked. The only window visible on the small, second-story threshold was covered by a thin curtain.

Bree hit the bottom step as Cindy's downstairs neighbor exited his apartment, carrying a bag of trash. "Excuse me. Hi. Do you know the woman in 2C?"

"Cindy?" he asked. "Yeah. Nice girl. Kind of quiet. Why?" He set the bag of trash down on the grass next to the walkway.

She fiddled with her keys. "She didn't come in to work this morning. Did you happen to see or hear her?"

"That's weird. She left at the normal time. I work nights, so I'm usually coming in as she's leaving. We waved as we drove past."

"Shoot. Thanks. If you happen to see her, would you ask her to call her boss?"

"Sure thing. Hope she's okay." He leaned down and picked up the bag.

Bree gave him a tight smile. "Me too."

She continued to think about Cindy on the drive home, and her mind flip-flopped between thinking Cindy was just sick and thinking she was lying in a pool of blood. Shit. Who could she call?

"Tim!" She sat upright in her seat. She was such a ditz. She checked her rearview mirror as she pulled to a stop at the intersection. Grabbing her phone from the console, she pulled up her contacts and thumbed Tim's number. His voice boomed out over Bluetooth and she adjusted the volume.

"Hey, what's up?"

"Hey. How long do you have to wait before filing a missing person report?" She checked for traffic and turned right onto her street.

"My brother missing in action already?"

Bree laughed. "No. Someone at work."

"Depends on the situation. Who's missing?"

"My medical technician." She pulled into her drive and shut off the engine. "She didn't come in or call." She grabbed her bag from the passenger seat and got out of the car.

"—the norm."

"What? Sorry, my Bluetooth switched off. I missed most of that."

"I said, I take it that's out of the norm."

"Yeah." She unlocked the mudroom door.

"When was the last time you heard from her?"

She dropped her bag on the bench beside the washer and hung her keys on the hook by the door. "Last Friday, when I left work."

"Where does she live?"

"Fayette—. Someone's here." She paused in the doorway leading to the kitchen.

"Here where? Where are you?"

"My house."

"Don't go in."

"I'm already in."

"Leave. Now."

"Oh, good. You're finally home."

CHAPTER 28

*C*indy stood by the kitchen counter, her blue hospital scrubs stained with large dark splotches. Blood. Blood also dotted her hands.

Bree set her phone on the counter to her left, still connected to Tim. "Cindy. What are you doing here? I've been trying to reach you all day."

"I've been waiting for you." She sounded…chipper. Excited. The same feverish excitement shone in her eyes. A whimper sounded from the dining room. Cindy's head whipped around to look over her shoulder, then back to look at Bree. "Come see." She walked into the dining room, to one of the ladder back chairs, and the person tied to it. She rocked the chair and turned it, revealing a petite blonde woman.

Katherine. Bree's heart pounded in her chest.

Cindy picked up the folding hunting knife laying on the table. "He left you on Sunday and went to her."

Katherine stared at Bree, beseeching. A gag was pulled tight against her mouth and tears streaked her face, mascara blending with blood that ran from a wound high on her temple. She struggled against the rope binding her arms to the chair. Bree scanned the cuts along her arms. They bled freely, but appeared to be superficial. Defensive wounds, maybe. Large spots of blood seeped through her pink top over her stomach, which worried Bree, unable to see the actual wounds.

Oh, Cindy. What have you done? Bree's gaze flicked to Cindy. "Who left me, Cindy?"

"Chad! Chad left you and went to her." She emphasized her words by pointing the knife between Bree and Katherine. "Did you know he slept with me?" She began to pace back and forth. Three short steps away. Three short steps back. "The night you met him. He told me I was beautiful. And special. Took me home with him."

What was she talking about? "Cindy, you weren't there that night." She continued to assess the situation as she took a small step closer to Cindy, edging her way between Cindy and Katherine. If she could distract Cindy while she was away from Katherine, she might be able to get the knife away.

"I was. I was there. I went to support you." Cindy shook her head, staring at the floor as she paced. "I wasn't invited. Snuck in. To see you. You were presenting, and I knew you were nervous. I heard you talking about it." She stopped and faced Bree. "But that's what makes you so wonderful. You did it for your grandmother. You always go out of your way for people."

"Why are you doing this, Cindy?" Bree spoke softly, trying to keep her voice soothing. *Keep her talking. Shit. Please Tim, get here soon.*

Cindy's face twisted and anger blazed from her eyes. "Because you don't deserve this." She pointed her knife at Katherine, who whimpered.

Bree flinched toward her, but Cindy only gestured with the knife. "I don't understand. Help me understand."

Cindy began pacing again. "I saw an article about you. When you got your medal. You're such an inspiration. You saved those people. You inspired me."

Is she talking to me or herself at this point? She took another small step forward.

"I followed you. In the news. There were a lot of articles about you at first, but they dwindled off."

God, she'd hated those news stories. Enlisted hero. Woman hero. She'd just been doing her job.

"Later, I saw an article about you graduating from Physical Therapy school and going to work at Fort Bragg." Cindy stopped again, her eyes bright with happiness. "Then, I found a job listing for a medical assistant at the hospital and I knew, I *knew*, it was meant to be. I'd only hoped to work near you, but I found out I was going to be your assistant. I was so happy." She clasped her hands together, the knife gleaming near her face. "And you're everything I knew you'd be. So nice. You encouraged me to take classes when you found out I dropped out of nursing school. Your patients love you." She pivoted sharply to glare at Katherine. "And those women *dishonored* you. *Disgraced* you." She took a step toward Katherine, the knife half raised in her hand. "With Chad."

She is batshit crazy. "Cindy." She looked at Bree, her head turning in slow motion. "It's not Katherine's fault."

Cindy's face fell. "You know her name? Why do you know her name?" Her voice was harsh.

"Chad told me about her. I know they're dating."

"And you accept that?" she screeched.

That was the wrong thing to say. Way to go, Marks.

"Why do you keep taking him back? He's a liar and a cheat. He's never going to love you!"

Calm. Calm. Keep her calm. Bree put her hands out in front of her. "Cindy, please. I didn't take Chad back. We're not together."

"You are! I saw you. I saw you hug him." She pointed the knife toward Bree. "You let him in your house. You let him touch you."

"He apologized, Cindy. That was all. I'm in love with someone else."

"You can't forgive him. You can't forgive *them*." She stepped closer to Katherine. "You have to understand. She has to pay." She pulled her arm back. Katherine screamed behind her gag.

"No!" Bree lunged forward and raised her left arm, blocking Cindy's thrust. The blade stung as it slid along her forearm. *Grab the shirt. Spin. Shift weight. Thrust hip. Leave it up to momentum.*

Forward motion and gravity threw Cindy forward. Her toe caught on the edge of the carpet and she tumbled to the floor, landing hard, and gasped. She tried to push herself up but collapsed, a pool of blood forming under her head.

"Cindy?" A wave of dizziness washed through Bree. What? Her arm. A four-inch gash ran across the inside of her forearm. Bright red blood spurt freely. Shit. She clamped her hand over the cut. Her vision began to fade, blackness encroaching from the edges.

Can't black out. Need to stop the bleeding.

Her knees buckled as Tim rushed into the kitchen, gun drawn. "Bree?" Detective Johnson and another officer followed behind.

Only a pinpoint of light was visible through the tunnel. "Tourniquet."

"MARKS! Get your ass back here. Damn it. Cover her!"

She crossed the expanse between vehicles, sliding on her knees behind the mangled rear bumper of the Humvee, the rear door wide open. She flinched, small pieces of metal ricocheting off the corner.

"Hold on. I'll get you out of there."

The soldier reached down and released his seat belt. He stepped out of the Humvee, uninjured.

"What—?" She stood and took a step back.

"You don't belong here, Bree. You have to go back."

She shook her head. "I can't. I have to save them."

"You saved everyone you could. It's time to let go."

"No. I have to get it right."

Beep.

"There's nothing to get right. None of this was in your control."

Beep.

"I should have been faster. I should have gotten to you sooner."

Beep.

"If you had gotten to me sooner, you'd be dead too. It wasn't your time then. It isn't your time now, Bree."

Beep...beep...beep...

The high-pitched, steady sound invaded her consciousness. She cracked her eyes open, struggling against the lethargy that fought to hold her under. She closed, then opened her eyes again. A narrow bed. White sheets. Her eyes closed again.

"Bree?" Her head was heavy, weighed down as she tried to find the familiar voice. "Stay with me, darlin'."

Jase. His voice was rough. Strained. She struggled harder to wake up.

"Open your eyes, baby." His warm lips pressed against her forehead. High on her cheek. Her lips. She cracked her eyes and he filled her narrow vision. His thumb brushed across her eyebrow. "There you are."

Her eyelids drooped. She moved her thick, dry tongue around her mouth, unable to work up any moisture. "Water." Her voice croaked. His touch left her. A sharp touch against her parched lips made her flinch.

"It's a straw, baby. Open your mouth a little."

Eyes still closed, she parted her lips. The cool water brought instant relief. The straw left her mouth all too soon.

She struggled to open her eyes again. To know for sure Jase was with her. She blinked several times, finally able to keep them open for more than a few seconds.

"Where am I?" She braced her arms on the bed to shift up and hissed in pain.

"Here, let me help you." He grabbed the control beside the bed and raised the back so she was upright. "You're in the hospital."

She looked down at her arm, bandaged from her wrist to her elbow. *Fuck.* "Katherine?"

He sat in the chair pulled close to the bed and held her hand. "She's in a room down the hall."

She nodded and swallowed. "Cindy?"

He brushed her hair back. "She didn't make it. The knife nicked an artery in her neck when you threw her."

Her eyes welled up. She turned her head and covered her eyes with her good hand, the I.V. pulling at her hand.

"Oh darlin', don't." His lips against her forehead. She heard rustling and then his long body wedged its way next to hers. She scooted toward the rail to give him some more space and turned her head into his shoulder as he slid his arm under her neck.

She soaked the material under her cheek. Sniffing, she tried not to rub her nose on his shirt. "Do they know why?"

"Detective Johnson has some ideas. He's been by every afternoon. You can ask him later." His fingers toyed with her hair. Her eyes drifted shut, tears leaking from the corners.

HER HEAD ROSE and fell with Jase's inhale and exhale. She should probably get off her side and arm, but she was comfortable.

"Jase," Denise hissed. "The nurses are going to lose their shit if they see you in bed with her."

"Then guard the door. And quit yelling."

"Why're you in bed with her?"

"She woke up. Got upset when I told her about whack job."

Bree opened her eyes. "Don't call her that."

Jase peered down his nose. "You fakin'?"

"Just woke up."

Denise poked Jase in the ribs. "Get out. My turn." They stared each other down for several moments. It was a pretty even match; no telling how it would go.

Jase sighed and pulled his arm from under Bree. She raised her head, and he eased to a sitting position. He swung his legs to the side and stood. Turning, he leaned down and brushed her hair back from her face. "Careful of her arm." Bree smiled.

"No shit." Denise pushed him out of the way and crawled up on the bed. She grasped Bree's fingers and moved her arm onto Bree's chest. She lay down on her side, facing Bree, her arm draped over Bree's hip.

"How're you feeling?"

"Weak." Her throat was still dry.

"That'll happen when you lose most of your blood."

"Is there water?"

Denise looked over her shoulder, but Jase already had the cup ready. He angled the straw so she could drink. She pulled away and nodded her head. "Thank you."

He set the cup down and walked around the bed. Shifting her knees, he sat on the end of the bed on her side.

"What's the rule?" Denise asked.

That was a loaded question. They had a lot of rules. One for almost every occasion–except for getting cut by your crazy medical assistant. They'd never come up with a rule for that. She shook her head.

"Don't take stupid chances."

Oh, that one. Jase squeezed her thigh. Apparently, he agreed. "Didn't have much of a choice. She was in my house when I got home."

Denise touched her forehead to Bree's. "You scared me," she whispered. "Don't do it again."

"Agreed."

"What do y'all think you're doin'?" An older nurse stood in the doorway, hands on her hips. Her salt-and-pepper hair twisted into a bun on top of her head, and she wore scrubs with a hearts-with-wings motif.

"Get off that poor girl." She stormed forward and waved her hand at Jase, as if shooing away a fly and smacked Denise on the leg. "Off. Bad enough someone tried to filet her like a fish, she doesn't need y'all piling on top of her."

Bree smiled as Denise and Jase did as they were told, grumbling the whole time.

"Nice to see you awake, dear." Her whole demeanor changed. "I'm Mary Ann. How're you feeling?"

She shifted onto her back and moved to the center of the bed. "Weak. Thirsty."

"That's to be expected with significant blood loss." Mary Ann raised the head of the bed so Bree was half reclining. She tried resting her arm on her chest, but it aggravated her wound. Laying it next to her on the bed, palm up, relieved most of the pain.

"How much did I have transfused?"

Mary Ann glanced at her as she checked the I.V. bag. "Fifteen units."

Bree's eyebrows rose. Denise hadn't been kidding when she said she'd lost most of her blood.

"I'm gonna take your vitals and change your bandage now that you're awake."

"Okay."

Jase stepped back from the end of the bed as Mary Ann rounded the bed, but never broke eye contact. His eyes were bloodshot, underscored by dark circles. His curly hair stood up in tufts, as if he had been pulling on sections of it.

"You look like crap," Bree said. He grinned and winked.

"I told him to go home and take a shower," Denise said.

"He wouldn't leave your side," Mary Ann added. "Called in the big guns when we tried to kick him out." Her look was disgruntled as she wrapped the blood pressure cuff around Bree's good arm.

"Big guns?" Bree asked.

"Gran," Jase said.

"Where is she?"

"She's coming back this evening," Jase said.

"Open back up." Mary Ann stuck a digital thermometer in her mouth. "Close." The machine beeped twice and Bree opened her mouth.

"I'll be right back with clean bandages." She patted Bree's uninjured arm.

"How long have I been here?"

"Three days," Denise said.

"Three days?" Her head rose from the flat pillow, but dropped again immediately.

"How much do you remember?" Jase asked.

"All of it. Right up until Tim and Detective Johnson stormed in. How's Katherine?"

"She was stabbed twice in the stomach," Denise said. "I think the doctors had to remove a kidney, but she's conscious. They have her a couple rooms down the hall."

"I'd like to go see her when I can."

Jase crossed his arms. "I'll wheel you down when the doctor says you can move around."

Bree glared. "My arm is cut, not my leg."

"Did Cindy—?" Mary Ann's arrival cut Denise's question short.

She carried an assortment of bandages on a stainless steel tray. "The doctor's right behind me. He's going to take a look at your arm before I wrap it back up."

Bree nodded. Mary Ann held her left arm in one hand while she gently unwound the gauze. The yellow-stained skin from the disinfectant… the purple-and-blue bruising around the edge of the gash… finally, the wound itself. The cut was almost straight across the fleshy part of her inner arm, the edge on the pinky side of her arm slightly higher than the edge on the thumb side. The tiny, black stitches were tight, precise, and evenly spaced. She stared at it dispassionately. As long as she didn't pull the wound open, the scar would be thin.

"How many stitches?" She didn't want to take the time to count them all.

"Thirty-two." Bree looked toward the door. An average-looking man in a white lab coat stood in the threshold. "I'm Doctor Walsh. How're you feeling?"

"Weak. How deep was the cut?"

"Quarter of an inch at the deepest." He pulled his hands out of his lab coat pockets and joined them in the room. It was getting crowded in the small space. Mary Ann stepped back to give him access to the bed. Denise shuffled to the side and joined Jase at the end of the bed.

"Radial artery?" she asked as he picked up her arm and palpated the edges of the wound.

"They warned me you were a medic. Radial artery. Do you remember telling the police you needed a tourniquet?" He squeezed her fingernails and released them.

Bree furrowed her brow and shook her head.

"It saved your life. Without it, you would have bled out before EMS got there. Squeeze my finger." He put his index finger under all four of her fingers. She tried to close her fingers around his, but hissed as pain shot through her arm.

"Don't worry. It's good you can close your fingers. I have hope there's no permanent nerve damage. You'll need to be assessed by a physical therapist after the stitches come out."

She gave him a baleful stare. "Are you kidding?"

He chuckled. "No. You can't assess yourself. Never a good idea to self-diagnose."

She sighed. "When can I go home?"

He squeezed her hand and motioned to Mary Ann. "I want to do another CBC to make sure your platelets are good. And you need to eat some solid food. Assuming everything comes back normal, tomorrow afternoon. Saturday at the latest."

She nodded. She wanted her own bed. Wanted her dogs. Oh, shit. Her eyes widened and the beeping of the machine next to her increased. "Charlie and Polly?"

Jase rubbed her feet. "They're fine. They were outside. If you need Polly, Tim can go get her from my house." She sagged into the mattress.

Knock, knock. Everyone turned as Detective Johnson stepped into the doorway. "Can I join the party?"

"You can have my spot," Dr. Walsh said. "Bree, I'll be back to check on you during my normal rounds." He maneuvered his way around everyone in the room and left.

CHAPTER 29

Detective Johnson took a few steps into the room. "How're you feeling?"

She quirked her mouth and her eyebrow twitched. "Okay, all things considered."

His gaze was sympathetic. He looked down at her arm, being rewrapped in clean bandages. "You up for answering some questions?"

"Sure."

"Not too long," Mary Ann said. "She needs to rest." She packed up the remaining supplies on the tray and left with a pointed looked at the detective.

He nodded and took up position next to Jase. Denise sat in one of the chairs by the door, thumbs flying across the face of her phone.

"Walk me through your day on Monday." He lifted a digital recorder and raised his eyebrows. She shrugged. Pressing a button, he set the device on the tray table next to the bed. "Start from when you realized Cindy wasn't at work."

"It was between seven-forty-five and eight, I guess. She's usually in by seven-thirty." Detective Johnson stopped her a few times as she recalled the events leading to the confrontation in her house, asking her to backtrack or clarify some part of the timeline.

"She landed on the knife?" Bree asked.

"The medical examiner determined she tried to break her fall, but didn't let go of it. She was still clutching it in her hand."

Her eyes and nose stung. She dropped her gaze to her lap to hide her tears. Jase lowered the bedrail and sat next to her hip. He pulled her hand into his lap, careful of the IV taped to the back. His thumb brushed her cheek, catching a tear.

She swallowed hard and looked back at Detective Johnson. "Have you been able to figure out why? She wasn't making a lot of sense. She rambled more than anything."

He sighed and grabbed the recorder off the tray. He turned it off and slid it into his coat pocket. "She had several scrapbooks full of news clippings about you. Most of them look like they were downloaded from the internet. Even if the content was the same, if it was from a different site, she saved it."

"What kind of articles?" Jase asked. His thumb brushed back and forth along the meaty part of her hand.

"They start from the time Bree received her Bronze Star."

"She mentioned that," Bree said.

"From there, it was anything and everything she could find," Detective Johnson said.

"How much is there?" Denise asked.

"Not a lot after the hoopla of her medal died down. A few articles here and there, mostly in conjunction with events her grandmother supported." He turned to Bree. "There were a lot of pictures after she started working at the hospital with you. Some of them you're looking at the camera." He scratched at the back of his neck. "Some were of you at your house or shopping. You seem completely unaware the pictures were being taken."

Bree suppressed a shudder. Cindy had followed her? Stalked

her? Something didn't fit. "But why did she kill those women? I don't understand that part."

He pointed at the vacant chair. "Do you mind?" Bree shook her head. He pulled it closer to the bed and rested one ankle over the other knee. "We have a theory about why she started killing. We found journals she kept, going back about five years." He pinched the bridge of his nose. "They were from around the time her husband left her for another woman."

Bree's eyebrows rose. "She was married?"

"Divorced. You didn't know?"

"I had no idea. I feel like such a shitty person. That's a pretty significant thing not to know about someone."

"It doesn't make you a shitty person," Denise said. "You said more than once she was a little weird."

"Still, something that should have come up in the two years I knew her."

"Not necessarily," Detective Johnson said. "We pulled her personnel file. She checked *Never Married*."

"Why?" Bree asked.

"What we've gathered from her journals is the divorce, and her husband cheating on her, destroyed her world. We've got a psychologist going through them as well. His preliminary assessment is that she lost her sense of self-worth. Then, she found you."

"I don't understand."

"She hero-worshipped you. In her own words, you were everything she wanted to be. Strong. Independent. Self-reliant."

"What did that have to do with Bree's ex?" Denise asked.

He glanced over his shoulder, then turned back to Bree. "She wrote about finding out Chad cheated on you. The entries became disjointed from that point forward. She'd refer to Chad, but a few sentences later, use her ex's name. The psychologist thinks finding out about your situation triggered a psychotic break. She was unable to distinguish between what happened to you and what happened to her. In the end, she took all her anger she felt from her divorce out on the women involved with Chad."

Bree stared up at the white ceiling. How did this happen? Could she have prevented it? She squeezed her eyes shut, and her fingers clenched around Jase's. Tears streamed from her eyes. Such a waste. So many dead.

Jase jostled her as he shifted forward on the bed. Her left arm lifted, and she felt Denise crowd her on that side. They surrounded her. Comforted her. Protected her.

"Bree." Detective Johnson's voice was soft, laced with empathy. "Nothing you did brought this on. Cindy was very troubled."

She peered over her human security blanket and nodded. Jase and Denise sat back.

Denise wiped Bree's cheek with the back of her fingers. "Just think of all the new stuff you'll have to talk to Dr. Tailor about. She's probably sick of hearing about the same old shit."

Bree snorted and blew out a snot bubble. Denise threw her head back and laughed while Bree glared at her. She put her hand over her nose and sniffed. "Get me a tissue, you cow."

Jase grabbed two from the box by the bed and held them out. Bree replaced her hand with them. "Can you leave the room while I blow my nose?"

He chuckled. "No."

"Fine. Don't blame me if it grosses you out." She blew her nose, then laid the wadded up remains on the corner of the table tray.

Detective Johnson approached her bed. A smile played at the corners of his mouth. "Thank you for answering my questions."

"You're welcome."

"I may have more later. We're already coordinating with hospital administration at Fort Bragg to talk to the people you work with."

She sighed. Maybe she could talk Jase into running away to Aruba and not deal with it.

"Take care." Detective Johnson touched two fingers to his forehead and left.

A yawn overtook her, and she covered her mouth with the back of her bandaged arm.

"I'm heading out," Denise said. "Gran texted while you were talking to the detective. She'll be here around two. Plenty of time to take a nap."

"Okay."

Denise laid her forehead against Bree's again. "I'm glad you're safe."

"Me too."

Denise kissed her cheek. "Later, Jase."

"Later." He didn't look away from Bree. He raised her fingers to his lips, his eyes twinkling over the back of her hand. "I love you. Snot bubbles and all."

Her face flamed. So undignified. Never mind she'd been lying in a hospital bed for three days.

His smile faded. Her breath caught in her throat as his look became grim. "You can't ever leave me, Bree. For any reason. You hold my heart together."

Tears welled up again. She blew another snot bubble.

EPILOGUE

"Happy birthday…tooooo yooouuu." The final line of the song trailed off. Everyone clapped and cheered as Gran took a deep breath and blew out her candles. All twenty-nine of them.

Bree squeezed her tight. "Happy birthday, Gran."

"Thank you, darling girl." She kissed Bree's cheek before she turned to accept more hugs and well wishes.

Bree left the cake-cutting to the catering staff and made her way to the side of the large party room where Jase stood with his parents and Denise. Several extended family members and friends stopped her along the way, and it took several minutes to reach the small group.

Denise broke off as she approached. "I'm getting a refill." She shook her empty wine glass. "You want one?"

"God, yes. I was going to get one on my way here, but my aunt Amelia is at the bar and I know she'll ask awkward questions about my sex life."

Denise glanced sideways at Jase. "Especially when she gets a good look at him."

"I'm surprised she hasn't tried to corner him already."

"I'll head her off if I see her walking this way."

"Thanks."

The resemblance between Jase and his father was uncanny, although he got his eyes from his mother. Bree walked right under his outstretched arm and wrapped her arm around his waist. "Thank you for coming, Mr. and Mrs. Larken. I'm glad you were able to fit this into your trip."

"Nonsense. We're honored to be invited. I think it's fabulous your grandmother celebrates the anniversary of her twenty-ninth birthday."

Bree grinned. "She's been doing it for as long as I can remember. When I was little, I didn't understand why she stayed the same age."

"And please, call me Melissa." She tilted her head to her husband, who rested a hand on her shoulder. "You can call him whatever name he's earned at the time."

Bree pulled her lips between her teeth and tried to suppress her smile.

Jase let out an exasperated sigh. "What'd you do this time, Dad?"

He opened his mouth to answer.

"He was complaining about how all his children are involved with Air Force people," Melissa said.

"That's all right, Melissa," Bree said. "We all make mistakes in life and have to learn from them. Some have to learn the hard way." A grin spread across Jase's father's face until Bree continued. "By joining the Army."

Melissa threw her head back and laughed. Jase kissed Bree's temple, probably to hide the smile she felt.

Jases's dad cast a glare at his giggling wife. He held his hand out for Bree to shake. "Bill. You can call me Bill."

Bree smiled and shook his hand. "How was your drive?"

"Long," Melissa said. "He insisted on taking back roads the whole way here. The drive took twice as long as it should have."

"It wasn't twice as long, woman."

"Three-and-a-half hours is almost twice as long."

Bree leaned close to Jase. "Are they always like this?" she asked under her breath.

He put his mouth close to her ear. "Pretty much. I don't know what they'd do if they didn't have something to argue about."

His voice sent shivers down her spine. Was immediately after blowing out the candles too soon for them to leave?

She watched his parents argue, but it was easy to tell there was no heat or anger behind the words. "At least I know you came by your bossiness naturally."

He smirked. "Yup. Got it from Mom."

She looked at him like he was crazy. "So not was I was thinking."

Denise rejoined them and handed Bree a glass of wine. "Ms. Mary is shagging."

"What?" Jase asked.

Bree blinked twice, then laughed. "Did someone tell you to tell on her?"

Denise stared at her blankly. "No. Ms. Mary told me to tell you, she's shagging."

"Why is old people having sex interesting?" Jase asked.

His mom and Denise laughed. "What? No…" Bree shook her head. "Not…" She faked a shudder. "I need to go bleach my brain, now."

"Shag dancing," Bill said. "Lots of shaggin' on the Carolina coast." He winked at Bree.

"Bree!" Her name rang out across the room, and she glanced over her shoulder at the small wood dance floor. Ms. Mary waved her arm. "Come shag with me."

A wide grin spread across Jase's face. "My mind isn't wired to think of that as anything other than an invite to—"

Bree slapped a hand over his mouth. "Quit talking. I'm going to go dance and make sure she doesn't throw out a hip." She removed her hand and planted a kiss on his mouth.

"Oh, yeah. I like her," she heard Melissa say as she walked away. Her smile was instantaneous. Yeah, she liked them too.

Ms. Mary decided to lead. They danced for two songs before the DJ switched to sixties music, and people wanting to shake their tail feathers and twist overran the dance floor. Maneuvering through the crush of bodies, Bree approached the bar and asked for a glass of water. She scanned the room until she found Jase sitting with Gran.

They were in an intense conversation. Jase leaned forward with his elbows resting on his knees. His look was serious, fierce even.

Her heart pounded in her chest and the blood rushed in her ears. Not again. "Fuck." She set her glass on the bar and almost missed the edge. "Fuck. Fuck. Fuckity-fuck." She made a beeline for Denise, grabbed her wrist, and dragged her into the far corner of the room, dropping f-bombs the entire way.

"Holy shit, woman. What is wrong?"

Bree felt light-headed. "Jase is talking to Gran."

Denise's nose scrunched and she frowned. "Okay?"

"Look at them." She paced back and forth in the corner.

"What am I looking at?"

"I'm having flashbacks to last year. I can't do it again." She put her hand over her chest. "Fuck. What am I going to do?"

"Stop." Denise grabbed her shoulders. "He knows how it went down, right?"

"Yeah."

"All right. One, he's not an asshat, so he's not going to do the same thing. Two, if I'm wrong and he is an asshat, then I'll grab you and we'll run out of here. Okay?"

That made sense. She was overreacting. Even if he was going to ask her to marry him, he wouldn't do it here and now.

Although his parents were here.

Did she even want to be engaged again?

To Jase?

Absolutely.

"Are you calm?" Denise asked.

She swallowed around the lump in her throat and nodded.

"Right. Let's do a shot."

"Shots are good."

Denise linked her arm through Bree's and led her back to the bar. Two lemon drops later, Bree relaxed enough to stop freaking out, but spent the rest of the evening waiting for Jase to make some grand gesture.

Melissa tracked her down an hour after her freak-out to tell her they were leaving. "I can't tell you how delighted I am to see Jase so happy." She hugged Bree tight and whispered in her ear. "Thank you. For bringing him back to us."

Tears pricked the back of her eyes. "Lunch tomorrow?"

Melissa held her at arm's length and smiled, not fooled by Bree's deflection. "I'll call Jase in the morning so we can figure out a time." She kissed Bree's cheek and walked toward Bill standing near the exit with their coats.

Bree jumped as a hand slid across her hip.

"Are you okay?" Jase asked.

"Yes." She smiled brightly. "You just startled me." She rested her hand on top of his.

He kissed the top of her head. "You 'bout ready?"

"Yeah. Need to say goodbye to Gran."

They wound through the remaining friends and family to where Gran sat with several people. "We're headed out." She leaned down and hugged Gran. "We're having lunch with Jase's parents tomorrow, if you'd like to join us."

Gran kissed her cheek, then rubbed her thumb over the same spot. "I'd love to. Give me a call in the morning."

"I will. Love you." Bree returned her kiss.

"Love you, too." She waved her fingers at Jase. "Drive safe."

"Yes, ma'am."

~

FINGERS BRUSHING across her cheek woke her. Bree yawned wide and turned her head to Jase.

Jase brushed a strand of hair off her shoulder. "We're home, darlin'." She nodded and unbuckled the seat belt, and Jase helped her out of the truck.

She hung her keys on the hook next to the kitchen door and kicked off her heels.

Jase stopped her from going farther into the house. "What's wrong?" he asked. "You've been quiet since you went to dance. Did something happen?"

Bree shrugged and averted her gaze. "Just tired."

"I know how you act when you're tired. This isn't it."

She sighed. "I saw you talking to Gran."

His thumb rubbed across the top of her hand. "Okay. And?"

"I thought…" She shook her head. "It's not important."

He sat on the padded bench and pulled her between his legs. "You thought I was going to propose."

She laid her hands on his shoulders, not meeting his eyes. Her face warmed. Her expectations were ridiculous. As much as she didn't want him to propose at the party, she still felt dejected when he hadn't. She couldn't get the thought of marrying him out of her head. *Brianna Larken* had a nice ring to it. She may as well get a notebook and draw hearts with their initials inside them.

One of his hands ran up and down the outside of her thigh. "I was explaining a couple of things."

Did she really want to know? "Like what?"

"That I'm not going to ask you to marry me."

She gasped. Nope. She didn't want to know. Her heart plummeted to her feet and she tried to step back. His fingers dug into the back of her legs.

"Let me go." God, this hurt. Why was he even with her if they didn't have a future?

"No. Listen to me, Bree." One arm wrapped around her hips. She pushed at his broad shoulders, but failed to budge him. "I said I'm not going to ask you, not that I don't want to marry you."

She quit pushing. "I don't understand."

"I don't ever want you to doubt why I'm with you. When we get married, it's going to be because *you* asked *me*."

Her brain struggled to play catchup. "Oh."

He raised his eyebrows, a smile tugging at the corners of his mouth. "Oh."

She bit her lip and dropped her gaze. *Well, this is embarrassing.* Maybe she had overreacted a little.

"But I am telling you this." She looked back into his hazel eyes. "We start talking kids, or you get pregnant, deal's off. I'm dragging you to the closest altar I can find."

"Oh." Her breath left her in a rush at the image of a little baby Jase.

He stood and picked her up in one move. She tightened her grip on his shoulders and wrapped her legs around his hips. He nipped at her shoulder where it met her neck.

"Where are we going?"

He strode through the kitchen. "I'm putting you where I want you."

AUTHOR'S NOTE

Writing this book has been such an exciting and, at times, cathartic journey. Bree and Denise are a mosaic of many, many of my friends and fellow women service members. They are the women I love and respect, and know I can rely on, no matter what.

The Cultural Support Teams grew out of the Female Engagement Teams when the Marines and Army, operating in Iraq and Afghanistan, realized there were certain things male service members couldn't do, due to cultural issues. I've had the privilege of meeting and knowing several during my own deployments to Iraq and Afghanistan. If you'd like to learn more about them, Gayle Tzemach Lemmon's article The Women of the Army Rangers' Cultural Support Teams (2014) is a great read.

Veteran suicide is a very serious issue, one that has affected me as a friend, co-worker, supervisor, and Wingman. If you, or someone you know, is having thoughts of suicide, please reach out. Please get help.

Veteran Crisis Line: ***www.veteranscrisisline.net***

Military One Source: ***www.veteranscrisisline.net***

ACKNOWLEDGMENTS

There are so many people I want to thank, I'm having a hard time figuring out where to start.

To all the wonderful authors in RWA and WRW who have provided guidance, insight, encouragement, and shared their experiences. I would not have gotten nearly as far without your help.

To the Scribophile author community for providing feedback and critiques, but especially to Deidre and Kristina who (through no fault of their own) became my critique partners and stuck with me until the end. I promise I will catch up.

Kristy and Toni, thank you for being the first to read the whole book in it's final version.

To my wonderful editor Denise (it's purely a coincidence), who managed to turn around my manuscript while packing up her family and moving half-way across the country.

To my framily (friends and family) for your encouragement and support in everything I do, even when you're not jumping for joy about some of the roads I take.

To the women who have cried with me and laughed with me;

bled with me and healed with me; and always, no matter what, gave me a safe place to be me.

HALF-BROKE HEART EXCERPT

Chapter One

Desire punched Chris in the gut. If sexy had a sound, it would be Denise's laugh. She wiped a finger under her eye as she trailed off in a deep chuckle.

"Chris has a somewhat questionable past," Jase said.

Denise turned off *Magic Mike*, shutting Channing Tatum down mid-hip grind. "Nothing wrong with that."

Grabbing his bag from where he'd dropped it on the floor, Chris raised his eyebrows before following Bree and Jase down the hall to Bree's guest bathroom. Glancing over his shoulder, he watched Denise cross the open living room into the kitchen. Her cut-off shorts were demure by today's standards, ending a few inches below her butt cheeks, but they showcased her long, tanned legs.

Looked like agreeing to go to Bree's for Chinese after camping instead of going home to grilled cheese was going to have more benefits than just the food. He'd been worried he was going to be the uncomfortable third wheel. Now he was uncomfortable for an entirely different reason. He pulled at the front of his cargo pants and shifted his hip a little with his next step.

Bree stopped in the middle of the hall. "There's towels and normal soap on the counter."

His lips quirked up. "Normal soap?"

"Not perfumey."

He smiled. "Ah. 'Preciate it."

Jase pulled her farther down the hall. "You're welcome," she said over her shoulder.

Chris shut the door and thumbed the lock, dropping his bag on the small wooden stool next to the vanity. Unzipping the bag, he pulled out clean gym shorts and a t-shirt. No underwear. Oh well, he'd just have to keep his mind on innocent topics and off the way those shorts hugged Denise's perfectly formed ass. *Not helping.*

He turned the shower knob all the way to the left and steam filled the room as the water heated. Untying the laces of his boots he kicked them away before pulling his shirt and pants off. He stepped into the shower and ducked his head under the spray, letting the pulsing, hot spray run over his shoulders and back, loosening muscles tight from sleeping in a tent for the last three nights. Not the worst place he'd slept, but definitely not the most comfortable either. He grabbed the bar of soap and worked up a lather, running his hands over his shoulders and chest.

Denise's laugh echoed in his mind, sending blood rushing to his groin. He closed his eyes and tugged on his semi-erection, picturing her long, tan legs wrapped around his hips. *Fuck.*

His eyes snapped open and he released himself. He couldn't rub one out in Bree's shower. Had to get that under control. He lathered up more soap and ran it over his close-cropped hair and three days' worth of beard.

His phone chirped twice in quick succession in his pants pocket. Running his hands over his head one more time, sloughing off the last of the soap, he shut off the water. The towel was soft as he ran it over his body and reminded him he needed to get more laundry detergent. Wrapping it around his waist, he dug in his pants for his phone.

Mtg 0800 Mon

New TF. You're lead.

His gut clenched. If his boss had decided to stand up a new task force, they'd gotten the intelligence they needed. Or shit had gone all to hell. He hoped it was the first option.

Order Half-Broke Heart today to keep reading!